In Need of a Cowboy

In Need of a Cowboy

LINDA LAEL MILLER

HEATHER GRAHAM

kensingtonbooks.com

KENSINGTON BOOKS are published by

Kensington Publishing Corp.
900 Third Avenue
New York, NY 10022

ISBN: 978-1-4967-5112-6 (ebook)

ISBN: 978-1-4967-5111-9

First Kensington Trade Paperback Printing: February 2025

10 9 8 7 6 5 4 3 2 1

Printed in the United States of America

Contents

Ask Me Again

LINDA LAEL MILLER

Chapter 1

Diamond Creek Ranch
Northern Arizona

The kid sat sullenly on the edge of the crumbling water trough in front of the barn, arms folded, face flushed, eyes averted. A battered army surplus backpack slumped at his feet.

Blindsided by the sudden discovery that he was the father of a twelve-year-old son, Jack O'Ballivan stood stock-still, as inescapably stuck as if he'd planted the soles of his boots in quicksand, and shifted his gaze back to the boy's mother, Loreen Baker.

Loreen, blonde and thin, stood well within Jack's personal space, and it was all he could do not to put out his hands and shove her into the manure pile behind her.

"You can't deny it, Jack," she said smugly. "The kid looks just like you."

That much was obvious. When Jack looked at the boy, it was like looking at a much younger version of himself—same dark hair, same blue eyes, same stubborn jawline.

For once in her miserable, screwed-up life, Loreen was telling the truth.

Jack lowered his voice. "'The kid'?" he challenged, in a raspy growl. "Is that what you call him? Or does he have a name?"

Loreen took a step back, and her cheap sandals made a squishing sound as they sank into the muck. She made a face.

"It's Gideon," she said, less confident than before. "His name is Gideon."

Jack leaned in a little. "And you waited *twelve years* to tell me about him?"

Loreen looked away, hugged herself nervously. "I had my reasons."

"Like what?"

"Like I was married a couple of months after we broke up, and my husband thought Gideon was his."

Jack thrust out a furious breath. "I see," he said, and now it was a real effort to hold his temper in check. He had a child—*a child,* and he'd missed more than a decade of knowing him. Loving him. And *protecting* him—something the boy had badly needed, from the looks of things.

"And now—?" he seethed.

"And now it's your turn to raise the kid. I've done my time."

Jack glanced in the boy's direction again, praying he hadn't overheard Loreen's words, then glared into her upturned face again.

"Are you on drugs, Loreen?" he asked bluntly. Her teeth were bad, and that wasn't a good sign. Neither was the grayish pallor of her skin.

She'd changed a lot since they were together, back in college; she'd been beautiful then, and lively, if a little wild at times.

For a while there, Jack had believed he loved her.

Until he'd caught her beating his dog with a stick because it had thrown up on her new shoes. He'd wrenched the stick from her hands, flung it away, and yelled at her to get her things together and get out of his apartment *and* his life.

Whatever he'd felt for her had died instantly, killed by the knowledge that she could be so vicious and so cruel as to deliberately hurt a helpless animal.

Loreen had cried and begged and said she was sorry, then dropped to her knees and tried to embrace the dog, Hobbs, who had sidestepped her to hide behind Jack, still whimpering from the pain and the sudden, fierce betrayal of a human being he'd trusted.

Now, remembering that scene, Jack felt a stabbing chill.

Had she beaten Gideon, too, in fits of anger?

"No," she replied stiffly, in belated answer to his question. "I'm *not* on drugs."

He shoved a hand through his hair. Reassessed this woman as calmly as he could, under present circumstances.

Her hair was straggly, overprocessed, and in need of washing. Her clothes, worn short-shorts, and a low-cut top that revealed a grungy bra, made her look like a hooker. Hell, for all he knew, she'd traveled that route.

"I don't believe you," he said flatly.

"What if I am, then?" she snapped. "All the more reason I shouldn't have to raise *your son.*"

"Will you keep your voice down?" Jack retorted. "The boy can hear you!"

Loreen shook her head. "No big deal if he does," she said, and the shrug in her tone only increased Jack's sense of outrage. "He knows how I feel. He's a brat and I'm sick of being around him. He always *wants* something, *needs* something. It's a total drag."

Jack closed his eyes for a long moment, shook his head.

When he opened them again, Loreen was grinning at him.

Grinning.

"You're rich now," she said. "Just write me a nice check, and I'll be out of your life—and Gideon's—for good."

Jack didn't bother to ask himself how she knew he had money; he made a point of living simply and keeping a low financial profile. At thirty-two, his fast-track days were behind him; he was all about living simply now, and he felt good about that.

"As if I'd trust you, Loreen."

For all the attitude she was dishing out, she looked hurt.

He didn't care.

For the moment, all his concern was for the son he hadn't known he'd had.

"You're going to have to sign custody of our son over to me, Loreen," he said, speaking as reasonably as he could. "*Permanent custody.* You're clearly not fit to care for him, and proving that to the authorities would be no trouble at all. A little digging and I'll have all I need." He paused, looked over at Gideon. The boy's head was down now, but he was petting Jack's German shepherd, Trey, with one faltering hand.

Jack's throat thickened, and the backs of his eyes scalded.

"Abandoning a child won't win you any favors with the law, either," he added, turning back to Loreen, and his voice was a hoarse croak that time.

Loreen's narrow, bony face tightened in fresh irritation. "Fine," she said sharply. "Then I'll just take Gideon and hit the road again. I thought it would be better to leave him with you than dump him on the foster system, but I guess I was wrong!"

When she whirled to walk away, Jack caught a firm but not bruising hold on her right elbow.

She shook him loose.

Just then, the child let out a roar of angry sorrow, and when Jack turned in his direction, he saw that Gideon had wrapped both arms around Trey's furry neck and buried his face in the dog's gleaming hide.

Jack was done arguing with Loreen. He strode over to the boy and crouched before him.

"Gideon?" he ventured, his voice gruff with emotion.

He could hardly believe he'd gotten out of bed that morning thinking he had an ordinary day of hard work ahead of him—rounding up stray cattle, checking fence lines, overseeing the renovation of the house and the completion of the new barn. Instead, he'd learned that he had a son, and now his heart had been torn wide open with a crowbar.

He knew little or nothing about the boy, but he already loved him fiercely. It was as if a switch had been flipped the moment he realized Gideon was bone of his bone, flesh of his flesh.

"I hate her," Gideon cried, while Trey stood patiently by, offering what comfort he could, a lick to the boy's cheek, a paw raised to brush the side of his knee. *"I hate her!"*

Tentatively—after all, he'd been an absent father, and the fact that he'd had no clue that Gideon existed would make little difference to the child—Jack rested a hand on the kid's trembling shoulder.

Gideon was small for his age, and downright skinny.

Just as Jack had been, when he was twelve.

At sixteen, the growth hormones had kicked in.

Now he was still lean, but he stood six feet tall and he was muscular from years of working out, followed by months of manual labor on the rundown cattle ranch he was determined to restore.

He had plans for this place. Plans that had nothing to do with getting richer.

"That's okay," Jack said, at something of a loss. He wasn't Loreen Baker's greatest fan, but he didn't hate her, and he didn't think Gideon did, either.

"You didn't want me," Gideon accused, lifting his head from Trey's neck to glare at him. "Why didn't you want me?"

The question sundered Jack O'Ballivan's very soul. "I didn't know about you, son," he replied hoarsely. "If I had, I would have been part of your life from day one."

Something shifted in the child's freckled, tear-streaked face.

Suspicion? Hope? Jack couldn't tell.

Behind him, Loreen shouted, "Fine, then! No money, no kid! Come on, Gideon—we're getting out of here! *Let's go!*"

"Do you want to go with your mom?" Jack asked, very quietly. It seemed important to let the boy know he had *some* choice in the matter, even though Jack had no intention of letting him leave. "Because if you don't, you can stay right here, with me."

"Seriously? I can stay with you. And—and this dog?"

"His name is Trey," Jack said, with a slight grin. His emotions were scraped raw. "And, yes, we'd both like that a lot. If you stayed, I mean."

"I'm not an easy kid," Gideon warned solemnly. "I can be a lot of trouble."

Jack swallowed his grin and tried to look serious. "Is that right? Well, I wasn't an easy kid, either, so I guess you took after me."

Gideon's little face brightened a little. "Is this your ranch, or do you just work here?"

"It's mine."

"It's not in very good shape," the boy remarked, taking in the ancient ranch house and outbuildings before looking over at the nearly finished barn.

"*Gideon!*" Loreen screeched. "Get. In. The. Car! *Now!*"

Gideon's gaze slipped past Jack's face and found Loreen, though he didn't move, or answer her demand. Then he looked at Jack again. "I think you need help getting this place fixed up," he said solemnly. He paused to bite his lower lip. "I guess I'd better stick around and give you a hand."

Another lump formed in Jack's throat, and he had to swallow hard—and painfully—before he could make a reply. "That would be good," he said. "Really good. I could use another ranch hand, and I think you'd do just fine."

Loreen was coming in their direction; Jack sensed that, stood, and turned around, standing between Gideon and his mother.

When she opened her mouth and sucked in a breath to yell again, Jack cut her off.

"Get yourself a room in town for the night," he said evenly. "I'll arrange to meet with my lawyer tomorrow, so we can get the documents ready."

Briefly, very briefly, her expression lightened. Then she narrowed her eyes and said, "What about the check?"

"Trying to sell a child is illegal, Loreen," Jack replied. "Do you want to go to jail?"

"She's been in jail lots of times," Gideon put in. He was standing beside Jack by then.

"Shut up!" Loreen hissed, bending to glower into her son's face.

"And she's already *got* a motel room," the boy went on. Evidently, he felt safe speaking up, with his newfound father standing beside him. "It's dirty, and it smells like mildew."

"I told you to *shut up,*" Loreen shouted.

The kid wasn't backing down. He lifted his eyes to meet Jack's. "Her boyfriend, Brent, is there right now. He told her to make sure she got some money out of you and not to bring me back with her if she didn't want more trouble than she knew what to do with."

Loreen closed her eyes and rocked back on her heels. Swore copiously.

Just about then, three of the ranch hands rode in on mud-splattered horses, and they didn't even pretend not to notice the standoff in front of the barn.

With a flash of corny humor, Jack thought, *This ranch ain't big enough for the both of us, Miss Loreen.*

"Everything all right over there, Boss?" called Tom Winter Moon, the foreman and Jack's good friend.

"It's fine," Jack replied good-naturedly, raising his voice enough to be heard from a distance of a few hundred yards. "The lady was just leaving."

Loreen looked as though steam might shoot out of her ears, like in a cartoon. "I can't go back to that motel without money!" she cried, actually stomping one foot in frustration. "Brent will kick me out!"

Unhurriedly, Jack took his wallet from the back pocket of his jeans, extracted five twenty-dollar bills from it, and held them out to her.

Loreen snatched the money immediately, though she made it plain she wasn't satisfied. She gave her son a scathing once-over and told him, "Don't get too comfortable, buddy boy. If I don't walk out of that lawyer's office tomorrow with a check in my hand, you and I will be out of here before you can say Jack's-my-daddy."

Gideon moved a little closer to Jack, pressing into his side.

Trey gave a little yelp and positioned himself like a furry wall between Jack and Gideon and Loreen, who seemed to have forgotten that she'd wanted to dump her son and be foot-loose and fancy free, as the old saying went.

Jack bent far enough to ruffle the dog's ears. Trey was in protection mode, but he was scared, too. He wasn't used to the kind of energy Loreen was putting out; Diamond Creek Ranch was a safe place, a refuge.

"Go," Jack said, holding Loreen's frenzied gaze. "If you don't, I'll call the police. I'm pretty sure they'll take a genuine interest in you, Loreen. That Brent yahoo you mentioned, too, most likely."

Loreen paused, looking as though she was about to launch herself at Jack, claws out, and rake him bloody.

She opened her mouth, closed it again, and then turned and stomped off toward the driveway, where her rattletrap rust-bucket of a car was parked.

Jack held his breath, hoping the damned thing would start, and exhaled heavily when the motor sputtered to life and then roared as Loreen revved the engine. After shifting gears—a loud, grinding sound resulted—she made a snappy three-point turn and sped for the gate.

The rig fishtailed on the dirt road, flinging up dust in all directions, and tore away.

Jack squeezed Gideon's shoulder. "You okay, son?" he asked.

The boy looked up at him. Smiled sadly. "I think she was expecting you to follow her orders."

Jack smiled down at his son, ruffled his shaggy hair. "Hope she isn't holding her breath," he said.

Chapter 2

Harper Quinn opened the front door of the cottage she'd inherited from a distant relative—it was a fixer-upper by any definition—and felt a strange, sweet frisson of—*something* as she took in the man standing well back from the welcome mat, hands in the hip pockets of his battered blue jeans. His long-sleeved chambray shirt was open to reveal a worn T-shirt beneath, and the stubble on his chin matched his dark, longish hair.

He was accompanied by a young boy, ten to twelve years old, similarly clad, and a German shepherd with a graying muzzle and gentle eyes.

Ollie, Harper's teacup Yorkie, scrabbled at the heels of her sneakers, wanting to slip past and greet the visitors.

His yapping was making her low-grade headache worse, and the shepherd was big enough to swallow Ollie whole, so she stooped to gather him up. He squirmed and wriggled in protest, but at least the barking stopped.

"This is Trey," the boy said, patting his dog's head.

Benignly, Trey plunked himself down on the weathered

boards of the porch, tongue lolling, and in that moment, Harper would have sworn the critter was smiling.

Harper smiled, too, looking at the boy. "This is Ollie," she replied, taking one of his tiny paws between her thumb and index finger and waggling it briefly.

The man laughed, and the sound was rich and masculine. "Now that the dogs have been introduced," he said, still keeping his distance, "I'm Jack O'Ballivan, and this is my son, Gideon."

"Harper Quinn," Harper said, a bit puzzled. She was a city girl, unused to neighborly visits. In the Seattle high-rise where she'd lived until a few weeks before, she had only a nodding acquaintance with one or two of the other tenants.

"My dad owns all that land across the road," Gideon said, his expression solemn and his tone vaguely hesitant, as if he wasn't quite sure of his own words. "You can't see much from here, except maybe the barn roof, because of the trees. It's called Diamond Creek Ranch, and it's almost a thousand acres."

"Gideon," Jack said, in a tone of gentle reproof. "We're here to welcome Ms. Quinn and offer help, not to brag about the size of our property." He rested a hand on the boy's head and ruffled his hair, and Harper's discouraged heart warmed at the sight; in her former life as a social worker, she'd seen so many children neglected and abused that she'd almost forgotten how it looked when a parent showed such easy affection for their child.

Gideon smiled, but his mouth wobbled with the effort.

His father seemed to sense the boy's reticence, and pulled him to his side, held him there for a moment or so. His intensely blue eyes were fixed on Harper's face, and the lopsided grin on his attractive face held a modicum of sadness.

"Obviously," Jack O'Ballivan said quietly, "you were on your way out, so we won't keep you. We're throwing a shindig next weekend—a big bonfire, a barbecue, some games and even a dance, to celebrate finishing the new barn. If you'd like to join us, that would be great—half of Copper Ridge will be there, so you'll have a chance to meet a lot of the locals." With that, he tilted his head back and took in the sorry state of the cottage, with its sagging shutters and peeling paint. "And I can recommend a few contractors, if you're planning to renovate."

Harper *was* planning to renovate; it had been years since anyone had lived there, and the neglect showed. After the surprise notification that she'd been left a house and several acres of land in northern Arizona, she'd applied for and gotten a counseling job with the Copper Ridge school system.

"Ummm," she said, biting her lower lip. She wasn't sure she was up for a party, even if it would allow her to meet the attendees, some of whom were bound to be teachers, or parents of the children she would be working with in a month or so, when school started. "Okay. Thank you."

"Is that okay, you'll come to the party, or okay, go ahead and send over a contractor or two?"

Harper felt her cheeks flush. Her feet felt rooted to the floor. Jack O'Ballivan wasn't classically handsome; he was rugged and strong, and though he was lean and muscular, he seemed to take up a lot of space.

Maybe he knew he had that effect on some people, and had taken care to maintain a small distance so as not to overwhelm the newcomer to the neighborhood.

She recovered quickly and replied, "Both. The party sounds like a lot of fun, and as you can see, this place needs a ton of work. I've been here a week now, and I've done a lot of cleaning and painting, things like that, but the roof is in poor shape and the fireplace chimney"—she gestured toward the side of the cottage—"is crumbling. In fact, half of it is lying in the yard. So I do need to hire someone as soon as possible."

Bringing the place up to speed was going to take a chunk of her savings, but of course, she didn't share that.

Gideon and Trey were already walking away, toward the broken front gate. The picket fence zigged and zagged and stuck out in every direction but straight up.

Mr. O'Ballivan lingered, one foot on the ground, one on the porch step. He gave her a thumbs-up and smiled again.

"I have most of the construction workers in the area occupied, working over at my place, but I can spare a few guys."

Straining in Harper's arms, Ollie started wiggling and yapping again, most likely wanting to follow the boy and the other dog. Maybe Harper's best friend Devon had been right, and she should adopt a second dog to keep her Yorkie company.

Devon ran an animal rescue organization back in Seattle, where Harper had lived and worked until she'd made the decision to leave the city and make a whole new start in a state she'd never even visited before.

With the deed to her cottage in hand, she'd scanned the internet for job opportunities in the area.

She'd been interviewed for the position in Copper Ridge via Zoom and, much to her relief, had been hired almost immediately.

Then, after breaking the lease on her condo in Seattle and sending the few things she'd decided to keep on ahead to be stored in the cottage, she'd loaded Ollie and a couple of suitcases into her compact car and headed for Arizona.

It had seemed a practical plan at the time—the property, unsaleable as it stood, was worth fixing up, in her opinion, though it would be a lot of work. Ultimately, if things didn't work out there and she wanted to move on, it would probably be easy enough to sell the place.

All around, the restoration would make for a good long-term investment and, since it was only ten to fifteen minutes from the school buildings in town, the commute would be easy.

On top of that, the surrounding countryside was spectacular.

More difficult in winter, though. Elliott Parker, president of the school board, had warned her that the Arizona high country was considerably different, weather-wise, from the desert farther south.

Heavy snowfalls, even blizzards, were not uncommon in this part of the state.

Returning from her woolgathering with a jolt, Harper set Ollie down inside the house and shut the door behind her so he couldn't escape. He'd never lived in the country before, and she'd had to chase him through the underbrush twice since they'd arrived. Since his brain was roughly the size of a lima bean, he couldn't know he'd make the perfect snack for hawks and coyotes and a number of other wild creatures.

"I'm on my way to town to shop for groceries," she said, adjusting the shoulder strap of her handbag resolutely. "Do you need anything from the store, Mr. O'Ballivan?"

"Jack," he corrected her, looking amused. "We're neighbors, after all. Your place is right across the road from mine." A pause, a shake of his head, in response to some thought he evidently didn't plan to share. "Thanks for the offer, but with the party coming up, I'm planning to hit Costco, up in Flagstaff, and we're okay until then."

Harper nodded. Watched him walk away, stop at the edge of the wide dirt road between their properties, look both ways, and then follow his son and his dog to the other side, turning to wave once before he started up the long gravel driveway toward the house.

Behind her, Ollie barked; like most dogs, he didn't like being left behind.

He had plenty of food and water, though, and after a few

minutes, he would surely curl up in his velvety-soft little bed in a corner of the kitchen and snooze until he heard her pull into the limestone driveway beside the house later on.

Not for the first time, Harper questioned her decision to completely reinvent herself, moving to a new place, finding a new job.

It was a whole different way of life, rural and somewhat isolated.

Her old job had been a meaningful one, even if it had left her burnt out and broken.

She might have managed to return to work after she fell into a state of mental exhaustion, if her then-fiancé, George Carrington, hadn't decided to hook up with one of her coworkers, a woman named Brittany Summers, whom she'd considered a friend, if not an especially close one. George and Brittany had been involved for more than six months when Harper accidentally stumbled across the truth.

The romantic bubble had burst one evening when Harper had arrived home from an out-of-town conference a day early, planning to surprise George with his favorite meal, in honor of a recent promotion and his birthday, combined.

George worked hard as a real estate developer, and he loved surprises.

The shower in the adjoining bathroom was running when Harper walked into the master bedroom and tossed her suitcase onto the bed to unpack later.

She'd been on the verge of stripping down to the skin and joining her man under that warm spray of water when she heard a familiar laugh—a *female* laugh.

Fully clothed but barefoot—Harper hated wearing heels, so she'd kicked them off as soon as she stepped into the condo—she'd stood absolutely still for a few long moments, unsure whether she ought to barge in and confront George and the other woman, whoever she was, or turn and flee the scene.

She could have spent the night at Devon's place, or stayed with her older sister, Adelaide, and elderly aunt, Sylvia, her only living relatives.

But she'd been leaning on Devon too much lately, and she wasn't all that close to either her sister or her aunt.

In the end, she'd decided to stand her ground, face the facts, and deal with them.

She'd opened the bathroom door, stepped into the steamy room, and caught George and Brittany, a fellow social worker, naked and laughing as they lathered each other in the shower.

They'd spotted her right away, unsurprisingly, and both of them had frozen in place, their blurry images visible through the condensation on the glass door.

Belatedly, Brittany had covered her silicone-enhanced breasts.

George had hesitated, then reached for a towel and wrapped it around himself before stepping out onto the mat and uttering the classic trope, "I can explain everything. . . ."

On top of the pressures of her work—Harper was confronted with heartbreaking situations virtually every day—the affair was too much.

She'd been strong that night. She'd thrown her engagement ring in George's blandly handsome face and told him to take his bimbo and get out of her condo.

They'd dressed quickly and fled, while Harper had stood, arms folded and jaw tight, in the kitchen, trembling with shock and fury.

But in the coming days and weeks, despite her best efforts to hold it all together, she had gradually fallen apart.

She'd resigned from her job, holed up in her condo, and wallowed in depression for way too long.

Her friends had tried to help, and actually, so had Adelaide and Aunt Sylvia, but Harper had only withdrawn further into the darkness that seemed to swamp her very soul.

A few dreary weeks had passed when Devon had appeared

one sunny afternoon, with a very small dog prancing ahead of her on a leash.

"His name is Ollie," Devon had said, in her direct way, decisively opening the window blinds. "He's been abandoned—wait till you hear why—and he needs you as much as you need him."

Strangely, Harper had felt an instant connection with the puppy. He was so small that he literally fit in the palm of her hand.

She hadn't thought of herself as a dog person, but that was before she met Ollie.

"Normally," Devon had gone on, setting two bags with pet-shop logos on the floor, "I wouldn't place an animal without the usual protocol, but it isn't as if I don't know you, and the minute that woman walked into the center with Ollie peeking out of her designer handbag and said she wanted to re-home him, my mind was made up."

Harper's lethargy had abated enough for her to nestle the tiny fellow in the curve of her arm and ask, "Why didn't she want him?"

Devon had begun to laugh then, very softly, but at the same time, tears had glimmered in her bright brown eyes. "Are you ready? Because he *poops.* He made a mess in her Hermès bag, and she's going to have to have the silk lining replaced. Obviously, that will be expensive."

"Well," Harper had responded, with a lightness she hadn't felt in weeks, "that's a first-world problem if I've ever heard one."

"I can't stand people who think of animals as accessories instead of living creatures," Devon had declared. "And you wouldn't believe how many purebred dogs and cats land on the doorstep at the center because of things like this. Dogs that bark. Cats that throw up on the Persian rug. It's ludicrous."

Just then, Ollie had climbed onto Harper's shoulder and tentatively licked her cheek.

"He's adorable," she'd said.

Devon had sunk into a nearby armchair, looking relieved. "You'll keep him, then? If you need a trial period—"

But Harper had shaken her head and stroked Ollie's black-and-tan fur. "No trial period. Ollie is my dog now, and he's not going anywhere."

Harper returned from memory lane with a snap and tightened her grip on the steering wheel of her small hybrid. She'd driven all the way into Copper Ridge with her brain wandering around in the past.

She pulled into the parking lot at the supermarket—there were only two in the entire town—and went inside.

While shopping, she encountered Dot Mansfield, one of the teachers she would be working with in the Copper Ridge school system. They'd met two days before, at a little tea party held by the superintendent and his wife, and Harper had taken an instant liking to the woman, a trim and active person in her fifties, and a lifelong resident of the town.

"Don't forget to come to the book club," Dot exclaimed, after a hearty hello in the aisle containing cleaning supplies. "We're meeting tomorrow night at seven, at my place." Here, she repeated the address, which Harper committed to memory. "And we always have a potluck supper."

Harper smiled. "What if I haven't read the book you're discussing?" she asked, loading a set of mop heads into her cart. "Maybe I should wait until next month to join."

"Nonsense," Dot replied, beaming friendliness like a lighthouse on a dark pinnacle. "Seven o'clock. We'll be discussing—oh, dear, the title escapes me, but it's something about a highway."

Harper guessed the title, but kept it to herself. It was a recent bestseller, *The Lincoln Highway,* about two young brothers on the road, and their adventures, and she'd read it months ago.

"I'll be there," she confirmed.

Dot wasn't through with the impromptu chat. "Have you met Jack O'Ballivan yet? The man who owns the land just across from your cottage? He's a relative newcomer, like you. Plans to turn that rundown old place into a working ranch—but he'll also be helping out with a foundation that specializes in horseback riding therapy for people of all ages. And he's throwing a party this coming weekend—seems like half the county is invited, and the other half can show up anyhow, if they want to."

"I met Mr. O'Ballivan today. Him and his son, Gideon."

"Gideon," Dot murmured, looking genuinely sad. "That poor child's been through a lot. Rumor has it that his mother dropped him off at the ranch and signed over custody the very next day. She's a wild one—carried on something terrible in front of the whole town, her and that boyfriend of hers, before they finally left." Here, Dot paused, brightened. "Well, Gideon will be in my class, and I've got a feeling I'm going to like him, though he's sure to be a handful."

Harper straightened her back and smiled, thinking of the boy, and the pride he took in the land his father owned. The way he'd stroked his dog and asked about Ollie.

"Maybe so," she said. "But we're up to the challenge, aren't we?"

Dot's high-wattage smile flashed again. "You bet we are," she replied.

Chapter 3

Sound asleep, Gideon resembled a ragamuffin angel, Jack reflected, with both sadness and love, as he stood beside his son's bed, full of silent wonder. And he was still scrambled emotionally.

In the week since Loreen had literally dumped their son at Jack's feet, he'd done his level best to keep things on an honest, healthy course, but it hadn't been easy.

Not that he'd expected it to be, but he hadn't quite anticipated the degree of difficulty, either.

Leaving the unfinished room in the new part of the house—like the rest of the space, it was under renovation—Jack found his dog waiting patiently at the end of the hallway. It was getting dark, but Trey was always up for exploring the property, and Jack himself felt the need of fresh air and open spaces.

"Let's go," he said, with deep affection, bending to ruffle Trey's floppy ears.

Trey gave a yip of good-natured enthusiasm and scrabbled at the door with one paw.

Jack chuckled. "Right," he muttered, moving in that direction and not bothering with the seldom-used leash. Trey never wandered so far that a shrill whistle wouldn't bring him bounding back to Jack's side in moments. "Come on, then. We'll head down to the creek for a few minutes, your favorite place to hang out."

Trey padded happily along behind as they left the house.

In the backyard, which, like most of the property, was covered with construction materials, equipment, and the three small house trailers that, combined, served as a temporary bunkhouse arrangement for Tom and the other ranch hands, Jack drew in a deep, restorative breath.

Tom Winter Moon's mother, Sadie, who lived in town but visited the ranch a lot, was sitting in a lawn chair in front of her son's trailer, smoking a cigarette.

"You going off someplace and leaving that boy all alone?" she asked, without preamble. Sadie had a few rough edges but, basically, she was a good person.

"He's asleep," Jack answered, slowing his pace. Smiling and patting his shirt pocket. "Anyway, I bought him a phone, and if he needs me, all he has to do is call or text, and I'll be with him in a flash. He knows that."

Sadie shook her head. "You do remember that his mom used to go off and leave him all by himself for days at a time, right?"

Inwardly, Jack bristled a little, though his smile held. Trey, already at the edge of the old orchard, stopped and lifted his hind leg alongside the gnarled trunk of an apple tree. "Yes, Sadie," Jack said patiently, "I'm well aware of that. It's one of the many reasons why he's living with me now."

"What if he wakes up and you're nowhere around?"

Jack sighed. "He'll be fine, Sadie. He's twelve years old, not two. And, yes, he's got a lot of problems, thanks to Loreen, but he's also pretty self-reliant. That's a trait I want to encourage."

Sadie tossed her cigarette down and ground it out with the

heel of her thick-soled shoe. "That's all well and good, but he's still a kid—an *insecure* kid."

Before Jack could frame an answer to that, his friend and foreman, Tom, stuck his head out the trailer door and said, "Mom. Rein it in, will you? Jack knows what he's doing."

At that, Sadie subsided, but by the way she tilted her head toward the main house, Jack knew she would be right there, watching and listening for trouble until he got back.

That was fine with him.

Beside the creek, which flowed just on the other side of the neglected orchard, the fish were jumping at mosquitoes and other flying insects, and the closer he came to the water, the more he had to slap at his bare forearms and his neck.

Trey, covered in fur, was, of course, impervious to mosquito bites. He sniffed the ground, checking the premises for unauthorized visitors, like squirrels and field mice, and when a crow landed in one of the nearby cottonwood trees and squawked a complaint, he barked.

Between sudden fatherhood and all the work of restoring the ranch to its former glory, Jack had been busy—too busy. He had a semitruck load of cattle arriving in the next few days—the first of several—and he needed to hire more help.

On top of all that, there was the upcoming party.

He'd probably jumped the gun, setting that big of an event in motion when so many other things were going on, but getting to know the locals was part of his plan to leave the financial rat race behind and establish an authentic, boots-on-the-ground life—or better yet, a boots-in-the-stirrups life—for himself, and now, of course, for Gideon, too.

Ready to return to the house, shower, and make it an early night, he whistled for Trey and headed in that direction. Obediently, the dog bounded along behind him.

Trey was getting up there in years, but he was still spry.

As he made his way through the deep grass and underbrush,

Jack decided he'd bring the boy down to the creek when time allowed, so they could do some fishing.

That had been one of the ways Jack had bonded with his own father, while he was growing up. An only child, Jack had lost his mother to pneumonia when he was seven, and after that, it had been him and his dad against the world.

For all that he'd missed having a mom, like most of the kids he knew, Jack had been raised in a loving home. Andrew O'Ballivan, his dad, now gone, had seen to that.

They had gone fishing together. Built furniture in the well-equipped basement of the family home. Taken road trips, stopping at every weird roadside attraction along the way.

See the Two-Headed Cow, 50 Cents!
World's Longest Snake, $1.00!

There had been dozens of them, each one a scam, each one fun simply because he and his dad were checking it out together.

I miss you, Dad, he thought. *And I want to be the same kind of father to Gideon that you were to me.*

If he never accomplished anything else, Jack was determined to raise his son to be strong, honest, secure in his own skin, able to cope with whatever came his way.

Of course, given the damage Loreen and her boyfriends had done to the boy, bringing him up was bound to be a major challenge.

He and Gideon were already in counseling—Jack had made that a priority, and they'd already had two intense sessions—but that was only the bare beginning of all that needed to be done.

Gideon didn't seem to mind being alone at times, but he had the inevitable abandonment issues. He'd been yanked out of school so many times, whenever Loreen decided to hit the road again, that he'd probably be in special-education classes when school started.

By his own admission, Gideon had never had friends, and it was easy to figure out why: he'd never lived in one place long enough to make any. That, along with the constant uncertainty and upheaval, meant he'd never developed social skills appropriate to his age and, according to the therapist, he might even be on the autism spectrum, though he was clearly high-functioning.

Whatever other struggles he might be dealing with, Gideon was smart. *Very* smart.

Approaching the house through the gathering dusk, Jack saw that every light in the place was on.

Sadie was no longer sitting in her lawn chair, keeping her vigil. No doubt, the mosquitoes had driven her back inside the trailer, despite her best intentions.

Jack quickened his step a little, opened the back door, and found Gideon sitting glumly at the kitchen table.

Like the other rooms in the house, it was a bare-bones space, with a plain wooden floor and drywall on all sides.

"Where did you go, Jack?" the boy asked.

"That's 'Dad' to you, buddy," Jack replied, though gently. He approached the table and sat down next to his son. "What's up?"

Sadie's concerns came to mind, and he felt a pang of guilt. He'd been so sure Gideon would be okay on his own, but here the kid was, out of bed, pale and wide-eyed, with the house lit up like a jack-o'-lantern.

"I needed a drink of water," the boy said, in a strangely detached tone of voice. "So I got up and I came out here to the kitchen, because I don't like to drink bathroom water, and you weren't here. You weren't anywhere. And Trey was gone, too."

At the mention of his name, and perhaps because he sensed Gideon's mood, Trey moved close to the boy's chair and laid his muzzle on his lap.

Distractedly, Gideon stroked the dog's head.

"I told you things would be different with me," Jack reminded the child gently. "I'm not going to leave you. Not ever."

"Mom used to say that, too," Gideon pointed out. "Then she'd disappear. Once, when she took off with one of her boyfriends, I didn't have anything to eat but dry cereal for a whole week."

"I'm not your mom, Gideon."

The boy's expression was a little obstinate, and under other circumstances, that would have amused Jack, because it was like looking into his own much younger face. "Where did you go?" he asked.

"Just down to the creek." Jack indicated the direction with a motion of his thumb. "No farther than that."

In that moment, he wished Gideon was small enough to hold on his lap, but he knew any such move would be a mistake, because being touched was another of the boy's issues. As far as the therapist had been able to discern, Gideon had never been molested, but he *had* been jerked around, slapped, and shaken, possibly from infancy.

God only knew how deeply he'd been scarred.

"I guess you wouldn't go off and leave this ranch and all the cattle and horses and everything."

"I wouldn't go off and leave *you,* Gideon. You're more important to me than any of those things."

Gideon looked hopeful and skeptical, both at once. His blue eyes were huge in his small, freckled face. "Where *were* you, though? Why did you leave me with her?"

"We've been over this, son. Your mother was expecting you when we split up, but she never told me. I had no idea you existed until the day she brought you here."

"You don't have a wife," the boy reasoned. "You don't have

any other kids. So maybe you didn't want a family. Maybe you're just being nice and you don't want *me,* either."

"I don't have a wife, or other kids, because I never met the right woman."

"I can help you find a wife—how about Harper Quinn?" Gideon surmised solemnly, looking more like a little college professor than the scrawny preteen boy he was. "She's pretty, and she's nice."

"Whoa," Jack said, with a chuckle. "Ms. Quinn *is* pretty, and she's nice, too, it would seem. But we hardly know her. For all we can tell, she already has a man in her life, or doesn't want one."

Gideon shook his head. "I don't think so."

"Why's that?"

"Because she's *lonely.* And she's sad about something. *Really* sad."

We're all sad about something, Jack reflected, with a silent sigh.

"Maybe, maybe not," he said aloud.

"You just have to look in her eyes," Gideon persisted. "You'll see."

"That's kind of a stretch, isn't it? Reading somebody's feelings just by looking?"

"No, it *isn't* a stretch. I'm an expert."

Jack suppressed a startled chuckle that might have morphed into a guffaw. "Is that so?"

"I *told* you. I can tell what people are like by looking in their eyes."

"Okay," Jack said, folding his arms on the tabletop and leaning in a little, while keeping his eyes wide open. "What am I like?"

Gideon studied him very seriously. "You're strong," he concluded, after some moments had gone by. "And you like being who you are."

"You mean to say I'm conceited?" Jack was teasing, but

Gideon's expression didn't change. If anything, it was more speculative than ever.

"No. If you were somebody else, instead of you, and you met the person you are now, you'd be friends with him."

Jack paused to take that in. It made his head spin a little, to tell the truth.

"Want to know what I see when I look into *your* eyes?" he countered, when he found the words.

Gideon frowned. "What?" he asked.

Jack made a show of looking.

"I see a good kid," he said, at last. "A kid who's been through some rough stuff, but still cares about people. And dogs."

"How do you know I'm like that?" Gideon wanted to know. He'd brightened a little, though, as if pleased by Jack's assessment of his character.

"By the way you treat Trey, for one thing," Jack replied, with quiet conviction. "You're probably pretty angry at the whole world, deep down inside, because of the way you've been treated, and that turns some people mean. But not you."

Gideon looked down. "I think I'm a mess."

Jack reached over, gave the boy's shoulder a brief squeeze. "That's not what I see when I look at you," he said and, once again, the backs of his eyes burned something fierce. "When I look at you, Gideon O'Ballivan, I see somebody special. Somebody good and strong and smart."

Gideon blinked then, and his eyes glistened. "My last name is O'Ballivan? Just like yours?"

The appropriate paperwork had already been filed.

"Of course it is," Jack answered, his voice so hoarse he had to clear his throat before he could go on. "You're my son."

He hadn't needed a DNA test to know this was true.

Gideon was, as Jack's dad would have said, the spitting image.

Gideon sat up a little straighter. "What does that mean, to be an O'Ballivan?"

"It means you come from a long line of good, sturdy, strong-minded people," Jack replied. "And it means I love you."

A silence fell between them then, heavy but not sad.

When he'd recovered a little, Jack went on. "Let me tell you about your great-great-great grandfather, Sam O'Ballivan. There might be a few other greats in there, because old Sam lived way back in the nineteenth century. He was a genuine hero, an Arizona Ranger—"

Chapter 4

Harper had enjoyed the book club meeting at Dot's place, and she'd already ordered next month's reading choice from Amazon. Although the other members were still acquaintances, instead of actual friends, they were all interesting people, and she looked forward to getting to know them better.

Now a few days had passed, and it was almost time to cross the road and attend Jack O'Ballivan's party.

She was standing in her bedroom, which she had practically stripped bare, intending to peel off the dizzying wallpaper and paint. A new bedroom set, Country French in design, was to be delivered in a little over two weeks.

In the meantime, she'd been using a folding cot and a sleeping bag, and she had the sore muscles to prove it.

As she removed the third cotton sundress she'd tried on in the last half hour, Ollie watched her intently from the cot, his tiny ears perked.

"Don't judge me," Harper told her dog, as she reached for a fourth sundress—blue, with white polka dots and a few strategically placed ruffles. "I want to make a good impression on the other neighbors, that's all. It's not about Jack."

Ollie tilted his head to one side, as though questioning the veracity of her words.

The blue dress was flattering enough, but was it suitable for an outdoor party celebrating the completion of a barn? What if she arrived on the scene and found everyone else dressed country-style, in jeans and boots and the like, while she minced along in strappy sandals and a semi-frilly dress and sandals?

She'd feel like a fool.

She didn't want to come off as *citified,* even though she was.

Exasperated with herself, Harper plunked down on the window seat, which looked out over the front yard, the road, and the part of Diamond Creek Ranch where the house and the barn and several trailers stood. Everything was mostly hidden behind a row of tall pine trees.

All that day, various vehicles had been coming and going, churning up clouds of dust as they traversed Jack's driveway. So far, she'd spotted several catering vans, a truck pulling a long horse trailer, and two eighteen-wheelers, one full of bawling cattle, the other hauling what looked like an actual *carousel,* dismantled but probably ready for quick assembly.

The sounds of hammering and sawing weren't so unusual, given that the main house, which Harper had learned was under massive renovation, was constantly being worked on. Still, they were definitely extra.

All of it was extra, over-the-top extra.

And Harper was ridiculously nervous. So nervous that she wished she'd made up some excuse so she could stay home and watch Hallmark movies on her laptop instead of crossing the road and whooping it up with the locals.

It wasn't like her to be shy and self-conscious.

She was, after all, a qualified counselor with a master's degree in psychology, and she'd worked as a social worker in Seattle, a nitty-gritty job that had taken her into all sorts of settings and situations, many of which could be considered dangerous.

There was Pioneer Square, for instance. That section of downtown Seattle, once a place brimming with upscale boutiques, eclectic little shops, business offices, and specialty restaurants, was now the province of the city's growing homeless population, many of whom were addicted to drugs and/or alcohol. Thus, there were so many panhandlers around that a person couldn't walk from one corner to another without being hectored with aggressive demands for money.

Children were a part of this tragic equation, of course, and it had fallen to Harper and her colleagues to wade in and advocate for them, which, for the most part, seemed totally ineffective. Several times, with the much-needed help of the police, she'd had to remove frightened kids from back-alley tents and lean-tos or abandoned buildings where the desperate, young and old, took refuge.

Just remembering all she'd heard and seen in those places brought tears to her eyes, and she felt a pang of terrible guilt because she'd finally had to turn her back and walk away, when there were still so many people who needed help.

You can't save the world, she reminded herself now, and for the umpteenth time since she'd left her old life in Seattle.

Yet again, she summed up her blessings.

She had this little cottage, rundown as it was.

She'd hired a contractor to rebuild the fireplace and chimney first, then go on to make multiple other changes.

And she had a job; in just a few weeks, she would begin serving as a family resource specialist/counselor in all three of Copper Ridge's schools—elementary, middle, and high school.

She could make a difference in the lives of a lot of kids.

She was beginning to settle in, make friends.

So why was she sitting here, fretting over what to wear to a party, for heaven's sake?

Feeling better, she stood up, crossed to the cot, picked Ollie up in her arms, and nuzzled his furry neck.

"You're right," she said. "I'm being silly."

Ollie licked her cheek, then wiggled, wanting to be put down.

Harper hauled the sundress off over her head and, along with the others she'd tried on, returned it to the closet.

Then she kicked her sandals in after them.

When she set out for Jack O'Ballivan's forty-five minutes later, having waited until there were cars lining the driveway and both sides of the road, she was wearing jeans, sneakers, and a red tank top under a matching lightweight cotton shirt. Her hair, piled on top of her head before, was now in a ponytail, and her makeup was minimal.

She carried a plastic-covered bowl filled with freshly made Waldorf salad, although it was pretty plain from the delicious smells tinging the air that there would be no shortage of food.

It wasn't dark yet, but the party was in full swing when Harper reached the top of the driveway.

It was like stepping into a carnival.

People were playing horseshoes, and the clang of metal against metal rang out like the peals of a church bell. Other games, complete with prizes, were being played in various makeshift booths.

There were picnic tables everywhere, and in the near distance, the carousel emitted a merry tune as it turned, practically overflowing with children of all ages.

Parents attended the little ones, standing beside beautifully carved horses and giraffes, elephants, and in between, benches and life-sized teacups.

Harper was slightly overwhelmed, trying to take in her surroundings; she actually felt a little dizzy, and gripped her bowl of salad hard, lest she drop it into the sawdust-strewn barnyard.

She might have been gaping when she realized someone was speaking to her.

"Harper?"

Harper blinked. Refocused her scattered attention.

Jack was standing directly in front of her, and she wondered how she could have missed him.

He was wearing jeans and a green T-shirt with a logo on the front, a drawing of a faceted gemstone in the midst of a flowing stream.

Diamond Creek Ranch.

Well, duh.

"I brought Waldorf salad," she said, and handed it to him.

Jack pretended to stumble backward, gripped the bowl in both hands, and laughed. "Okay," he said. "Thanks and welcome."

Harper felt her cheeks burning. To her left were long buffet tables, brimming with food. To her right was the barbecue setup, and just beyond it stood a combination bar and soft-drink stand.

"I guess it isn't a potluck," she said, and felt lame for showing up with Tupperware.

Jack peeled back the lid and peered in at the salad she'd prepared earlier in the day. "My favorite," he said, just as Gideon appeared, with Trey at his side.

He was wearing a T-shirt just like his father's.

"Didn't you bring your dog?" Gideon asked, studying Harper with concern.

She instantly relaxed. She was always comfortable around kids.

"Nope," she said, with a smile and a shake of her head. "He's holding down the fort."

Jack nudged his son and grinned down at him. "Do me a

favor, will you, son?" he said, holding out the Waldorf salad in its sealed plastic bowl. "Take this to the house and put it in the fridge before somebody decides to help themselves. I'm greedy enough to want all of it for us."

Gideon looked pleased and a little relieved, and it occurred to Harper that she wasn't the only one feeling slightly intimidated by the event unfolding around them.

With a nod, he took the container and headed for the house, Trey galloping along behind him.

Jack sighed, watching the boy and dog disappear into the crowd.

"Is something wrong?" Harper asked.

Jack met her gaze, sighed again. "I'm thinking this get-together might be too much, too soon, for Gideon," he confided quietly. "He's still adjusting to having a father, living in a new place, all that."

Harper knew a little about the situation with Jack and his son, thanks to Dot—how the boy's mother had basically abandoned him in Jack's care a few weeks before—but that was the extent of it, since she hadn't encountered this intriguing man again since the day he and Gideon had come to the cottage to introduce themselves and offer the help of some of the construction people.

"The important thing is, he *has* a father," she said, at some length. "It's going to take time for him to learn to trust that."

"Yeah," Jack sighed.

People passing by stopped to greet Jack, slap him on the shoulder, thank him for inviting them to the party. He was friendly to all of them, but when they'd moved on, he was still standing square in front of Harper, and she hadn't moved, either.

"He likes you," Jack told her, his voice slightly gruff. "Gideon, I mean."

"I like him, too," Harper said. She didn't know the child

very well, but she was a sucker for kids. That was one of the reasons she'd stayed in a high-stress, heartrending job for so long.

And I like you, she added silently.

"Dot told me you'll be working as a sort of counselor for the school district starting in September."

"That's true," Harper said, beginning to wonder if she was right in thinking this conversation was headed in a definite direction that had nothing to do with barn dances and barbecues, bonfires and carousels.

Jack shoved a hand through his dark hair, looked away, looked back. "We're both in therapy," he said, after yet another sigh, "Gideon and I, but Gideon is still holding his cards close to his chest. And, as I said, he likes you. I was wondering if—well—if he wanted to talk things over with you, things he might not be comfortable saying to me—"

"He can talk to me anytime," she put in, when Jack's words fell away. In those moments, she felt sorry for both father and son; building a healthy relationship would be no easy task. Then she touched his arm. "But don't pressure him, Jack. Things like this have to unfold at their own pace. They can't be forced."

"I understand that," Jack said. "But it's killing me, just the same. I could have been there for him, and I wasn't."

Twilight was beginning to gather in the folds of the surrounding hills, all purple and apricot splendor, and somewhere beyond the whirling carousel, someone was tuning a fiddle.

People began to line up at the buffet tables and crowd in around the barbecue stand.

"It's not your fault, Jack. What matters is what you do now."

Jack smiled again, and then he took Harper gently by the elbow. "Let me show you around," he said.

Harper didn't hesitate. Just being close to this man felt

strangely, sweetly *right.* So she allowed him to lead her away from the center of the hubbub.

They started with the house, although they didn't go inside.

Though clearly in need of work, the structure had an innate appeal; it was a one-story home, built of gray stone, with mullioned windows and a newly constructed wraparound porch.

According to Jack, it dated back to the 1870s, and it had a colorful history.

He'd bought the property a year before, though the renovations had begun months later, and he hoped most of the work on the house would be done before winter.

"It's a pretty big place," Harper said, when they started back toward the party, which was really revving up by then, brimming with laughter and music and the clatter of plates and glasses. "Just for you and Gideon, I mean."

Jack took her hand, held it briefly, let it go again. "I'm planning on putting it to good use," he said. "When the buildings are finished, there will be a therapeutic riding school here, for one thing."

Harper's breath caught, even though she'd heard about the plan from Dot. "Really? Oh, Jack, that's a *wonderful* idea!"

"I've been lucky," Jack answered, with a shrug-like motion of one shoulder. "This is my way of giving back."

Harper was secretly relieved. She'd wondered if the place would evolve into a dude ranch, a tourist attraction. And the truth was, she'd dreaded that possibility, since it would have meant a lot of noise and traffic.

"It will be so good for Gideon to be part of something like this," she said, wishing he'd take her hand again, and suddenly too shy to take his.

Jack nodded in agreement. "It will," he said. "Naturally, now that he's part of my life, he's my biggest priority. But even before he showed up, I wanted a way to lend a hand. Leave the world a little better than I found it, when my time comes. And to honor my dad's memory, too, I guess. He was a good man."

Harper felt a twinge of sorrow for her own parents, who had died in a boating accident when she was thirteen, but she didn't dwell on the loss at that moment, because she was processing what Jack had just told her.

It made her want to know him better, and then better still.

She was still mulling that thought over when the yelling started.

Chapter 5

Jack recognized his son's voice instantly; Gideon was bursting with rage, out of control.

The words being shouted back and forth between the combatants were unintelligible from that distance, but the message was clear enough; here were two young boys bent on taking each other apart, stitch and seam.

Trey's anxious bark underscored the urgency of the situation.

Jack bolted in the direction of the ruckus—it was coming from behind the line of game booths nearest the carousel—and when he arrived, closely followed by Harper and a throng of other people, he saw that Tom Winter Moon had gotten there first.

Tom was holding the two boys apart, with a firm grip on the backs of their dirty shirts, and when he saw Jack, he relaxed his hold only slightly, because both kids were still straining to get at each other.

Gideon was a head shorter than the other boy; blood dribbled from the side of his mouth, and a bruise was already blossoming under his right cheekbone, but his eyes stormed with fury, barely contained.

Here we go, Jack thought grimly. So far, dealing with his son had been fairly easy, but now there was a definite hitch in the process.

What he did next would matter, he knew that, and the thought was sobering.

He had virtually no experience as a father—suppose he got this wrong?

There was no time to consider the question. He went directly to his son, facing him, torn between anger and an unreasonable need to send the other kid packing, tell him to get off the ranch and never show his face there again.

Of course, he didn't do that.

Tom let go of Gideon's shirt and moved away, but at the periphery of his vision, Jack noticed Harper standing nearby. Before he could speak, she reached out, laid a hand lightly and briefly on his right forearm.

"Breathe," she said softly, and through the blood pounding in his head, he heard her.

He sucked in a breath, let it go slowly.

"What just happened here?" he asked Gideon, his voice very quiet.

Gideon didn't answer; instead, he scrambled to get around Jack, clearly intending to pummel his opposition to the ground.

Jack caught him by the back of his shirt and pulled him back again.

"I asked you a question, son," he said evenly.

Having gotten a closer look, he could see that the small cut at the edge of Gideon's lower lip wasn't serious; no stitches would be needed. And he realized that what he'd thought was his own anger had actually been alarm, fear that this little stranger he loved so much might be badly hurt.

Gideon spat in the dirt, narrowly missing Jack's boot. When

the kid lifted his gaze to his father's face, his expression was defiant, and his eyes blazed a fiery blue.

It was at that moment that the other boy threw himself in Gideon's direction.

Young as the kids were, it took both Jack and Tom Winter Moon to restrain them and keep them apart.

"That's it," Jack said, forcing the words through clenched teeth. "Head for the house, Gideon. Right *now.*"

Tears welled in Gideon's eyes then, but they were plainly tears of frustration, not shame or regret.

As he and Gideon passed through the concerned crowd, Jack murmured apologies to those looking on, and reminded them to enjoy the party.

For the bystanders, at least, the drama was over.

For Jack and Gideon, it was just beginning.

When they entered the house through the back way, Jack let the screen door slam behind him. He'd seen Loreen's temper in action, and he wasn't going to let Gideon go down that trail.

"Sit," Jack ordered, in a near growl.

Gideon obeyed, but he made a lot of noise scraping a chair back from the table.

Trey, who hadn't been able to keep up, probably because there were so many people out there, pawed at the screen door.

Jack let him in, then went back to the drawer he'd just wrenched open and rummaged for bandages and disinfectant cream.

"I'll ask you again," he said. "What happened out there?"

Gideon said nothing, but the tears were still flowing, trickling between the flecks of sawdust on his face.

"You can stonewall all you want, bucko," Jack said, peeling a half dozen paper towels off the roll and wetting them under the faucet. "But you won't be able to outlast me, I promise you that."

Gideon was silent while Jack dabbed at his cut with the paper towel, patted the area dry, and then applied a dab of disinfectant.

The kid winced.

Jack applied a bandage, then handed Gideon the wet paper towel, and the boy wiped his eyes.

"I hate that kid," Gideon announced, after a few moments of fast, shallow breathing, and Jack realized then that he couldn't lay all the blame for Gideon's temper at Loreen's feet. He himself came from a long line of stubborn men and women.

Jack pulled back a chair, sat astraddle of it, and kept his gaze fixed on his son. "You don't know him well enough to hate him," he said. "Talk to me, Gideon."

Gideon bit his lower lip, winced again. It was starting to swell, and the bruise on his cheek was streaked with purple and green, with an odd glow about it.

"I'm in trouble," he replied, his gaze dropping to Trey, who was keeping a vigil beside his chair. "Go ahead and hit me."

Something plummeted deep inside Jack, and never hit bottom. He felt the now-familiar burning behind his eyes.

"I'm not about to hit you," Jack replied.

Gideon looked up, clearly surprised. "Really? I just got in a fight and wrecked your fancy party. If Tom had stayed out of the way, I would have whipped Riley Carlisle's butt!"

"You're giving yourself too much credit," Jack said matter-of-factly, fighting back a grin. "You're not badass enough to wreck this party all by yourself." A pause. "Just listen. Hear the music? The laughter? The clanging of the horseshoes against the iron pipes Tom drove into the ground yesterday?"

Gideon slumped a little. Nodded grudgingly.

"You realize," Jack went on, when the boy stayed mum, "that you and that Carlisle kid will probably be in the same class at school, come next month?"

The kid straightened his spine, jutted out his chin. "Yeah," he said, with lots of bravado. "And if I can't tear him a new one today, I'll do it on the playground, first time I see him."

"So," Jack said, in a speculative tone, stretching the word a little, "I guess you want to grow up to be like—what was his name again? Your mom's boyfriend? Oh, yeah. Brent. You want to be like that guy. A thug." Here, he heaved a heavy sigh. "Poor old Sam O'Ballivan must be rolling over in his grave."

Gideon's eyes widened, and color flared in his cheeks. "*No!*" he protested, with a vehemence that pleased Jack, though he didn't let it show. "Brent's a jerk, and he's mean!"

Jack raised his eyebrows, pretending to be confused. "Well, son, if you go around hating people, and looking for chances to knock their lights out, you're going to wind up like Brent and a few other guys you've probably gotten to know, living with your mother."

"No *way*!" Gideon practically howled the words.

"Way," Jack replied.

"Are you saying you've never been in a fight?" Gideon challenged, leaning forward a little in his chair.

"No," Jack answered. "I'm not. I *will* say, though, that unless a man's defending himself or somebody else, fighting is wrong. It never leads anywhere good—jail, maybe, or the emergency room at the nearest hospital."

"I *was* defending myself," Gideon said fiercely. His color was still high, and his eyes flashed.

"And?" Jack prompted, with hard-won patience.

Gideon shuffled his feet back and forth, kicking the legs of his chair. Damn, but he was a bull-headed kid. Turn all that hard-headed will in the right direction, and Gideon O'Ballivan would grow up to be a fine man, a force for good in the world.

Finally, he opened up. "He said it's all over town that my mom is a whore and you probably aren't really my dad. So *I* said he was stupider than a clod of dirt and couldn't find his own ass with both hands if he tried."

Jack felt his heart fracture. Again. "Is that what started this row? Riley calling your mom names? Saying I'm not your dad?"

Gideon shook his head, looking forlorn now. "No," he said. "I told him I was getting my own horse, and you were going to teach me to ride. That's all. But he got real mad and shoved me and said some kids have all the luck. Then he told me him and his mom live in a shack on the other side of Copper Ridge and he never gets anything but hand-me-downs and grub from the food bank. I told *him* what it was like living with Mom—you know, to show him it wasn't just him going through hard stuff, and that things can change, like they did for me. That was when he hauled off and popped me one in the face. Then I got mad, too, and we started hollering and swinging at each other."

"I see," Jack said thoughtfully. This was the most Gideon had ever said to him at one time, and he didn't want to staunch the flow by saying too much.

"So, like I said, I'm in trouble, even if you aren't going to hit me?" Gideon asked. He didn't shrink from the answer; his manner was forthright and, at the same time, innocent.

"Not this time," Jack replied. "But if you go after the Carlisle kid when you see him again, you'll be grounded until three weeks after the Second Coming."

"What's that?" Gideon wanted to know, wrinkling his nose comically. "The Second Coming of what?"

Jack wasn't about to attempt an explanation, not then at least, but he made up his mind in that moment to start attending church again, and see that Gideon got to Sunday school.

He needed to set a good example for his son, and it wouldn't hurt him to up his spiritual game a little, either.

"Can I go back to the party?"

Jack answered with questions of his own. "You want to? You're ready to show some manners, act like a host instead of a brawler?"

Gideon shrugged his narrow shoulders. "As long as Riley

doesn't come at me again. If he does that, I'm going to punch him out. You can't expect me to just stand there and let him wail on me."

Not for the first time, Jack had to suppress a grin. "Just stay clear of him, and remember one thing."

Gideon was on his feet. "What's that?"

"I *am* your father."

"I know," Gideon replied, somewhat to Jack's surprise.

"You do?"

"Sure."

They hadn't had a DNA test done yet. "How?" Jack pressed quietly.

"Look in a mirror, man. We're the same, except you're big and I'm little. Everybody says so." The kid grinned his slanted O'Ballivan grin. "Except Riley Carlisle, anyhow."

Jack had to look away for a moment, and his voice was hoarse when he spoke. "Go and wash up," he said. "You look like you've been rolling around in the barnyard. Which, of course, you have."

Gideon was out of his chair, and halfway across the kitchen, heading for his room, when he suddenly stopped, turned, and ran back to Jack.

The boy threw his arms around Jack's middle, squeezed once, and then left the room, with Trey trotting happily behind him.

After splashing his face with cold water at the kitchen sink, Jack went outside again. There, he circulated, greeting people, shaking hands, and keeping an eye out for Riley Carlisle, in case he had to get between him and Gideon.

He was filling a plate at the buffet line when a woman came his way, herding a reluctant boy along in front of her.

It was no great leap to guess the kid's identity; his clothes were covered in dirt and sawdust, and there was a first-class shiner blooming around his left eye.

Jack stepped out of line, acknowledged the woman with a

nod. He didn't know her personally, though he'd seen her before; she worked nights at a gas station/convenience store in town, where he usually stopped to fill the truck.

He waited politely.

"This is my son, Riley, and he has something to say to you." The woman gave the boy a little shove from behind.

"I'm sorry," the kid croaked out, and when he lifted his face, it was flaming with embarrassment. "For getting into a fight with your son, I mean."

Jack didn't acknowledge the apology, since it didn't precisely belong to him. "You like horses, Riley?" he asked presently.

The boy caught his breath, and Jack thought, *Bingo!*

"Yeah," Riley said earnestly. "But I've never been on one."

"Maybe you'd like to come out here again one day soon, and give it a try," Jack suggested. "Riding, I mean. Lots of people around who could show you the ropes."

Now, Riley's bruised face was alight. "For sure?" he asked, as if he couldn't quite believe it.

"For sure," Jack confirmed, and Riley's mom smiled at him over her boy's head. "I'm Shannon Carlisle," she said. She offered her hand, and Jack juggled his plate to shake it. "Thank you," she added.

Then she smiled again, turned, and walked away.

The boy followed, but he kept turning around to look back at Jack in happy amazement.

Jack returned to the buffet line, made a few more selections, and scanned the picnic tables for Harper.

She was finished eating, he guessed, since the plate in front of her was empty, except for plastic cutlery and a crumpled napkin.

Jack drew a deep breath, exhaled it slowly, and headed in her direction.

Chapter 6

"How did it go—your talk with Gideon, I mean?" Harper asked quietly, as Jack swung a leg over the picnic table bench and sat down beside her. "Is he okay?"

By then, the other diners had drifted away, empty plates and cups in hand, and a soft breeze whispered through the leaves of the cottonwood trees rimming that part of the yard.

Jack's heart tripped over a beat as he met her gaze. "He's fine. A little worse for wear, as my dad used to say."

She smiled, scanned the crowd, and pointed. "There he is, watching the horseshoe competition."

Jack looked in that direction, picked up his plastic knife. "Gideon's on his honor to keep the peace," he said, after buttering a biscuit, taking a bite, chewing and swallowing. He hadn't realized how hungry he was—breakfast had worn off a long time ago, and he'd missed lunch, too. By then, the caterers were gearing up to serve supper. "He wasn't seriously hurt. I doctored him up and, hopefully, got him thinking about how we need to cut other people—and ourselves—some slack now and then."

Harper's pretty green eyes glistened a little, and her smile was both gentle and, somehow, sad. "You're going to make a very good father, Jack O'Ballivan," she told him.

His throat thickened, and he took a swig from the draft beer he'd snagged earlier as he passed by the bar. Without it, he figured, he might have choked on the forkful of potato salad he'd just swallowed.

"You think so?" He paused. Sighed. "I sure hope you're right."

"You have doubts?" she asked, touching his arm again, the way she had when he was about to break up the fight between Gideon and Riley.

Jack shrugged, wishing she'd hadn't pulled back so quickly. "Sometimes," he admitted. It was strange, how easy it was to confide in this woman, even though he barely knew her. "It isn't as if I've had a lot of practice raising kids. Especially angry, damaged ones, like Gideon. I didn't even know I *had* a son until Loreen showed up wanting money and a place to dump the kid."

"You have full custody, though?" Harper paused then, and a look of chagrin crossed her face. "I'm sorry—that was intrusive. Too personal."

He turned and regarded her in fond silence for a few long moments. "Truth is," he replied, "it's good to have somebody to talk to besides the therapist. So, yes, I have full custody—"

Harper was beautiful even when she frowned. "But?" she prompted.

"*But,*" Jack replied, resigned, "we probably haven't seen the last of Loreen, unfortunately. I gave her a little cash the day she came here, and, on the advice of my lawyer, a fairly good-sized check, after the papers were signed. Soon as she's run through that—and it won't take long—she'll be back."

Harper nodded with glum conviction. "I'm sure you're right."

"You sound as though you speak from experience."

She smiled wanly, and it was clearly an effort. "Not personal experience—I've never had children of my own, never even been married—but from a professional standpoint, yes. I'm familiar with this kind of situation."

Jack merely raised an eyebrow in question, unable to speak because his mouth was half full.

"I was a social worker," she told him.

"'Was?'" Jack asked, when he'd finished gulping down the bite of pulled pork he'd just shoveled in.

"I wimped out," Harper said, in the tone of someone making a shameful confession. "There were some other things going on in my life when my brain went into overload. Too many toddlers carried away, screaming and straining for their oblivious mothers, most of whom were high on coke or meth, and screeching obscenities. And that's just one of about a thousand similar experiences."

"My God," Jack muttered.

"Yeah," Harper agreed.

"And you think you 'wimped out'?" he asked.

She nodded. "These children, and their parents, too, need *more* people who have the guts to step up and do something about the problems they're facing, not fewer—not quitters like me."

Jack put down his knife and fork and turned to face Harper Quinn head on. "I don't know a whole lot about you," he said, "but I'd bet dollars to road apples that just about the *last* thing you are is a quitter."

Harper said nothing, though her cheeks turned pink.

"Sometimes," he went on, after waiting in case she wanted to answer, "a person has to step back. Untangle themselves and regroup. You'll be working with kids again as soon as school starts, right?"

"Right," she managed to reply, in a voice so soft that he sensed her response, rather than heard it.

"Sounds like a contribution to society to me," Jack said. "There are all kinds of ways to help out, Harper. Maybe you ought to just do what's in front of you, for now, and leave the toughest kind of social work there is to people who feel called to do it."

Tears welled in Harper's eyes then, and Jack wanted to take her into his arms and comfort her, bury his face in her rich chestnut hair, whisper words of reassurance, but that would be too much, too soon, he knew that. And he didn't want to make a wrong move.

Something special was happening between him and Harper Quinn, and he meant to let it unfold in its own way and time.

She sniffled, worked up a rather watery smile. "You're a good man," she said. "Did you know that?"

He grinned. "Not for sure," he replied.

"What were your parents like?" Harper asked, out of left field.

"My mother died when I was little, and I don't remember her very well," Jack responded. "My dad was a regular hard-working guy with a big heart. He would have walked through fire for me, and I never doubted that. He loved me as much as any father ever loved a son, and that was more than enough."

"I knew it," Harper said, with a kind of proud modesty. "When it comes to being a father, Jack, you've had the best possible training. It's isn't going to be easy, but if you raise Gideon the way your dad raised you, everything will turn out all right. Loreen or no Loreen."

Jack wanted to kiss Harper more than he'd ever wanted to kiss a woman before, and that was saying something, considering his lively romantic history, but this was different. *She* was different.

So he held back.

"Tell me something," he said, and his voice was a little on the husky side.

"What?" Harper asked.

"Is there a man in your life? I'm not asking about your Uncle Bob or that nice old fella you always run into in the post office or at the supermarket. I mean—"

Harper laughed, a little nervously, but an old sorrow rose in her eyes, then, mercifully, faded away again. "I know what you mean," she interrupted. "And the answer is no. I was engaged once, but it didn't work out."

Jack's heart surged upward like a beach ball held too long under water. "That's good," he said.

"Fair is fair, Jack O'Ballivan," Harper challenged good-naturedly. "What about you?"

Jack shook his head. "Totally single," he said. "Like you, I've never been married. Which is not to say there haven't been plenty of women—Loreen included, to my profound embarrassment."

"You're a confirmed bachelor?" Harper teased.

A whimsical image entered Jack's mind just then, out of nowhere. He saw himself and Harper engaged in a lively pillow fight on top of a mattress.

No great mystery where *that* would lead.

He was glad he was sitting at the picnic table and thus covered where it counted.

"Nothing of the kind," he replied. "I'd like nothing better than to have a wife and family—brothers and sisters for Gideon, et cetera. But so far, I haven't clicked with a woman in the right way. And for me, that's vital."

Harper was thoughtful. "I guess my former fiancé and I didn't ever really 'click,' as you put it. We had very different ideas about some very basic things. In fact, looking back, I realize I wasn't in love with George at all. I was in love with the person I thought he might turn into, given enough time and encouragement."

Jack chuckled. Picked up a potato chip and crunched on it, well aware, the whole time, that he was stalling.

"I think that probably happens a lot," he reflected, eventually.

"Me, too," Harper agreed.

By then, it was getting dark.

All over the grounds—the barnyard, in real time—fairy lights flickered on.

Music rose and fell as people headed in the direction of the low wooden platform that would serve as a temporary dance floor.

Gideon appeared, with Trey, as Jack was gathering the refuse of the meal he'd just eaten and trying to figure out what he ought to say next.

He didn't want this time with Harper to end.

Didn't want her to walk away—go home—or head for the dance floor and wind up slow dancing with some other guy.

"Can Riley spend the night?" Gideon asked eagerly.

Sure enough, Riley was there, right behind Gideon. And just as eager.

Jack made a point of looking stern, though he was pretending, of course. "Well, now," he said, rubbing his chin in a considering way. "I thought you two were sworn enemies."

"We're over that," Gideon said dismissively, as though the battle had occurred years ago, rather than a few hours back.

"Yeah," Riley agreed. "That's old news."

"I see," Jack ruminated. Slanting a sideways glance at Harper, he saw that she was smiling up at him, obviously pleased by this development.

And he took her hand, careful to keep a loose grip, just in case she was about to walk away. "You're sure you two can get along for a whole night?" he asked the boys.

They nodded vigorously.

Jack emitted a dramatic sigh. "If it's all right with Riley's mother, it's all right with me," he said.

Gideon and Riley whooped in celebration and ran away.

"That's the boy Gideon fought with earlier, isn't it?" Harper queried.

Jack smiled. "Yeah," he said. "That's him."

"What did you *do*?" Harper asked, giving Jack a pretend poke in the ribs.

"Nothing special," Jack replied. "I just pointed out that the two of them might just be more alike than different. I guess that did the trick."

"You're amazing."

"In that case . . ." Jack began, as the music drifted over them, carried by the night breeze. They were alone again, under the cottonwood trees.

"In that case what?" Harper asked.

He dumped the plate and cup into a nearby trash bin, returned to Harper, and extended a hand to her.

She looked at his hand, then his face, apparently confused.

"May I have this dance?" he asked.

Harper hesitated, bit her lower lip. "Here?" she wanted to know, after casting a glance in the direction of the dance floor, where couples were already coming together, laughing, talking, enjoying the warmth of a fresh summer night.

"Here," Jack confirmed.

After another moment—the longest moment Jack could remember—Harper smiled up at him and moved into his arms.

It seemed perfect that the first of the evening's fireworks whistled high into the navy-blue sky and burst there, spilling multicolored light.

Chapter 7

By the time she set out for her first day of the new job, on a crisply cool morning in early September, Harper was sure she was in too deep, romantically speaking. Ever since the night of the big party across the road almost a month before, when she and Jack had slow-danced together under the whispering leaves of a cottonwood tree, the man had been on her mind day and night.

It was unsettling.

She was powerfully attracted to Jack, she could admit that, if only to herself, but the landscape of her heart was still ravaged, and raw to the touch.

George had hurt her, and badly.

A repeat performance would be devastating.

Surely what she felt for Jack was only friendly affection, though, not love. It was way too soon after that train wreck of a breakup with her ex-fiancé for anything like that.

Wasn't it?

Her best friend, Devon, claimed it was high time she got back in the game, once Harper had told her, via both email and

Zoom, about meeting Jack when he showed up unexpectedly at her front door that day, and then about the huge party he'd thrown.

Devon said she ought to go for it, because Jack sounded pretty darned good to her, and there was no telling if Harper would ever get another chance like this one.

Harper had explained that, though she and Jack had shared suppers and enjoyed movie nights in both houses, and even gone on a few horseback rides together—she was inexperienced *and* awkward, since she'd never ridden before—they hadn't discussed the nearly visceral and vibrant pull between them.

By Harper's reasoning, the phenomenon could well be one-sided. Jack seemed to enjoy her company, and there *had* been moments when he'd drawn tantalizingly near to her, as if he meant to kiss her—once when he was teaching her and Gideon to fish, down by the creek, and another time when they found themselves alone in Harper's kitchen, side by side, doing the dishes.

He'd paused and turned to her, and the pause had been electrified, but just as Jack was about to zero in—unless that had been mere wishful thinking on Harper's part—Gideon had bounded into the room, waving his phone. He'd just reached the next level in his favorite video game.

Now, as she drove toward town, and her small office in Copper Ridge's middle school, Harper chided herself for dwelling on the situation.

Or, more properly, the *non*-situation. Her relationship with Jack felt more like a standoff than a budding romance.

Was she even ready for romance?

Even though Devon swore she *was* ready—Devon was chronically optimistic and securely engaged to a man who clearly loved her deeply—Harper's doubts lingered.

Maybe she was on the rebound.

If that were the case, getting involved with another man so

soon after ending things with George, even though it had happened months ago, might lead to catastrophic failure.

Harper wasn't sure she could endure that kind of emotional pain again.

On the other hand, Jack O'Ballivan might be her last chance at real, lasting love, just as Devon warned.

Harper was in her late twenties, after all and, trite as it was to say so, her biological clock was ticking. If she wanted children of her own—and she most certainly did—time was definitely a factor.

She was pondering the possibility that she might be putting all her dreams at risk if she didn't come to an understanding with Jack soon, when Ollie leaped from the back seat, landed briefly on the console, then settled himself comfortably on the passenger side.

Startled, Harper reproved, "I thought we agreed that you would stay put in the back."

Ollie gave a little whine and studied her with liquid brown eyes.

Harper laughed and reached over to pat his tiny head. "Silly dog," she said. "You'll have to behave better than that if you want to come to work with me three days a week."

Ollie tilted his head to one side, as if considering a response.

Harper had been given permission to bring her dog to work when she chose, as long as he behaved, and she'd settled on the three-days-per-week plan. A few days before, she'd brought a small dog bed, a duplicate of his favorite toy, a purple alligator, and various other supplies to the school and arranged all of it in a corner of her office, close to her desk but out of the way, too.

"This is a test, buddy," she told him, as she pulled into the school parking lot and then the spot she'd been assigned. "Misbehave, and you'll have to stay home alone on work days. Got it?"

Again, Ollie whined.

"Good," Harper responded. Then she reached across the console and reattached his leash. Ollie was something of a rascal, though a sweet one, with a tendency to rush off in sudden pursuit of small animals, and Harper was taking no chances.

Losing Ollie, she reflected, with a touch of surprise, would be far worse than losing George had been. Ollie was her companion, her snuggle buddy. And, unlike George, he was entirely devoted to her—as she was to him.

It was a short walk to the entrance nearest her office, and Ollie trotted merrily along beside her, stopping just once to lift his leg against one of the bushes lining the sidewalk.

When they entered the building, Dot Mansfield was standing in the wide hallway, directing students toward their assigned classrooms.

She smiled at Harper, and at Ollie, now nestled against Harper's chest and seemingly fascinated by the number of children passing before him. He probably thought it was a parade in his honor, Harper decided, with a grin and a nod of greeting for Dot.

"Bet you've got a full schedule for the day," Dot confided quietly, when the hall was empty except for a few strays. "There was a fight on the school bus, and poor little Ellie Bennet is waiting in the principal's office. It seems things aren't going well at home and she's refusing to set foot in a classroom because her clothes aren't brand-new, like most of the other kids'. I feel so sorry for that child."

Harper sighed, hoping the Bennet family wasn't as bad as some of the ones she'd encountered during her career as a social worker. If Ellie was neglected, or in any kind of danger, she would, of course, be duty bound to report the matter to the proper authorities, and the results of taking such direct action might be difficult indeed.

Several times in Seattle, she'd received death threats from parents and other relatives of children who had been removed from their custody and placed in foster homes, and others had taken more direct revenge. She'd had the windshield on her car shattered, and her tires slashed more than once, and as if those things weren't worrying enough, she'd acquired a stalker, who'd followed her for weeks before the police had finally nabbed him.

Sure enough, he turned out to be another angry parent. He couldn't seem to make the connection between his own behavior and the loss of his young daughter; everything, in his opinion, had been *Harper's* fault.

She shivered slightly at the memory, and Dot, being perceptive, took notice.

"Are you all right?" she asked. "You actually went pale for a few moments after I mentioned Ellie."

Harper drummed up a smile. "I'm just fine," she said brightly, wondering if she should have signed on with one of those personal counseling apps and worked remotely, instead of accepting this job. Several of her former colleagues had done this, and they not only had flexible hours, they were earning good money.

Just then, while Harper was reconsidering her employment choices, a bell sounded shrilly, signaling the start of classes.

Harper waved to Dot, and they parted, Dot entering her classroom on the other side of the hall and Harper heading into her office.

She'd just settled Ollie, now unleashed, in his dog bed and turned to uncover her desktop computer when a timid knock sounded at the door.

Harper breathed a silent prayer for kindness and wisdom.

Then she called, "Come in," in the most cheerful and welcoming voice she could manage. She was expecting Ellie Bennet.

She sank into her desk chair when the visitor proved to be Gideon O'Ballivan instead.

His head was bent as he entered.

"Have a seat, Gideon," Harper said gently, troubled to see that his shirt was torn and his hair mussed.

He obeyed without lifting his head. Said nothing.

"What's up?" she asked, keeping her tone light. And remembering Dot's earlier reference to the fight on the school bus that morning.

Still nothing.

"Gideon," Harper prompted, after a few long moments, "look at me, please. And answer my question."

Gideon's responding sigh seemed to involve his entire body, but he did meet Harper's gaze, finally.

"There was a fight," he said miserably.

"So I've been told," Harper replied. Ollie rose from his bed, walked over, and stood on his hind legs beside Gideon, scrabble-pawing at one leg of his blue jeans.

Automatically, and very gently, Gideon bent, lifted the little dog into his lap, and stroked him distractedly while he struggled for what he ought to say.

"I didn't start it," Gideon said, after another silence, and he sounded sad now. He looked at her with Jack's eyes, and they were brimming with tears. "I really didn't, Harper."

"You'll have to call me Ms. Quinn during school hours," she pointed out, though, again, she spoke gently. "On the ranch, or at my place, I'm Harper."

Gideon gave a nod, still petting Ollie. "Okay," he said, his tone dismal.

"Once again, Gideon," Harper persisted, "what happened on the bus this morning?"

"There was this kid named Justin, and a couple of his friends, who started giving me a hard time as soon as I got on."

"About what?" Harper suspected she knew the answer—Gideon had been taunted about his mother in the past, and told that Jack probably wasn't his father. Jack had mentioned that to her before.

"I missed a lot of school, when I was living with Mom," the boy said miserably, "so I'm in special classes, until I catch up."

Harper nodded. Jack had been tutoring Gideon in reading and math since his arrival at Diamond Creek Ranch, she knew, but the child was still far behind in his studies. In fact, the only alternative to joining the assigned classes was to go back a grade, or even two.

It was, she thought, a choice between two different but equal humiliations, and she felt sorry for Gideon. Wanted to hug him, ruffle his hair, get the little sewing kit out of her purse and mend his torn shirt.

But she could do none of those things.

Not here, not now.

"Go on," she urged, when Gideon had fallen into yet another silence.

His face was muffled by Ollie's fur when he gave a hiccuping sob and muttered, without looking up, "Justin said I was too dumb to be in seventh grade, and I ought to go straight on back to kindergarten."

Harper did her best not to dislike the unknown Justin; that wouldn't be fair. Nor would it be professional.

"So who hit whom?" she inquired.

Gideon gave a quivering sigh, wiped his eyes with the back of one hand, sniffled, and looked up. "I hit Justin, and he grabbed hold of my shirt and tried to slam me against a rail. The bus driver—a really big lady called Miss Evans—hit the brakes and separated us. Justin had a bloody nose, so his shirt got ruined, too."

"I see."

"Do you still like me?" Gideon's voice was vaguely plaintive.

"Of course I do," Harper assured him. "Which is not to say I think it's all right to hit people, even if they're teasing you.

Didn't something like that happen at the party, between you and Riley Carlisle? And now he's your best friend."

"He takes a different bus," Gideon explained. Ollie had begun to squirm, so he set him down carefully, and the dog trotted back to his bed, curled up with his purple alligator, and went to sleep. "If Riley had been there, things would have gotten a lot worse. He would have torn into Justin like a buzz saw."

"That's all beside the point, Gideon," Harper said reasonably. "We need to work on other ways of settling disagreements than punching people, you and I. And that's probably going to mean regular sessions in my office, before and after school."

"My dad is going to be so pissed," Gideon said.

"Language," Harper reminded him.

"I don't know how to behave right," the boy erupted, not angrily, but with passionate frustration. "Mom didn't care what I did, as long as it wasn't something *she* had to deal with. And I went to all these different schools, all over the place, and I never got a chance to make friends. I *had* to fight, because I would have been bullied and teased if I didn't—kids made fun of my clothes and my mom and the way I always had to go to classes for dummies!"

Again, Harper had to suppress the urge to rise from her chair, round the desk, and haul this troubled boy onto his feet and into her arms.

You're not his mother, she told herself. *You're a neighbor, a friend of his father's, a counselor, that's all. So stay in your own lane.*

"I think you've learned a lot about good behavior since you came to live with your dad," Harper said. "And you aren't a dummy, no matter what anybody says. You just need to catch up a little, and I know you can do that. I hope you know it, too."

"My dad says I'm smart," Gideon conceded, looking and

sounding chagrined again. "I think he's just trying to make me feel better, though. I think Mom and those kids who picked on me were right. I'm about as *smart* as a box of rocks."

"Not true," Harper said.

"Can I go now?" Gideon asked.

"Yes," she replied. Evidently, Jack hadn't been contacted, told to come to the middle school and collect his son. "Time to go to class, but stop by the boys' room and splash some cold water on your face first. And keep your temper, Gideon."

Gideon nodded, looking a little less frazzled, but still upset.

Harper made a mental note to speak to Jack about the school-bus incident herself, even though she was pretty sure someone from the principal's office would have notified him by now.

Gideon crossed the small room, opened the door—revealing a small blond girl dressed in mismatched and none-too-clean clothes, with her hand raised to knock—and looked back at Harper.

"Will you help me explain this to my dad?" he asked. "Please?"

"Yes," Harper said. "I definitely will. Now, get going. You don't want to miss class."

Gideon nodded, eased around the child who was surely Ellie Bennet, and disappeared from sight.

"Come in, Ellie," Harper said, taking in the little girl's appearance.

Ellie was a pretty child, and she would undoubtedly be a beautiful woman when she grew up. The question was, what kind of woman would she grow up to be, given the start she was getting?

Harper meant to do her part to make sure the girl was set on the trail to a bright future, though she knew her efforts would be limited by the usual legal tangles and red tape.

Shyly, Ellie sidled into the office, letting the door swing closed behind her with a soft whoosh.

"I didn't do anything wrong," she said, with a touch of preparatory defiance.

"I'm not saying you did," Harper pointed out smoothly. "Sit down, please, and tell me a little about yourself."

Chapter 8

Harper's brain was still buzzing as she and Ollie arrived home that afternoon, when the workday was supposedly over. She'd consulted with four different students, including Gideon and Ellie Bennet, *and* two parents, both of whom had been either cowed or angry and defensive.

The first was the father of one of the school-bus bullies, Justin Parks.

Evan Parks seemed to hate the whole world, starting with his ex-wife and certain government officials, and he apparently blamed everyone but Justin—or himself—for the boy's behavior. Justin, Harper had quickly realized, wasn't the problem.

Clearly, the kid was absolutely *inundated* with negativity and foul energy at home, and Harper had sympathized with him as deeply as she had with Ellie, whose main problem seemed to be not so much bad parenting—though there was certainly room for improvement in that area—but plain old garden-variety poverty.

She was ashamed of her second-clothing, minor speech impediment, and learning problems. Turned out, the girl suffered from mild dyslexia and she, like Gideon, was in special classes.

Ellie's mother had come to the school to retrieve her semi-hysterical daughter, and paused to speak with Harper, on the advice of the principal.

Becky Bennet, it soon became apparent, was basically a good person. She loved her daughter, but she was chronically unemployed, primarily because she was afflicted with one of the worst cases of depression Harper had ever seen.

And that, considering Harper's job history, not to mention her own experience with the problem of depression, was saying something.

Becky was tiny, with enormous hazel eyes and hair the same shade of blond as her daughter's. She fell into the chair facing Harper's desk, rather than sitting down, and it didn't take long to understand that the woman was literally dragging herself from one place to the next, so deep was the inertia she dealt with every day.

She'd confided, in fact, that these days, she usually didn't even have the energy to get out of bed in the mornings; Ellie had been making her own meals and then cleaning the tiny house they shared all summer long.

Harper had empathized, certainly, but her first concern was the child's well-being.

Now, back home, and having exchanged her crisp linen blouse and sharply creased black slacks for jeans and a T-shirt, soft with age, Harper continued to ruminate on the concerns she'd encountered that day.

First, Gideon and his temper.

Then Ellie, in her worn-out, thrift-store clothes.

Justin Parks, who was actually a good kid, in Harper's opinion. He dealt with a lot of anger at home, and he probably needed a way to vent. Hence, the bullying.

Not that his personal troubles were an excuse.

But they *were* a reason.

And after Justin, two other children who, thankfully, had less severe problems, were sent to Harper's office. One, a girl named Susie Svenson, who had recently come to Copper Ridge to live with her divorced father, primarily because her mother had recently remarried and she now had step-siblings and the blended family thing wasn't working out.

Then, finally, there was Marcus Desmond, a thirteen-year-old living with his grandmother. He'd been caught leaving the grounds during school hours and snagged by one of the teachers, who'd sent him Harper's way.

Marcus had simply wanted to go home on his lunch break to make sure Grandma took her allotted midday medicine. She was forgetful, Marcus explained, and the medicine was important. She could die without it.

The kid had had good reason for what he'd done, obviously, though leaving the school grounds before the last bell, unless in the company of a parent or guardian, *was* strictly against the rules.

Harper hadn't come up with a solution yet—not for any of the kids and certainly not for the parents, and that bothered her.

Frankly, she hadn't expected the job to be as hard as it was, and she was momentarily overwhelmed.

Ideas of what to do about all these pressing difficulties chased each other round and round in Harper's head as she fed Ollie and, when he was finished gobbling down his grub, she snapped on his leash and stepped out the back door for a walk around the yard and, perhaps, as far as the creek—the same one that ran through Jack's property.

The stream curved around in a wide loop through the countryside, flowing under a small wooden bridge three miles up the road, and then tumbling and whispering its light-splashed way right through Harper's five acres and on toward Diamond River.

Harper loved that creek, and so did Ollie, which meant she had to keep him on the leash. On their last visit, she'd let him off, thinking it might be good to let him wander just a little, like a normal dog, and he'd jumped straight into the creek, which had spun him around twice and carried him far enough downstream that Harper had to run along the bank and finally splash into icy, knee-deep water to rescue him.

He'd been soaking wet, of course, and seemingly proud of himself.

The ways of Ollie were past finding out.

When they reached the little clearing beside the creek—where a huge, mossy, and flat boulder, probably the mere tip of a stone iceberg, provided a nice perch for sunning oneself, or reading—the dog stopped and looked hopefully up at his mistress.

She shook her head. "No way you're getting off-leash," she said firmly. "Remember what happened last time?"

Ollie must have understood, because he sighed so forcefully that his entire body, miniscule as it was, heaved with the expulsion of breath. Then, when Harper took a seat on the rock, he pranced to her side and sat down within petting distance.

Sitting there, in the waning light of a September day, Harper shivered slightly. There was definitely a nip in the air, and she wished she'd brought a light jacket along, or worn a sweatshirt instead of a tee.

Finally, her brain began to offload the problems of the day, and she was in an almost meditative state when she was startled by the sound of something rocketing through the dense brush on the other side of the creek.

She tensed, and automatically reached for Ollie, ready to flee, or defend him if the intruder turned out to be a coyote or anything else that might represent a threat.

Turned out, it was Trey, the O'Ballivans' dog, and he was about to leap into the creek and swim across to greet her when a shrill whistle sounded from a copse of pine and spruce trees behind him.

"Trey! Whoa!" It was Jack's voice.

Harper felt a thrill, and a light blush rising to her cheeks.

Jack came out of the trees and grinned over at her.

She set Ollie down again, reassured that he'd be safe. He and Trey were canine buddies, used to each other because of the regular visits back and forth, between Jack's place and hers.

"Hey," he said. "I know I'm trespassing, but you weren't at the house, so Trey and I tracked you down."

Harper smiled. "Are you here to talk about Gideon?" she asked.

Jack nodded, walked downstream about twenty yards, and crossed the creek by moving gracefully, arms out from his sides like a tightrope walker, over the trunk of a fallen tree.

Trey trotted happily along behind him.

Reaching her, Jack sat down next to her on the big rock. Like her, he was wearing jeans and a T-shirt, and his dark hair was damp from a recent shower.

"So," Jack began, after huffing out a breath of resignation, "Gideon—and the principal—told me about the incident on the bus."

"Where's Gideon now?"

"At home, in his room. He's under house arrest for the time being. No video games and no TV. Just his homework."

"He's a good kid, Jack," Harper said, though she knew it was unnecessary. Jack O'Ballivan was invested in understanding Gideon, and he was well aware that the boy, for all his need to catch up on schoolwork and learn to interact with others more effectively, was intelligent and basically well-intentioned.

Jack turned to look into her face, and there it was again, that feeling that he was about to kiss her.

He didn't, though.

"Any recommendations, Ms. Quinn? If so, I can probably use them."

On an impulse she never could have explained in a million years, Harper laid a hand on Jack's warm, muscular shoulder. He smelled deliciously of fresh air and soap, though he'd probably been pounding nails or herding cattle all day. His was a working ranch, not a hobby farm.

"Mostly, I think Gideon needs time to adjust. He's learning to trust you, Jack. He wants to, but he's been let down so many times, mistrust has become a habit. Besides therapy, and you're already getting that in Flagstaff, it's going to take patience."

Jack sighed again, and grinned. "So, no magic formula, huh?"

She laughed. "No magic formula."

"He trusts you," Jack pointed out quietly. "Why not me?"

"Gideon's got no skin in the game, where I'm concerned," Harper answered, her hand still resting on Jack's shoulder. "To him, I'm just the woman across the road, the counselor he sees at school. You, on the other hand, are the main pillar of his life. He's feeling his way along, making sure you mean what you say."

Jack nodded a little sadly. "A few days ago, I woke up in the morning and found him sleeping on the floor, in front of my bedroom door," he told her. "I guess he was making sure if I took off, he'd know about it."

Harper closed her eyes for a moment, feeling Gideon's pain, his fear of abandonment. And Jack's need to reach his child, to somehow convince him that he had a home and a father now. That he was loved and valued.

"Did you talk with him then?"

"I tried," Jack replied. "Basically, he said he went to the bathroom in the middle of the night and fell asleep on the way back." He paused, grinned. "He's not a very good liar, and I find that reassuring. Call it clutching at straws, but there you have it."

"How about going back home for Gideon and then coming to my place for supper, the two of you? And Trey, of course. I'm going to heat up a container of frozen lasagna, so the meal won't be fancy, but—"

"But," Jack interrupted, and his voice had turned husky, all of the sudden, "you could serve dry oatmeal, Harper Quinn, and I would eat it happily, with gratitude, if it meant sitting across a table from you."

She couldn't answer, and for some ridiculous reason, her eyes welled up.

And that was when it finally, finally happened.

Jack cupped her face in both hands, tilted his head to one side, and bent to touch his mouth to hers, softly at first, then more firmly.

The kiss deepened, and everything inside Harper melted.

Except her doubts.

She'd been right, thinking she might be getting in over her head, spending so much time with Jack O'Ballivan.

And she wasn't ready for the things that kiss promised.

But that didn't mean she didn't want them.

All of them.

When Jack finally drew back, it was only to rest his forehead against hers. His eyes were still closed.

"Wow," he breathed. "Is it just me, or did we just get hit by lightning?"

Somehow, the remark eased the tension—Harper didn't try to delude herself about what *kind* of tension it was—though she still felt a burning ache in a particular part of her anatomy.

This was *not* going to turn into sex, she reminded herself silently. She'd been an old-fashioned kind of gal before she met George, and now she was one again.

Maybe it was trite and stupid, but uncommitted sex was out of the question for her now. She'd been down that road, and it hadn't led anywhere good.

Jack got to his feet, scooping Ollie up and holding him in the curve of one arm while he helped Harper up with the other.

"Don't panic," he said, with warmth and uncanny perception. "I know you're not ready to take this further, but I think we should talk about it at least. Don't you?"

Harper had to gulp back the lump in her throat before she could answer. "Yes," she said simply. "I think we should talk about it, but not tonight. It's nothing Gideon needs to overhear."

"Right," Jack agreed. Still gripping her hand, he started pulling her back toward her little house, carrying Ollie the whole way. Trey zipped ahead of them, forging a path through the trees and underbrush. "Suppose we go horseback riding, just you and me. Saturday, maybe? Gideon can stay with Sadie and Tom, so we'll have some privacy."

Harper stopped, making Jack stop, too.

He looked down at her, patiently curious, one eyebrow raised, a slight grin tipping his mouth to one side. "What?" he asked reasonably.

"We can't have sex. On Saturday, I mean."

Jack's grin broadened. "Yeah, I figured that," he said. "We're going to *talk,* Harper. I promise you, that's all. With the proviso that kissing is not off the table."

Harper suddenly felt silly, like some prissy old maid, and she laughed. "That sounds fair," she said.

An hour later, the lasagna was ready to come out of the oven, the salad was made, and the dogs were curled up together on the hooked rug near the back door, snoozing.

For a silly moment, Harper actually envied them. They looked so unruffled, so tranquil.

Jack was setting the table, while Gideon sat in the chair he usually occupied, head down.

Once the plates and silverware were in place, Jack reached over and ruffled Gideon's hair.

"Chin up, scout," he said. "There are no lectures forthcoming."

Tentatively, Gideon looked up. Glanced from his father's face to Harper's, then back again. "Am I in trouble, though?"

"Yep," Jack replied, pulling back Harper's chair and waiting politely while she set the just-baked lasagna in the middle of the table. "No video games and no TV for a week."

Gideon groaned dramatically. "A whole *week*?" he all but howled.

"Longer, if you lose your temper again." Harper was seated by then, so Jack drew back his own chair and sat, too.

"I was defending myself," Gideon protested, but weakly.

"The bus driver reported everything to the principal," Jack reminded his son easily, "so there's an eyewitness testimony. The other kid was giving you a bad time, but you threw the first punch."

"If I'd just told him to shut up," Gideon reasoned, "he wouldn't have. So I had to sock him one."

Jack sighed, rubbed the back of his neck. Exchanged glances with Harper.

She smiled. "Who wants salad?" she asked.

Chapter 9

On Saturday morning, Jack was awake even earlier than usual.

He let Trey out the back door, filled the dog's food and water bowls, and looked in on Gideon, who was still sleeping.

His son looked so young—younger than twelve, certainly—and so vulnerable that Jack's heart ached with both love and concern.

Harper was right, he thought. Turning Gideon's life around was going to be a tall order, and it would take time. Loreen and her boyfriends had done a lot of damage, damage he was determined to undo.

With a soft sigh, Jack closed Gideon's door and turned to head back to the center of first-thing-in-the-morning operations, the kitchen.

It was still half finished, that room, a strange amalgamation of brand-new top-of-the-line appliances and worn linoleum, fancy tract lighting in the framework ceiling, windows in need of replacement.

Jack started a pot of coffee brewing, poured himself a mugful as soon as there was enough in the carafe to do so. He took it black and, since he hadn't gotten all that much sleep the night before, he was glad it was strong.

Trey returned, scratched politely at the screen door, and came in when Jack opened it, going straight to his kibble, gobbling it down with a lot of heavy-duty crunching, and then moving on to lap loudly at his water.

Jack chuckled and leaned down to pat the dog's head. "Anybody would think we've been starving you," he observed, shaking his head.

He was considering what to make for breakfast when his cell phone rang in the pocket of his shirt.

In the early-morning quiet, the noise was jarring.

A tightening in the pit of his stomach warned Jack that this was a call he didn't want to take.

Nevertheless, he did. Avoiding problems wouldn't solve them.

The caller ID panel read, *Unknown*.

He thumbed the *accept* icon.

"Jack O'Ballivan," he said briskly.

"It's me," Loreen blurted. Even though she'd spoken just two words, Jack knew there was a lot more she wanted to say.

"What do you want, Loreen?" Jack asked evenly. His backbone had stiffened, and his shoulders were bunched around his ears.

He took a deep breath and released it. Relaxed a little, though everything in him was on red alert.

"I need money," Loreen said sheepishly. The tone was unexpected; the request wasn't.

"What else is new?" Jack retorted.

"Listen, my car broke down, and I'm stuck in Crap Creek, Nevada!"

"Where's Brent?"

"Don't be an asshole about this, Jack. You loved me once, and I gave you a son, remember? It won't hurt you to peel off a couple of hundred bucks and send them to me—there are apps for that." She paused, and he could hear her breathing. It was rapid and shallow, which meant she was stressed, and possibly in need of a fix. He strongly suspected that heroin was her drug of choice. "Brent's gone. He's—he's in jail."

"So you want money for bail?"

"Get real!" Loreen burst out. "That would take more cash than I can even *dream* of having. Besides, I wouldn't do it. I'm asking for money because I don't have anybody else to turn to, Jack."

Jack knew she was telling the truth about that last part. Loreen had undoubtedly burned a lot of bridges since she'd started using. "What happened to the check I wrote you? It was sizable, as I recall."

"It was gone in a few days," Loreen said defensively. "I owe some people—some not very *nice* people—a *lot* of money. If they catch up with me—"

Jack wasn't heartless; he knew Loreen was messed up, that a lot of what she did could be chalked up to her habit and to the fried neuropathways in her brain. She did rotten things, yes, but she was sick, not evil.

None of which meant he wanted thing-one to do with her.

"If your life is in danger, Loreen," he said reasonably, "go to the police."

"*The police?*" She let out a raw and bitter laugh. "Not gonna happen, cowboy! I probably have warrants!"

Silently, Jack counted to ten. Then he said, "Here's what I'll do. I'll pay for your stay in any rehab facility you choose, as long as it's legitimate. One hundred percent. But you have to stay for the whole show, Loreen, and you can be sure I'm going to vet the place first."

Loreen began to cry. "You'd do that? It would cost *thousands,* Jack. If you can do that, you can give me enough to get out of trouble, once and for all, and I'll never bother you again. Call it back child support."

Jack huffed out a scoffing breath. "That's the one thing I can't understand. Why you didn't come after me for child support a long time ago."

"I told you," Loreen said, almost whining the words. "I was married when I had Gideon. The guy thought the kid was his. And you haven't answered *my* question. Why would you want to spend so much just for rehab?"

Just for rehab.

Jack's voice had a definite edge when he replied. "Why would I pay top price for you to get treatment? Because you're Gideon's mother. And for that, if nothing else, I'm grateful to you. *But* it's rehab or nothing, Loreen. If you need cash so badly right now, go and wait tables or tend bar somewhere. Even in Crap Creek, they must have bars, if not casinos."

"I can't *do* that, Jack! I've been wearing the same clothes for three days and sleeping in my car. Now that it's broke down, I can't even get to the YWCA or a shelter for a shower and a meal!"

Jack almost gave in, because it bothered him when people were down on their luck, and Loreen surely was. On the other hand, she could be lying through her teeth, holed up in a motel room with Brent or somebody just like him, more concerned with scoring the drugs she needed than anything—or anyone—else. He was betting on the latter.

She hadn't even asked about Gideon.

He was about to call her on that, and on her real reason for calling, when he heard a noise behind him and turned to see his son standing in the doorway, looking miserable and afraid.

"I've got to go now," Jack said into the phone, gesturing for Gideon to come in and sit down at the table. "Let me know if you decide to get treatment. If you don't, then don't bother me again."

In the background, he heard a man's voice uttering a gravelly curse.

"Jack, wait—" Loreen protested, sounding desperate now.

Jack ended the call.

Turned to his son.

"Was that her?" Gideon asked, stroking Trey, who, as usual, had come to sit beside his chair.

Her. Not *Mom*, but *her*.

"It was Loreen," Jack answered, refilling his coffee cup.

"I'm scared," Gideon announced, surprising his father.

"What's to be scared of?"

"What if she comes back? What if some stupid judge says I have to live with her?"

"Whoa," Jack said, going to the table, easing Trey aside, and crouching to look up into Gideon's face. "I have custody, bud. Full and *permanent* custody. And your mother has a drug habit. You're not going to be sent away."

Gideon's face contorted; he was trying so hard not to cry. "I heard you say you'd pay for her to get treatment. What if she gets well and she gets her parental rights back?"

"You're borrowing trouble. Try to stay right here, in today, where everything is all right. It's going to be a nice day, and I'm giving you time off from being grounded to go fishing with Tom, so you can have some fun."

"You're going riding with Harper," Gideon said, and his tone was flat, giving nothing away. It was anybody's guess how he felt about what amounted to his father going on a date.

"That I am," Jack said, standing up again. "Do you have a problem with that?"

The question was a sincere one. Jack really wanted—needed—to know the answer.

Gideon shook his head. "Just don't get too far away, okay?

Because if you're far away, and Mom decides to come around, I might get kidnapped. I might never see you or Trey again if she snatches me!"

"Your mom is a long way from here," Jack said. "And she's up to her—eyeballs in trouble right now. She isn't going to 'snatch' you, buddy."

"Did you tell the people at the school not to let her pull me out of class and take me away?"

Jack realized he hadn't, and made a mental note to do so. In fact, he'd tell Harper today, just to make double sure the principal and Gideon's teachers got the word. Having let the duty lapse, he wasn't going to depend entirely on his memory.

"That's taken care of," he said, which was a hedge, if not an outright lie, but honest as he was, Jack couldn't bring himself to let the boy worry.

"For real?" Gideon pressed.

Jack let the question slide. "What do you want for breakfast?"

"Some of that trout we caught last weekend," Gideon answered. Clearly the ploy had worked, and he'd been distracted from the idea of being stolen by his drug-addicted mother, if only for the moment. "It's really good, rolled in flour and fried in hot grease. That's how Sadie makes it, when she comes out here to cook for Tom and the others."

"Dude," Jack reasoned. "It's frozen."

"Then zap it in the microwave."

"You don't give up easily, do you?" Jack teased.

Gideon puffed out his unremarkable little chest and sat up very straight in his chair. "Nope," he said. "I'm an O'Ballivan and you said it yourself. O'Ballivans don't give up. Not *ever*."

The remark made Jack feel slightly less guilty. If it hadn't been Saturday, he'd have called the principal's office at the middle school right then and there, and told them that under no circumstances was the boy's mother allowed to take Gideon off the premises.

He took the package of cleaned and frozen fish from the freezer above the refrigerator, unwrapped it, and shoved the whole thing into the microwave to defrost.

The meal was tasty, especially supplemented with hash browns—also frozen to start with—and bowls of fresh blackberries Gideon had picked himself. The thorny bushes grew in plentitude all over the property.

Gideon was more than ready to go fishing when Tom tapped at the back door, around eight thirty. Looking at Gideon but speaking to Jack, the foreman said there would be plenty of time for a run to town to do some bowling, if they got tired of fishing, or caught their limit too quickly.

Message received.

Tom was telling Jack he could take all the time he needed, riding with Harper. He, Tom, would take up the slack.

It was close to ten o'clock when Jack saddled his favorite gelding, a buckskin he called Samson, along with the tame little pinto mare, Dapples, he'd chosen for Harper's mount.

Harper had a natural talent for riding—she'd ridden with him and Gideon a few times since the night of the big party—but she hadn't had a lot of practice, and she still lacked confidence.

Jack was playing it safe. Keeping *her* safe.

The way he meant to keep Gideon safe.

It was a short ride down the driveway and through the gate—he had to dismount to open and close it—then across the road to Harper's cottage.

The place had been improved considerably since she'd moved in, he observed, as he swung down from the saddle and tethered both horses loosely to the fully restored, bright-white picket fence surrounding the sizable yard.

The fireplace chimney had been rebuilt, the roof shored up, the shingles painted.

The front steps still sagged a little, but that was okay.

In time, that would be taken care of, too.

The door opened, and Harper appeared, looking hell-too-cute in jeans, a long-sleeved cotton shirt, and newly purchased boots, but the crowning touch, literally, was her western hat.

It was bright blue, like the shirt, and banded in shiny silver circles, like coins but without the imprints. Over one arm, she carried a large wicker basket with a lid.

"Sandwiches," she said, grinning as she lifted the basket a little way, "plus deli potato salad, cupcakes, and two bottles of wine."

Jack laughed and took the basket from her while she opened the gate and passed through. Teasing, he lifted the lid and peered inside.

"All that," he joked, "and no Ollie."

Harper rolled her beautiful eyes. "He's miffed, but he'll be just fine, lazing about and playing with his toys."

Jack closed and latched the gate behind her, then held Dapples' bridle while Harper jabbed a booted foot in the stirrup and hauled herself up.

Plunking into the saddle, she sighed and said, "I need to work on my upper body strength."

Jack chuckled, shook his head, and mounted Samson, deftly managing the picnic basket as he did so. But he made a point of pretending it was outrageously heavy.

"I was planning on taking you to town for lunch or dinner—depending on how long we're roaming the countryside—but it looks as if we're all set. It'll be a picnic." He paused. "Without the blanket."

Harper blushed a little at the image that reference probably brought to mind, but she kept right on smiling. "Jack O'Ballivan," she said, "you promised to behave yourself."

"But I didn't promise not to kiss you."

She seemed to consider that as they started their ride, traveling in the direction of the wooden bridge down the road. Jack pondered all the soft earth and green grass on either side of that bridge.

What he imagined doing there, on the shadowed banks of the creek, went well beyond kissing.

"No," Harper finally answered, after due consideration. "You didn't promise that."

Chapter 10

Watching Jack ride horseback and wrangle the picnic basket with such ease impressed Harper, caused her to imagine how deft and skilled he might be at doing other things, and when they finally dismounted, after an hour of following an old dirt road up into the foothills on his ranch, her knees were weak.

She told herself it was because of the ride, but she knew that wasn't the whole story.

The spot Jack had chosen for their picnic was in a small clearing, near the remains of an old log cabin, long abandoned and shaded by several oak and maple trees, planted years before.

Once her legs felt sturdy enough to walk instead of leaning against her horse, Harper approached the cabin.

"Do you know who lived here?" she asked, as Jack came to stand beside her.

He considered his answer before offering it. "They were most likely the original homesteaders," he said. "The place has been added to again and again, and unlike a lot of ranches, it didn't remain in the same family—it's been sold and resold a number of times."

"It's beautiful," Harper murmured, taking in the wild landscape surrounding them. They'd splashed across a shallow part of the creek on the way up the trail, and passed a herd of cattle, roaming free, grazing on acres of lush green grass. Now that they were nearer the treeline, the air was cool and crisp. "What a fantastic place to raise children."

Realizing the possible implications of that last statement, Harper blushed and averted her eyes. The truth was, she'd been picturing several children besides Gideon, children born to her and Jack, and she was mortified to realize he'd guessed what she was thinking.

The soft, amused look in his blue eyes indicated that he had, but instead of saying so, he tilted his head to one side for a moment, then indicated the copse of maples and oaks. "Suppose you set up the picnic while I secure the horses?" he asked.

Harper nodded, reclaimed the picnic basket, and quickly turned her back. She hadn't known Jack O'Ballivan long enough to be thinking about *having children* with him, for heaven's sake.

Finding a piece of soft ground under the trees, she opened the basket and took out the thin blanket she'd packed, along with the sandwiches, potato salad, cupcakes, and wine. She spread out the blanket and knelt to begin removing the food, most of which she'd prepared very early that morning.

Meanwhile, Jack tethered the horses loosely to the old but sturdy-looking hitching rail alongside the cabin. There, they were in the shade, and there was plenty of grass for them to nibble on. The animals had drunk their fill of creek water earlier, on the way up, and Jack had assured Harper that they would be fine for the time being.

Well, the *horses* would be fine.

Harper wasn't so sure she would.

Despite the peace and beauty of the place they'd chosen for their picnic, the attraction she felt for Jack was building momentum, like a wildfire blazing through tinder-dry grass.

He'd promised to limit their physical interactions to kissing, and Harper knew that was for the best, but a part of her—a *big* part of her—wanted something else entirely.

They sat cross-legged on the blanket, facing each other, as Harper carefully arranged the containers of food—after using hand sanitizer from the small bottle she'd tucked into the basket, an action that made Jack grin.

She kept her attention focused on the food, hoping Jack wouldn't see the blush heating her face. With luck, he'd mistake it for sunburn.

The occasional surreptitious glance, however, proved he was aware of her jangled senses and maybe even the fire spreading through her body.

He selected the white wine from the insulated basket, rummaged for the corkscrew, opened the bottle, and poured a portion into each of the two plastic wineglasses provided. Waited until Harper stopped fussing and fidgeting to hand one to her.

"Easy does it, cowgirl," he teased, as she spilled some of the wine onto her jeans. "I'm a man of my word. As badly as I want to make love to you, right here and now, I won't."

Harper's face felt downright inflamed, but she made herself meet his eyes. "You want to make love to me?" she asked, and then silently berated herself for asking such a stupid question. Jack O'Ballivan was a strong, healthy red-blooded *man*—of *course* he wanted sex. Didn't all men?

He gave a mock sigh. "Will you just chill out, Quinn?" he asked. "Nothing's going to happen between us unless you're one hundred percent in agreement." With that, he touched his wineglass to hers, then took a sip.

"You don't actually think *I* think you'd force me?" Harper asked, horrified that she might have given him that idea.

"You know I don't think that," Jack replied casually. "But I have to admit I'm wondering why you're so nervous."

Harper was a long time answering, but when she did, she was honest. "I'm nervous," she began, "because I kind of wish you hadn't promised—well, what you promised."

Jack made a low, growling sound, then laughed. "Let's talk about something else," he said. "At least until you calm down."

"You *did* say we needed to talk," Harper reflected, as a breeze rustled the leaves over their heads.

"That I did," Jack agreed. He used the hand sanitizer, then reached for one of the chicken-salad sandwiches Harper had set out. He took a bite, chewed thoughtfully, and finally swallowed. "There's a lot we don't know about each other."

Harper didn't have an appetite by then, though she'd been hungry only minutes before. So she nibbled at one corner of her own sandwich and waited.

"For instance," Jack began, after drawing in a deep breath and exhaling it slowly, "what are you looking for in a husband?"

Harper considered the question for a while, though the answers were ready and waiting at the forefront of her brain. "Commitment," she replied quietly. "Integrity. Emotional availability." She paused, swallowed, then searched Jack's face with sad eyes. "I trusted my fiancé, and he lied to me. Blatantly. He told me he loved me, that we were going to get married and have babies and live happily ever after, but all the while, he was cheating. I came home from a conference one day and caught him and one of my friends from work in the shower together. Turned out, they'd been an item for months, and I never had a clue."

Jack reached across, gently smoothed back a tendril of her hair, which had come loose from her ponytail at some point.

The touch of that man's work-roughened hand did things to Harper that went beyond the havoc her imagination was wreaking.

"I'm sorry," he said.

Harper sucked in a deep breath, mainly to keep herself from bursting into tears, and held Jack's gaze. "I'm over it," she said. "I've finally realized that losing George, hard as it was, was one of the best things that could have happened to me. As they say, I dodged a bullet. It would have broken me if we'd been married, with children, when he cheated."

"But you still worry about getting mixed up with another guy like him," Jack ventured.

"Well, obviously I wouldn't want that, but I'm stronger now. Maybe even smarter."

"Oh, you're definitely smart," Jack pointed out. "Could be, you've even picked up on the fact that when it comes to fidelity, I'm a sure bet. As far as relationships go, I'm either all in or all out. I don't do shades of gray, and that's not always a good thing—I can be opinionated as hell, and twice as stubborn."

"Have you ever been in love?" Harper asked, surprised by her own forthrightness. Maybe it was the wine.

"Early on, I thought I loved Loreen," he replied solemnly. "We met in college and lived together until I caught her beating my dog. For me, that was the end."

Harper shuddered at the image. "That's awful."

"I was semi-serious about a few other women over the

years, but when it came right down to it, the connection I wanted—needed—just wasn't there. So I guess the answer to your question is, no, I haven't been in love, at least, not deeply enough to make a lifetime commitment."

"Okay," Harper said, because she didn't know what else to say at that moment. There was loneliness behind Jack's words.

"Are you thinking I'm too damned choosy?" he asked, grinning now.

"No," Harper responded. "I'm thinking you're smart. I knew, deep down, that George and I weren't right for each other, but I went ahead with the engagement anyway, because I thought I could turn him into the person he *should* have been."

"Do you have regrets?"

"Yes," she answered, without hesitation. "I regret the time I wasted. I guess I just wanted a home and a husband and a family so badly that my judgment was skewed. Makes it hard to trust myself."

Jack put his sandwich down and balanced his wineglass on the lid of the picnic basket, then reached out to cup her chin in his hand. His thumb moved gently over her cheek. "Listen," he said quietly, holding her gaze. "You *can* trust yourself, Harper. We all make mistakes—it's choosing to learn from them that matters. And you know what? I've wanted a home, a wife, and a family for as long as I can remember, so we're on the same page there."

"Really? You want more children, besides Gideon?"

"Yes," Jack responded, without hesitation. "And before you say it's too soon to talk about the future, Harper, hear me out. Something is happening between us, something powerful and right and good. It has the feel of a once-in-a-lifetime thing, at least for me. So there are times when waiting *isn't* the best thing to do. When it's better to go for it."

Harper opened her mouth, then closed it again.

Then, at the same time, both she and Jack shifted to their knees, and in the next moment—and for some moments after that—they were kissing. *Really* kissing, deeply and with fervor.

By the time that kiss ended, Harper felt like a figure skater, poised on the tip of one blade and spinning into a blur.

She loved Jack O'Ballivan, and that was a fact.

Time had nothing to do with it.

Jack gripped her shoulders, as if to stop the spinning, though of course he couldn't have known it was happening.

Or could he? He was one of the most perceptive people Harper had ever encountered.

He leaned forward, eyes still closed, and rested his forehead against hers, like he had that other time, beside the creek. "Harper," he said, his voice gruff with emotion. "Maybe you won't believe this, but I've been waiting for you for a long, long time."

Harper spread her fingers through his dark hair, then tilted her head slightly and kissed him. "I believe you," she whispered, when that kiss, too, had ended. "And it just so happens that I've been waiting for you, too."

Jack opened his eyes, his hands cupping her face now. "I'm taking this a step further," he said. "I'm about ninety-nine percent sure I love you."

Harper tipped her head back and laughed for pure joy, and Jack began nibbling at her neck.

Within five minutes, he had her wanting him so badly that she was ready to throw all constraint to the wind, but Jack was determined to keep his word, it seemed.

He held her wrists gently and said, "We're going to wait, Harper."

She stared at him, less mirthful now. Confounded, even. "*Why?*"

He touched her lips with his, just barely grazing them, and

fire shot through her system as if from a flame gun. "Because you're worth it," he said. "We're going to do this the old-fashioned way, Quinn. The *right* way. When I take you to bed, we'll be husband and wife."

Harper had nothing to say to that. She was, actually, a little disappointed.

He laughed and kissed her again, and everything around them seemed to vanish—the landscape, the horses, the old cabin, even the half-finished picnic and the spilled wine.

Harper was lost as she had never been lost before and, at the same time, completely and wholly *found.* She seemed to dissolve into particles, now a small, separate universe, now melded, cell for cell, with Jack.

All that, without actually making love.

During the slow, quiet ride down the hill, back to level ground, Harper marveled at the strange new feelings shifting and swirling within her, around her.

Jack glanced her way now and then, but he seemed to be lost in thought, as well. Happy thought.

When they reached the barn, she helped him put away the horses, removing their saddles and bridles, brushing them down, filling their feed troughs.

Inside the house, they washed up at different sinks, then met in the kitchen.

They'd decided not to go out to dinner, but to stay in, together.

Jack, having been single for so long, proved to be a very competent cook.

He whipped up a meal of fried chicken, mashed potatoes and gravy, and green beans boiled with onions and bacon.

It was all delicious.

Gideon and Tom returned from their adventures about midway through supper, having caught six sizable trout between them. Trey was with them, and he was exhausted, gobbling up his supper of kibble, lapping up what seemed like a gallon of water, and then collapsing, with a big doggie sigh, into his bed.

Gideon looked from Jack to Harper and back again.

Then, without saying a word, he grinned.

Like his father, Harper concluded, Gideon was perceptive.

He knew something had happened between Harper and his dad, and he was happy about it.

Thank heaven.

Chapter 11

Gideon walked by the side of the road, head down, kicking at rocks and gravel and dirt clods as he went. His dad would be mad at him, he knew, not just for missing the school bus, but for not calling him, or at least waiting to hitch a ride home with Harper.

He'd been expecting her to come along, stop and pick him up, but so far, he hadn't seen a single car or truck on the road, and he was beginning to regret his decision to avoid Justin and his buddies by hiding in the schoolyard until the bus was gone. After all, he'd been walking for almost an hour, and he was still a long way from home.

Home.

The word made Gideon smile.

He finally had a home, a real one. He had a dad and a dog and a horse and a few friends, which was pretty much all he'd ever wanted.

He maneuvered his backpack off his shoulders, opened the flap, and dug through the contents until he found his phone.

He'd never had his own phone before, and this one was

high-quality. He played video games on it whenever he got the chance, and it made him feel safe, knowing he could connect with his dad or Harper or Tom Winter Moon if he needed help.

Gideon let his thumb hover over his dad's name in the contact list, but he didn't press the digital button. Skipping the bus ride was going to get him into the kind of trouble that would last a while.

He was just about to put the fancy gadget away and keep walking when he heard the car.

Everything within him stilled, and he felt as though the soles of his feet had grown roots, ones that tunneled deep into the hard dirt of that country road. He knew the sound of that car.

Before he could dive for the brush lining the sides of the road, the old, rusted-out wreck roared around a corner and came to a dust-flinging stop right beside him.

Loreen stared at him from behind the wheel for what seemed like several minutes, though it was probably only a few moments, and Gideon still couldn't move. He couldn't even speak, let alone run for it.

His mother leaned across the bench seat and pushed open the passenger-side door.

"Get in," she said. Her hair was mussed, with three inches of roots showing, and her makeup was smeared, blurring her features.

Gideon still didn't move.

It was all over. All the good things in his life would be gone soon, and he would never see his dad again.

"N-no," he managed.

"What are you doing out here all alone, anyhow?" Loreen demanded. She was high; he could tell by the dullness in her eyes and the twitch of various muscles in her face and along the length of her skinny neck. "Damn it, Gideon, *get in the car.* I'm taking you back to your fancy-ass ranch and your rich daddy, so let's get going, okay?"

He shouldn't have believed her; he knew better.

But he was scared, and he hung on to the hope that she really meant to take him home. She was probably back in the area because she needed money; he was just a pawn in the game.

So he got into the car, closed the door, fastened his seat belt.

Loreen immediately jerked the phone out of his hand. He'd forgotten he was holding it.

"Now isn't this a pricey little gizmo?" she said.

Gideon grabbed for the phone, but she dropped it into the holder in her door.

He moved to undo his seat belt, intending to jump out and take off running, phone be damned, but Loreen's energy must have been spiking, because she laughed like a crazy woman, made a wide U-turn, and tore off in the direction she'd come from minutes before.

He slumped in the seat, the bulk of his backpack notwithstanding, and silently called himself ten kinds of idiot.

"You're not taking me home," he said flatly.

It wasn't a question.

"Not just yet," Loreen said, and when they came to the crossroads—left turn to head back to Copper Ridge, right to go south, in the general direction of Phoenix. "I'm going to see what I can get for the phone first."

"Then take the phone and let me out of the car," Gideon suggested, though it was more of a plea than a suggestion. "I want my dad."

"Well, of course you do," Loreen spouted. "That big house. All that money. And look at you, wearing rich-kid clothes."

She was definitely high.

"Loreen," Gideon said, "stop the car and let me out. Please."

"Now that just wouldn't be *safe*," she trilled. The pitch of her voice made his ears hurt, and his stomach was jumping around so much, he thought he might hurl all over the grubby dashboard. "What was Jack *thinking,* letting you walk along a country road all by yourself?"

"He doesn't know I didn't get on the bus," Gideon confessed. "But he'll come looking for me, so you might as well give me back now."

"Oh, I'll give you back, don't you worry about that. If the price is right, that is."

"He'll press charges," Gideon said. "Kidnapping is a serious crime, Loreen. It's a felony, in fact."

"Where do you get off calling me *Loreen*? What happened to *Mom*?"

"You're not my mom. Harper's going to be my mom pretty soon, I think. Dad's in love with her, and she's spending a lot of time at our place. She's nice and she's pretty and she doesn't take drugs. She'll make a really good mom."

Loreen's knuckles turned white where she gripped the beat-up steering wheel, and she gunned the engine, her face contorted with anger.

Gideon sighed. He'd done it again. Said the wrong thing and set her off.

But then, *everything* set Loreen off, when she was like this.

Which was always.

"Mom," he said, "slow down. You'll get stopped for speeding."

Please, God, let her get stopped. Then the cops will take me back to Dad.

Loreen drove faster, her jaw clamped down so hard it looked as if it might snap.

Gideon moved his pack to the floor, sat back, closed his eyes, and did his best not to cry.

Harper was about halfway home when she met Jack, driving his truck. Trey rode shotgun, tongue lolling.

Jack brought the truck to a dust-billowing stop, squinting through the haze. "Is Gideon with you?" he asked grimly.

Having buzzed down her passenger-side window, Harper coughed and waved a hand in front of her face, instantly alarmed. "No," she called back. "For God's sake, Jack, *what's wrong*?"

"He didn't get off the bus. I was helping with one of the construction projects, and it took me a while to notice."

Glad she'd left Ollie home that day, Harper pulled over and got out of the car, locking it behind her with the key fob.

Without being invited, she scrambled into the truck, forcing Trey to leap into the back seat to make room for her.

Jack was staring at his phone, flicking through a series of apps.

"He has to be with Loreen," he said, dropping the phone into the console and jamming the gearshift hard before hitting the gas pedal. "They're headed south." He muttered the state route number and then added, "Call the police."

Harper was already doing that.

"They're alerting the highway patrol," she relayed to Jack, moments later. "They want a description of Loreen's car—and Loreen herself, of course."

Jack reeled off the requested descriptions and Harper repeated them for the police dispatcher on the other end of the line.

Forty-five frantic minutes later, they'd tracked Loreen—via Gideon's phone—to a service station along a two-lane highway. Trees towered behind the place, part of a dense wooded area.

There was one car parked at the pumps, and it was Loreen's.

Two highway patrol cars screeched into the lot seconds after Jack braked hard beside the rig that looked to Harper as if it might fall apart at any moment.

Loreen was nowhere in sight—she could have been inside,

paying for gas, or in the restroom. And, although the passenger door was wide open, Gideon wasn't there, either.

Harper felt everything within her deflate.

She loved Jack, and she loved his son.

The two patrolmen were inside the station before Jack and Harper got out of the truck, Trey leaping down after them.

Jack looked wildly around him, clearly afraid.

"Gideon!" he yelled.

One of the state troopers came out of the gas station, holding Loreen firmly by one arm. The other officer followed and began searching her car.

Jack was turning in circles, shouting his son's name.

Harper felt a pang of shared desperation.

"Where is he?" Jack demanded furiously, after striding over to face Loreen.

The woman's shoulders sagged, and her head was down. She was about to offer a response when Trey suddenly began to bark and darted away from them, streaking toward the woods behind the station.

Jack was right behind him, with Harper close behind.

There was a crashing sound behind them as one of the troopers joined the chase.

The barking stopped, but there was a lot of rustling in the brush before Gideon appeared, Trey at his side. Tears streaked the boy's face, but he was grinning.

Jack wrapped his arms around the boy, held him tightly, his eyes closed.

Harper rested a hand on Jack's lower back. His breathing was fast and shallow, and he was trembling just a little.

"I *told* her you'd come looking for me," Gideon all but crowed, looking up at his father, then over at Harper. "She's really stupid!"

"She's sick," Harper said, very quietly. Then, when Jack finally stepped back, she hugged the boy, too.

Loreen was arrested, partly because she'd violated her custody agreement with Jack, but mostly because the troopers found a small packet of heroin in her glove compartment. Then, of course, there were the warrants.

She was handcuffed and read her rights.

She looked back, her expression sad, as she was ushered into the back of one of the cruisers. Again, though she couldn't excuse what the woman had done, Harper felt sorry for Loreen.

"How did you find us so quick?" Gideon wanted to know. He was clearly relieved, and stuck close to Jack, who took out his phone and tapped the screen.

"Tracking app," he replied.

"Loreen took my phone," Gideon said. "I think it's in the side panel of her door."

Jack looked inquiringly at the remaining trooper. The car was about to be impounded and taken away, once the tow truck arrived, and the police would want to search it again, in case they'd missed anything the first time.

"Go ahead and take the phone," the officer said, and Jack did so. "Looks like there's a backpack in there, too." He smiled down at the boy. "That yours?"

Gideon nodded.

"Okay. You'd better get that, too."

Gideon immediately obliged.

"Will she go to prison? Loreen, I mean?" the boy asked, once he and Harper and Jack were all in the truck again. He and Trey were in the back.

"Maybe," Jack said, glancing at the rearview mirror. "That's not up to me."

Harper saw the muscles in his face relax.

"Are you going to press charges?" Gideon persisted.

Jack exchanged glances with Harper, then nodded. "You bet I am. Your mom needs to take responsibility for what she did, and who knows? Maybe, with some time to think, she'll get her act together one day."

"Whatever happens," Gideon replied, "I don't want to see her again. Not 'til I'm a grown-up man, anyhow. Then I'll be tough like you, and she won't be able to mess with me."

"In the meantime," Jack began, putting the truck in gear and pulling out onto the road, headed toward home, "I'd like to know why you didn't take the bus home like you were supposed to."

Harper looked back at Gideon, gave him a reassuring smile and a little nod of encouragement.

"I didn't want another run-in with Justin and his posse," Gideon answered, ducking his head. "Obviously, *that* was a major mistake."

Harper hid a grin.

"You've been making a lot of those lately," Jack said seriously, though when he looked Harper's way, she saw a twinkle in his eyes, along with heartrending relief.

"I know," Gideon confessed. "I suppose I'm grounded again."

"*Again* is the operative word, champ," Jack said. "We've got to get a handle on your behavior, sooner rather than later."

"What I need," Gideon announced, with rising enthusiasm, "is a *mom.* A real one—like Harper, for instance."

Harper smiled, reached over, and squeezed Jack's thigh lightly.

He smiled back at her. Winked. "You just might be right about that," he told his son.

The Cowboy

HEATHER GRAHAM

For Ashley and Allyson Somers,
great sisters who have been amazing to my family.
And in loving memory of Victoria Graham Davant—a
sister is a gift!

Chapter 1

Naturally, he was tall.

Broad-shouldered, striking, a man with a quick, charming smile and a lean, mean way of walking that was easy and amused. He wasn't *exactly* tall, dark, and handsome—his hair was a sandy red, not long but not cut so short that a waving thatch couldn't fall rakishly over his forehead.

But Vicky Henderson couldn't help but watch the man suspiciously behind the façade of the flirtatious smile she shared as he walked his horse just behind the fence where she stood with so many other audience members.

Was he the man who had taken Kasey Richardson and Melissa Martinelli? Used that charming smile and lazy swagger to make her smile and laugh, follow him anywhere. . . .

Was he the height of the man caught on video, leather jacket high on his neck, hat pulled low over his face, charming the young women who had disappeared? The man who knew the cameras were there and just how to avoid them?

"Victoria, you're there?"

Watching the man—down on the program as Adrien Anderson—Vicky Henderson paid heed to the voice of her superior, Assistant Director Frederick Eames, coming to her through the tiny earbuds she was wearing.

"Hey!" she said, as if the earbuds she wore were a phone connection. Well, technically, they *were* a phone connection, just in a very secure form of communication.

While she had always loved rodeos and games, Vicky wasn't here for the enjoyment of the occasion, but rather, she was working on a special undercover operation. Two women had recently been abducted from what their assisting FBI profiler termed the "equine scene" of South Florida, and it was thought they'd most probably both disappeared from the "Guts, Grime, and Glory" games being played at the riding center in Davie, Florida. The one clue on the center's video surveillance had shown Kasey last talking to a tall man in a cowboy hat—dozens of them, of course, attending the games—and she was walking toward the exit with him to the parking lot. No video there.

While the city of Davie also offered a rodeo, the games were something different. They were held on property owned by Dulaney Feed and Supply, one of the largest companies in the state or elsewhere to offer supplies for horse owners as well as those who raised cattle, goats, and other farm animals. Something of a surprise to those who saw South Florida as the beaches and the mega-cities of the coastline. There were many small—and also massive—ranches and farming areas between those heavily populated areas and the eastern edge of the Everglades.

And from those who did love and live a "horse" life to those who were city dwellers and tourists, the games were a big draw. Those who owned horses in the area loved them, because they usually loved their "pets" and were proud to show them off.

Then again, of course, they were simply fun. They were good for the economy—all of the vendors sold their wares at the games, and food trucks arrived in the dozens. The games were as much entertainment as they were contests. And so the games brought out would-be cowboys like Adrien Anderson. Strange name for a cowboy. It should have been "Tex" something, she thought.

"Still no sign of Melissa Martinelli or Kasey Richardson," Eames told her. "We've had teams combing the areas near the games, but we'd need search warrants to burst in on a few, so . . . anyone approach you yet?"

"Lots of people with things like 'hi' and smiles, a couple of would-be pickups; but they've been checked out. Now I'm watching a few people, but . . ."

"I'm watching the operation, and, yes, we've great, speedy tech folk behind us. And Brannigan is a huge support for you. Vigilant, you know."

She smiled at that. She was lucky. She loved her partner, Hank Brannigan. He was older and reserved, a married man with a great wife and family. He always had faith in her, as she did in him. He had never mocked her as a cop—and while her department tended to be good, there were many who didn't think that a young woman could be a decent detective.

Then there was the fact that she had been specifically selected for this operation. She was also a redhead, with hair that waved around her shoulders. Her eyes were green. She was similar in age, height, weight, and all else as the missing women.

And she knew Hank was there. When the long-haired twenty-something with the beer in his hand had suggested a date, Hank had been near. But the man had wandered off immediately when she had turned him down. Hank had followed him and reported soon after that the man had returned to a party of what appeared to be frat boys. And if they were a danger to anything, that danger would be to a keg of beer.

She'd spent a little time with a man who had claimed to own a ranch nearby, who had asked her to come riding, assuring her he had great horses, some spirited, some calm, that would fit her abilities and pleasure.

She'd continued to chat with him—with Hank nearby—but she'd quickly learned he had three teenaged daughters, and while she had been flirting, their tech department had discovered he had a solid alibi. He'd been out of town the last two weeks and couldn't be the man who had been seen with the women who had come to the games, met someone, and disappeared without a trace.

"Play it so far, but not too far, but we don't know if these women are dead or alive."

"I know, sir. But we must find out where he's going from here. If they are still alive, it's imperative we get to them—"

"I know. I just don't like risk to my detectives. Well, I know you're right. Oh, and you have even more protection. The Feds have decided to send an agent in, so he'll probably make contact at some point soon."

She was silent.

"Vicky, don't tell me that you don't want the help—"

"No, sir! Young women are missing, and I believe in taking whatever help we can get. I guess I'm just surprised. We don't know if we have abduction or abductions and homicides on our hands, and I thought three was the magic number for a 'serial' anything and that the Feds wouldn't be—"

"Personal favor, from what I understand," Eames said. "One of our victims is the niece of a U.S. senator from Virginia. He wants to know what the hell happened. He called the director. And this all came about really quickly, as in within the last hours, not leaving our agencies time to get it together before the games, before we could get him together with you and Hank. Just don't think he's the bad guy—we don't want to go shooting any Feds, okay?" Eames asked lightly.

"You got it, sir," she promised. Ending the call, she winced. "I'll try not to shoot any Feds," she promised.

Vicky knew Eames had to try to be light; both abducted women had loving families. They were both known for being wonderful and kind, working hard and giving to charities. The newspapers were highlighting the situation daily.

Hank thought the young women were already dead. He believed they would find what was left of their human remains somewhere in the Everglades. And Eames, she knew, had brought in everyone humanly possible—the city and county police departments in the whole of South Florida, including the Mikasuki and Seminole tribal police forces.

So far . . .

"Hey, ladies and gents, we are about to go for the true championship in all barrel racing!"

He was there again. Almost in front of her. The would-be cowboy, Adrien Anderson. Atop a handsome buckskin—an animal that had to be at least seventeen hands tall. He sat addressing the crowd, waving his western-style cowboy hat in the air.

His eyes lit on her, and she gave him her best, coquettish smile.

Then the announcer came on over the speaker, and the man was up. With a turn on a dime, he was headed out for the barrel course with his handsome buckskin. A cloud of dust arose as the horse dashed off. The sun was beating down, and the crowd was roaring and cheering.

Whoever he was, he could ride. Of course, when it came to barrel racing, it was the horse that mattered. He'd had the knowledge and talent to have the right horse. He still came off as a major jerk who apparently thought he was God's gift to women.

But Vicky didn't think he was the man they were looking for. Such a man would have been noted by the witnesses who knew that Kasey had spoken with—flirted with—a man. But none had been able to describe him other than saying he'd been fairly tall, mid-twenties to early thirties, and maybe he had dark hair or . . . maybe it had been light. The hat and . . . well, who had been noticing people who were just talking by a vendor stand when there was so much going on?

He wasn't the guy.

Vicky decided to move into the building area on the grounds and browse around the vendors. While many of the people attending the games might have horses, almost all had dogs, and the company's dog-food booth was always busy.

She glanced back as she left the crowd that was roaring with approval for the cowboy, Adrien Anderson. She saw Hank had been applauding, but he was aware of her movement and was following. Hank was wearing a cowboy hat himself, denim jeans, and a tailored denim shirt, and he fit right in with the other attendees.

Vicky headed to the booth where cans, bags, and pictures were displayed, along with refrigerators for those who wanted to give their canines the very best that could be bought. The pictures were great.

"What kind of pup do you have?"

She turned and smiled, aware that a man had come up beside her. He was tall, sandy-haired, wore the appropriate hat, and had an easy, charming smile. She noted as well that he was purposely situated on her right side, where he could avoid the camera.

He didn't seem to care if he was seen on video talking to a woman—as long as his face wasn't caught in that video.

She smiled.

"I don't have one yet. I'm trying to make sure that I'm prepared. I'm thinking I'd like to go to a shelter. I believe adopting a pet would be the right thing to do. What about you? What kind of dog do you have?"

"Dog?" he queried. "I have five. Three German shepherds and two rottweilers. I have a great place that's not far from here. Lots of room for them to roam." He gave her a charming grin. Then his smile faded. "Are you really thinking about getting a pet now?" he asked her.

"Yes, definitely. I'm alone, and I think a dog—"

"I think I can help you," he said.

"But—"

"My dogs are all rescues," he said. "I can't resist—when I know that an animal needs help, I take it in. But the last puppy—okay, she's full grown—but the last girl, Blue, isn't fitting in. The others are being a little too hard on her, and while she might finally get along, I think she'd be happier in a home where she's the star of the show."

"Oh! She's a shepherd or—"

"A beautiful, sweet, human-loving shepherd. I can take you to see her. I think that the barrel racing was the last game of the day," he said.

Was this it? The way he had conned two women into leaving with him? Could he just be a nice guy really trying to place a dog?

No. She was going to go with him, trusting in the fact Hank would be right behind her. And, of course, the fact she carried her 9mm. The county was looking into nonlethal weapons, supporting the carrying of batons and stun guns. But Eames had insisted she carry a firearm on this operation, since they had no idea if the women were dead or alive.

If she might agree to go with a man who meant to kill her, and even if Hank was right behind her, he still might try to carry out the deed.

She gave him her best, sweetest smile. "Wow. Thank you. Sure."

"Come on. Oh, do you have a car here?" he asked.

"I took a rideshare. Parking can be such a hassle—even out in the great green nowhere!" she assured him.

"Yeah, I hear you. I got here early. For that exact reason."

She made a point of walking with a bit of a sway, making sure Hank could see her, and that he had time to follow her carefully.

"Oh! I'm Vicky!" she said. "And you're. . . ?"

He smiled. "Loving dogs, right? We forgot the basics! I'm Jimmy Trent. And it's a true pleasure to meet you. Hey, are you from around here?"

"I am," she said. "Well, not exactly around *here,* but close enough. I'm from West Palm Beach—my whole long life. And you?"

He laughed. "Close enough, too. Originally, Fort Lauderdale. Then I bought a property out here. I love this whole area. I mean, they pass legislation to keep it rural, and you've still got the highways when you want more excitement, I-75, the turnpike . . . it's all good!"

"That's cool. I wonder. I never thought about living in the middle of nowhere."

"Well, it's really not the middle of nowhere, like I said. You can reach anything."

"Ah, but on the border of the Everglades? Do you get alligators in your pool? I've seen pictures, people out in the border cities—"

"Hey, come on. Waterways connect! You can get one just about anywhere. Hey, I saw one crossing I-95 one day."

"Yeah, after one of the storms, I saw one on the street, too. It was funny—the sucker was in Miami Springs and crossing with the light. I mean, I don't want to run into one, but they were here first. So I'm glad Animal Control was able to put it back somewhere and not need to euthanize it. It was just wandering around and never hurt anyone," Vicky said.

"I'm with you. I hate killing things."

Did he? She hoped so!

They reached his vehicle. It was a pickup truck, but he was

playing the ultimate gentleman, walking her around to open the passenger-side door for her.

She thanked him and slid up into the seat.

"It's not far. I really could have walked," he told her. "But I wouldn't want to make you walk—"

"Ah, walking is not that bad!"

"We're just about a mile. Still, I want you to enjoy meeting Blue."

"I'm sure I'm going to!" she said, smiling in his direction.

They left the many acres where the games had been taking place and pulled along a small back road. They passed a large cattle ranch and a smaller house with about two acres of land and several horses grazing in the fields.

He looked in his rearview mirror. With no other traffic, there was no way he couldn't see that Hank was following. *But Hank was driving a nondescript blue sedan. With any luck, Jimmy Trent wouldn't think anything of it.*

She glanced in the side mirror. She could see that Hank was playing his part; he pulled to the embankment, got out of the car, and pretended to be studying a map.

Jimmy Trent gave his attention back to the road.

"Almost there . . . see the drive ahead?"

She did. A small dirt driveway led to a gated property with a box attached to one of the fenceposts that obviously called for an entry code. She noted the fence around the property.

It was high, but not so high that Hank couldn't, with some effort, hike himself over it.

But hopefully, she wouldn't need Hank. She would find out where this man was hiding the kidnapped women and arrest him. With a little bit of luck, it would be that simple.

Unless, of course . . .

She didn't want to believe he had killed them already. And she could be encouraged by the fact that no bodies had been found yet.

He pulled the pickup truck to the gate, paused to fill in the numbers; but he keyed them so quickly that she was unable to get the code.

They pulled along the dirt road. The property offered a single-level house, a two-story barn, and another building—maybe once a smokehouse or simple storage.

There was a vehicle in front of the house. A white SUV.

"You have a roommate?" Vicky asked.

He shrugged. "Sometimes. A friend from college. He's from the Jacksonville area, and I let him hang here when he's in town."

An accomplice, or someone who might keep him from doing whatever he'd planned to do with her?

"Let me help you down!"

He was still the ultimate gentleman, hurrying around to give her a lift down from the passenger's seat of his pickup truck.

"Thanks!" she said sweetly.

There was, so far, no sign of Hank. But Hank would be smart enough to stay out of sight until they'd gotten into the house. Of course, they could be wrong, or she might have been wrong, suspecting this man when he was just a flirtatious dog lover.

No. Every intuition was warning her that she was right.

"Come on. I keep the dogs in their side of the house when I'm out."

"You have so much land. You don't let them run around?" Vicky asked.

"Naw, I've heard of too many cases where dogs get out, or where someone's bull breaks through a fence, and they wind up torn to shreds . . . I like them safe. I work from home, so . . . they have plenty of time to run around when I'm here and can keep an eye on things."

"You're so good! Are you sure you want to part with Blue?"

Jimmy Trent smiled. "I think she'll be happier with you. She's scared of her sisters and brothers. Come on—I'm actually a pretty good housekeeper!"

She grinned and followed him up the one-step to the small porch in front of the house. The front door also opened with a code. This time, Vicky caught the numbers.

6689

He opened the door and indicated she should step in.

He was, apparently, a good housekeeper. She entered a large living room containing couches, chairs, and an entertainment center, with the entire place appearing to be dusted, mopped, and clean.

"You can't even tell one dog lives here, much less five!" Vicky said.

He smiled. "You wait here. I'll be right back."

He left her in the living room. She quickly began to look about. He'd gone to the left, so she went to the right.

He had to be keeping the abducted women somewhere.

But the kitchen and dining room were empty and just as clean as the rest of the house. There were bedrooms, of course. And there were the stables and the storage building or whatever the other structure on the grounds might be.

"Vicky?"

She heard Eames through her earbuds.

"I'm in, but nothing yet. Six-six-eight-nine. Those numbers get you into the house. I'm not sure about the gate."

"We can ram a gate."

"No cause yet. I need to find something."

"I'll get the code to Hank. And Hank is near. He's just waiting for your word."

"Thanks."

She had wandered back to the living room when Jimmy Trent returned—with five big dogs at his side.

"Drop the bag," he said.

"What?"

"You heard me. Drop your bag. Now." He smiled and looked down at the dogs. "Blue, get ready. This one's for you if she doesn't behave."

One of the German shepherds bared her teeth and growled.

So, that was it. He did love dogs. And they were trained to keep control of his captives.

"No," she said flatly, reaching instantly into her bag for her 9mm.

But that made Jimmy Trent laugh and produce his own weapon, a Smith and Wesson.

"You're going to shoot me and five dogs in time to save yourself? Just toss down the weapon, and I'll forgive you for being such a bra-burning bitch. Do it *now*!"

"I'm a damned good shot," she said.

"So am I. And Blue . . . if I let her get to you and you don't shoot fast enough . . ."

"Drop it!"

The words came from behind her. Vicky spun around.

Apparently, Jimmy Trent's occasional roommate was his accomplice. He now had a weapon trained on her, as well.

Hank was coming, she reminded herself. But he wouldn't know he would be facing two people. And still, she was dead if she didn't agree, and if she did, she still had a chance to find out where they were hiding the women they had kidnapped.

If, indeed, they were still alive.

"Come on. Drop it, and let's go."

"If I drop it, you'll kill me," Vicky said, looking at the accomplice.

"Don't be ridiculous. If we wanted you dead, you'd be dead already."

Jimmy Trent's accomplice was about his age, but there was something harder about him, in the sallow contours of his face, perhaps in his eyes, eyes that seemed to have a strange light in them.

She could kill one of them, but she would definitely die.

Or she could play it out, and maybe she could find the young women, and maybe, just maybe, they'd all survive. Hank would have gotten the address out to others by now and . . .

"Drop it and let's go," the accomplice said, his eyes gleaming, smiling in a way that bared his teeth, making him resemble a growling dog.

She dropped her bag, and the 9mm.

"Out the front door, casually. Jimmy, take her arm."

The dogs obviously were Jimmy Trent's. They followed him like little lambs as he came forward and took Vicky's arm.

Jimmy Trent had the nerve to smile charmingly at her.

"You can pet Blue now if you want. She's only dangerous if I tell her she needs to be."

"I do love dogs," she murmured, pausing to stroke the shepherd.

He had told her one truth. The dog moved into Vicky, wagging her tail. She wasn't sure, but it seemed important to pet the animal. Blue might believe she was a friend if another command was given.

"Out, out the front door. We need to get her where she's supposed to be."

"You need to get me where I'm supposed to be?" Vicky protested. "I'm supposed to be home. I have a family. I have friends."

The accomplice ignored her, turned to Jimmy, and said, "You need to get back to those games. If anyone saw you—"

"I know how to avoid cameras!" Jimmy said.

"Right. But witnesses may remember you. Tell anyone who asks that you dropped her off at the gas station a few miles down, should it ever come up."

"Yeah, right, whatever," Jimmy Trent said.

The accomplice, name still unknown, was obviously the dominant one in their partnership.

Whatever that partnership might be.

Trent led Vicky out. His partner followed, after collecting her 9mm, her phone, and her bag.

They were out on the front porch when the accomplice suddenly started swearing. "You ass, Jimmy, you ass! She's a cop."

Damn! She'd had her I.D. and badge in a hidden zipper compartment of her shoulder bag. But he'd found it!

"What?" Still holding her arm, Jimmy turned to stare at his partner.

"Ah, hell!" The accomplice spat out. He walked around, grabbing Vicky by the upper arms and shaking her hard. "What the hell—who knows you're here? We've got to clean this up, Jimmy. Get the hell on out of here. This bitch has probably written back all about the address! Tell me, tell me, who the hell—"

"Hey jerk, let her go this instant and drop all weapons!"

Everyone spun around, Jimmy Trent and his accomplice both aiming wildly.

But there was no one to be seen.

Then a single shot rang out.

Jimmy's accomplice screamed in agony as his shoulder erupted with a spew of blood, and he fell to his knees.

As Jimmy Trent grabbed hold of her, Vicky managed to kick the accomplice's fallen gun far from the reach of either of the men.

"No!" Jimmy cried. "No, no, no! I—I—"

He fired wildly.

"Drop it or you're a dead man!" came the voice.

Then, at last, Vicky saw the speaker.

It was the Cowboy.

The giant buckskin came leaping over the fence, its rider

taking aim at Jimmy Trent all the while. The distance to the porch was nothing for the horse and rider, but as he advanced, Jimmy Trent shouted, "Blue!"

The dog began to growl.

It tore out, running for the horse, swirling around, confused.

Too late.

The Cowboy was there, at the porch, and the man leaned expertly from the saddle and reached for Vicky, sweeping her up and out of the path of the growling shepherd.

"All, all!" Jimmy began.

But the Cowboy warned in a flash, "One more word and a bullet goes through your mouth!" he promised. "I don't want to kill the dogs for your crimes. Call them off now!"

And Jimmy Trent did.

He dropped his gun as he spoke to the dogs.

The Cowboy eased Vicky back to the ground. Even as he did so, she heard sirens and saw Hank was at the gate, coming through, and that other police vehicles were arriving quickly behind him.

She heard Eames's voice through her buds. "Vicky, you all right? Are you all right?"

"Yeah," she said quietly, looking at the Cowboy, who was off the buckskin and cuffing Jimmy.

"Vicky, you're sure? Everything is under control?" Eames persisted.

"Oh, yes," she assured him. "I think I've met our Fed."

Chapter 2

It wasn't as bad as he thought it might be.

Sent in as he had been, Adrien had accepted the fact he might be resented by the local police. After all, the FBI wasn't usually called in on such a situation as this in which two young women had disappeared.

Of course, he prayed—as did they all—that the young women were alive.

Somewhere.

But even if they'd had known homicides, the local police would have expected to handle the matter themselves under most circumstances. Maybe it wasn't that unusual. After all, the FBI had field offices in South Florida, and it had been an easy thing for the powers that be to transfer him to a local field office to make it all the more palatable.

Of course, he'd been chosen because he knew the terrain.

It wasn't as bad as it might have been. Eames seemed to be an exceptional man who was capable of empathy in the middle of extreme professionalism.

And even the lead detective had somewhat proven herself.

Of course, if he hadn't come along, she might have found herself in a bit of trouble. Or she might have extricated herself, as well. Still, it was a good thing they didn't need to find out if that might have been true or not.

When he'd first seen her . . .

Well, she'd been dressed for the part, appearing as much the same as the kidnapped women as she could, her beautiful sweep of auburn hair curling delicately around her shoulders, face made up to enhance the emerald color of her eyes, perfect little figure clad in a sundress that emphasized long legs and a shapely form.

Fluff . . . a beautiful little piece of fluff.

Except there was nothing fluffy about her now.

EMTs were working on the man with the shattered shoulder, but Detective Victoria Henderson's manner had changed completely. The man who had been identified as James "Jimmy" Trent had been cuffed, and she was now grilling him after—rather amazingly—commanding one of the dogs to lead the others back into the house, where they were shut away in the "dog" half of the house while officers and agents searched the property.

"I can't believe the dog obeyed her!"

Adrien turned to see Detective Henderson's partner, Hank Brannigan, was standing at his side, shaking his head. Hank noted Adrien looked at him, and he smiled, offering him a handshake. "Welcome to our hell and thank you! You are our Fed, right?"

Adrien smiled. "I am your Fed."

"Where the hell did you learn to ride like that?" Hank demanded.

Adrien grimaced. "Here."

"Here?" Hank said, surprised.

"I grew up in Southwest Ranches," Adrien told him. "My brother took over my folks' house when they moved into a retirement village in Boca. He keeps Chaparral for me at his property and . . . well," he said, pausing to stroke the neck of his running quarter horse. "I got this guy when I was in high school. He's sixteen years old now, and one of the most amazing horses I've ever come across."

"Sixteen. Is that old?" Hank asked.

Adrien smiled. "Horses on average have a lifespan of twenty-five to thirty years. The oldest on record made it to sixty-two—Old Billy. So . . . I guess he's about middle-aged now."

"Well, I have to admit, I thought you were some jerky jock when I first saw you out on that field—a hell of a rider, but a jerky jock at that. Now . . . well, hell. You saved my partner when I should have been faster at that gate," Hank told him. "Don't judge a book by the cover, eh?"

Adrien laughed softly. "Hey, when I saw Detective Henderson, I thought she was a dumb twit, a girl who looked just like those being kidnapped and hanging out all sexy anyway. I didn't know she was with the department until they got my earbuds working, but I'd intended to go after them as soon as I saw him with her at the pet food vendor stand. Then when they left . . ."

"But you grabbed your horse, not a car."

Adrien shrugged. "A horse can leap fences. Cars can ram them, but not as quickly or efficiently."

"All right, then . . ." Hank began, breaking off.

Victoria Henderson's voice had grown loud. She wasn't yelling; she wasn't out of control.

But she was definitely threatening.

"Now, if you tell me where the two women are, you have a chance for a deal. I don't believe they're dead, and I believe you know where they are. In fact, hmm . . . just where were you taking me? To join them? If something has happened to either of those young women, you should remember that Florida has the death penalty. You know, frankly, I'm not sure how I feel about it. Because rotting in a few of our prisons where you might be shanked any day of your life might be a greater punishment. Then again . . ."

One of the EMTs looked at her, shaking his head.

Adrien knew his shot had done a hell of a number on the unknown partner's shoulder and arm. Apparently, he was out now.

Unable to answer.

Detective Henderson gave the EMT a nod and turned back to the cuffed Jimmy Trent.

"You weren't the alpha male here, my friend. Save your ass, please! Where are they? I mean, they're probably here, and we can pull the entire place apart, but if you want to cooperate . . ."

"Only one!" Jimmy Trent said.

"Only one what?" Hank asked, stepping forward.

Jimmy Trent looked from Victoria to Hank—and then over at Adrien. Adrien almost smiled. He scared the man, he realized. It was good to be tall—sometimes, his height alone could be imposing.

He let Chaparral's reins drop and took a few steps toward the man.

"Only one woman is here. That's what you're saying. Where is the other woman, and where is the one who is here?"

"The storage building?" Victoria Henderson asked him. "And hmm, let me guess. You've built up the land around it or someone did, and there's something that resembles a basement beneath the floorboards?"

Trent looked at her, his face white. He wasn't a great criminal. The man was horrified he'd been caught, and he was frightened.

"That's it," Adrien said. "Which woman—"

"I don't know!" Jimmy Trent said. "I don't. I wasn't here—he was coming this morning. That's why I was looking for a replacement. I mean . . ."

"Who is the 'he' who came for her?"

"Carl. Carlos, depending on . . . I mean, he's an American. His grandfather is from South America, and he has connections and . . . they can make him a lot of money," Jimmy Trent said. "Please, honestly, I swear, I never hurt anyone!"

"Carl or Carlos—who? What's his last name?" Hank demanded.

"I, um, sometimes, Miller, sometimes Gonzalez, I mean, I'm not sure what the real name is. Look, I'm cooperating. I'll tell you anything, but I don't know everything!" Trent wailed.

"I'm going to the storage shed. Hank—" Victoria Henderson announced.

"Oh, I've got this guy," Hank said. "I want to get him to the station, see what our people can discover online about this Carl or Carlos."

"I'll get to the storage shed with you, Detective Henderson," Adrien said.

She studied him for a minute, and he almost smiled. She'd thought he was a ridiculous womanizer, a jerk.

Now . . .

Was she grateful he'd come along? Was she ready to respect him? Or was her opinion of him still on the line?

But he couldn't worry about that right now. He had hoped they'd solved the case—that both young women might be returned to their homes—the senator's niece, and from what he knew, another young woman who was apparently an asset to humanity, intelligent, kind, caring, and generous to those who needed help.

Of course, whether he liked it or not, the senator would keep up the pressure if the young woman who was still missing was not his niece. Not that they wouldn't pursue anyone with the same ardor—but they could do it without political pressure.

She walked swiftly ahead of him. She wasn't really tiny, Adrien noted. She was probably a good five-eight, a respectable height.

He was just taller, and she had purposely made herself appear naïve and *fragile.* Easily taken because she always looked for the good in others, because she was trusting.

Just as the two young women who had fallen to the lure of Jimmy Trent and his rescue dogs.

"The dogs," she murmured suddenly.

"The dogs?" he asked.

"I don't believe the poor dogs did anything other than growl. I think they were used to scare people. I hope to hell some power out there doesn't determine they all need to be euthanized!"

"Well, when we find whoever is still hidden here, we can find out if they were used to chew anyone into submission. And if not—"

"They'll go to a shelter where they may wind up euthanized anyway. I just wish . . . wow, sorry, I mean, truly, I am desperately concerned for human beings first, but . . ."

"Gotcha. Let's find our victim first."

She nodded. She could move fast; he gave her that. She reached the shed, and she swore softly, seeing that it was secured with a padlock.

"No worries," Adrien told her. He slammed the bulk of his shoulder and back against the wooden closure.

It gave with a shatter.

She stared at him. "Damn! You are useful!" she told him.

"I try, Detective Henderson."

"Vicky, please, just Vicky."

"Adrien."

"I know. I read the program. Your real name?"

"Yeah. No reason not to use it."

"Did you win the barrel racing?"

"I did."

They had picked their way through the shattered wood and

stood in the middle of the structure. It wasn't big—perhaps twenty by twenty.

And there was nothing in it. Nothing at all, except for a covering of sawdust over the floor.

"There's a trap somewhere," Vicky murmured. "There!"

She hunkered down, moving sawdust aside with her hand. Adrien saw the floorboards matched up strangely, and he joined her in pushing sawdust aside.

Then he saw it; a metal hook.

He caught hold of it and pulled, drawing up a piece of the flooring that was about four by four in dimension. There was no ladder, there were no steps. And only darkness greeted them.

"Hoist me down, please," Vicky said.

"You got it," he told her, catching her beneath the arms as she lowered herself down, making sure she didn't fall flat on her face.

"Here! She's here, passed out on the floor. But she's alive! We need a medic. We need a medic, fast!"

Adrien was ready to drop into the small hole in the earth, but he didn't need to. Vicky Henderson apparently carried a fair amount of muscle in her slim frame. She was able to lift the young woman in the hole high enough for him to reach down and get his arms around the woman and lift her clear from the hole. His first instinct was to run with his human bundle, but he realized he'd be leaving Vicky Henderson in the hole. He remembered he wore earbuds and could be heard by Eames, Vicky, and Hank, so he spoke quickly.

"Help. We have a victim in the shed. Need a medic."

He had barely turned before Hank was in the shelter, followed by EMTs carrying a stretcher. Even as they arrived, the young woman began to moan softly and open her eyes. Her first response was a scream.

"No, no, no!"

"It's all right; it's all right! We're the good guys!" Hank told her quickly.

She began to sob softly. "They took her today, they took her today. They took Kasey today, and I don't know . . ."

Beyond a doubt, the young woman was traumatized. And if she was saying that they had taken Kasey, then she was Melissa Martinelli.

She was safe; she was cared for. Adrien turned and saw Vicky was holding the edges of the hole; he hunkered down again to catch her beneath the arms and pull her from the hole.

A bit of the flooring gave.

He fell back, and his body took the brunt of the fall.

And Vicky Henderson wound up lying on top of him, staring down into his eyes.

Miraculously, they both smiled at the same time.

"Thanks. I think!" she told him.

And he nodded. Then there was that second when they both just looked at each other, and he thought she had decided that he might be all right.

"Un, sorry!" she murmured, quickly scrambling up.

"You two okay?" Hank asked.

"Nothing a shower won't cure," Vicky told him. "Except—"

"You two want to go to the hospital with her," Hank said. "Of course. I'm going now—she's the only one here, right?"

"No one else in the hole," Vicky said. "I believe Jimmy Trent is telling the truth. He wasn't the dominant partner in any of this, and he's scared silly now. Someone has Kasey Richardson, and we must find out who has her and where she's been taken."

Through the earbuds, Adrien heard Eames's voice, as did Vicky and Hank.

"Vicky's right; Hank, get Trent here now. Vicky, you and Adrien follow to the hospital."

"Sir, we can't ride a horse to the hospital," Adrien reminded him.

"Our people are out there. Call for Officer Vickers—he'll get your horse home. And hitch a ride behind the ambulance—"

"I'd like to ride in the ambulance," Vicky said.

"Room for one," a young EMT told her.

"Go," Adrien said.

She did, following the EMTs bearing the stretcher that carried Melissa Martinelli.

"I know John Vickers. Good guy. He'll see that your horse is safely brought—"

"To my brother's house. It's not far—Southwest Ranches," Adrien told him.

"Come then, I'll introduce you quickly," Hank told him.

"Where's Trent?" Adrien asked.

"With an officer in my car; this will take about sixty seconds."

Hank was almost right; when they exited, he saw a young, uniformed officer was already talking to his horse. Hank introduced him quickly, and John Vickers assured him, "I know the area; I'll find your place. My partner will get me from your brother's place. If you need to call—"

"I'll let him know. Thank you."

"No, thank you, man, this is a cool horse!" Vickers said.

Adrien grinned and turned to find out about the ride he needed. There was an officer right behind him, ready to oblige.

When he arrived at the hospital, he found Vicky Henderson was in the waiting room.

"She's going to be okay," Vicky assured him. "They did a lot of threatening, but she said that they didn't hurt them. If they didn't behave, Trent told them he'd sic the dogs on them and let them chew them to ribbons. But the dogs never touched them. I know it's stupid to be worried about the dogs—"

"The dogs will be okay, and it isn't stupid. It means you're a decent person."

She smiled at that. She had been pacing the waiting room, but with his arrival, she sank into a chair at last.

"I didn't get much from her yet. The poor woman is truly traumatized. But she did see this Carlos person—briefly. And . . ." She paused and then looked at him. "I understand you were pressured into coming here."

"Not pressured. I'm here often; I have a brother here. I'm, uh, from here."

"Oh!" She studied him anew.

"Yeah. Grew up at Southwest Ranches, went to Florida State University College of Criminology, became a cop in St. Augustine and then opted for the bureau, went through the academy, and got assigned in Virginia . . . and then transferred down here."

"When?"

"Yesterday," he said dryly.

"Ah." She studied him for a minute. "Melissa Martinelli isn't the senator's niece, is she?"

He shook his head.

Vicky leaned back against her chair and closed her eyes for a minute. "I like to believe we'd do everything in our power to find anyone—man or woman—who had been abducted. But since I'm not a fool, and I know that powerful people can exert a lot of pressure, I think a part of me is glad we found Melissa first. Because they'll keep you—and every officer and agent in the state—on this now until Kasey Richardson is found."

"I can't argue that."

Eames's voice came through to them again.

"Vicky, I can hear you," he reminded them.

"Yes, sir," she murmured. Then she added softly, "And that's okay. I stand by my words."

"Okay, I didn't hear them," Eames said. "So—"

"Sir, as soon as they let me in, you'll know!" Vicky reminded him. "Has Hank—"

"Yes, Hank is here; he's in with Trent now, working him well, but . . . I don't know what else the man can give us. I think his role was just to be charming and lure the victims to the house. But he's working him. And Hank is good. We'll see."

"I'd like a crack at him," Vicky said.

"And you'll get it," Eames promised.

"Hey, the doctor is coming out," Adrien said, seeing that a dignified, mature man in a doctor's uniform was coming through the door to the waiting room, obviously ready to approach Vicky.

They both stood, waiting for his report.

He walked over to them, nodding in acknowledgment to Adrien's presence.

"She's going to be okay," he told them. "Physically. I have a feeling she may need therapy for many years to come, but she wasn't beaten, dehydrated, or starved. I think that being continually exposed to the darkness and small space caused a physical reaction to kick in. When she closed her eyes and passed out, she didn't have to face her circumstances. When they took Kasey . . . who had become her friend, there had to be a horrible breaking point for her."

"May we see her?" Vicky asked.

"Yes, physically, she's sound, but we'll keep her in the hospital overnight for observation, and until her family has been notified," the doctor said.

Vicky glanced at Adrien. He gave her a small nod, realizing her concern.

Someone was still out there. The someone who had taken Kasey Richardson. And that someone might not want her talking, and they might not be done with her. . . .

"Doctor, we're going to place officers and/or agents on guard for Miss Martinelli," Adrien said. "They won't disrupt—"

"Right. We'll let her go in the morning," the doctor said. He obviously didn't like what was going on, but he told them, "The man who was brought in, unidentified, no I.D. on him—and we were informed that no one knew him—is still in surgery. We want to have him transferred to a prison hospital facility as soon as possible."

"Of course," Adrien said agreeably. "For now—"

"Yes, you may go in and see Miss Martinelli."

He led them in and indicated the room where they would find Melissa Martinelli.

She was sitting up in bed, just staring.

"Melissa?" Vicky said quietly.

The young woman managed a weak smile. "You! You were with me in the ambulance. You—you got me out of the hole!"

"We got you out of the hole," Vicky told her. "Well, honestly, Melissa, the police and agents and the entire community has been looking for you, and we had lots of help getting you out of the hole."

"Thank you, thank you, thank you. . . ."

"I'm Detective Victoria Henderson, and this is Special Agent Adrien Anderson. And now, we need your help. We need to know everything—"

"I told you what I know in the ambulance!" Melissa said.

She was wide-eyed, trembling, so vulnerable. Yet even so, Adrien could clearly see why Vicky Henderson had made such a perfect choice for the undercover mission in drawing out the kidnapper. The two women had deep red hair, bright green eyes, and slender, well-proportioned facial structures, as well as similar body types. Of course, he had seen pictures of Kasey Richardson, Senator Peter Connery's niece. Whoever Carlos was, there was a type he was demanding. And Vicky, like Melissa and Kasey, fit the bill.

"Melissa, would you tell us everything, from the beginning?" Adrien asked gently.

Melissa took a deep breath. “He seemed like such a nice guy. He saw me buying dog food. He told me about his rescues. Some rescues!” she said, wincing.

“The dogs never hurt you,” Vicky said, glancing at Adrien.

“What? No, no. He just talked about what they could do, chew us to pieces so that we'd be begging to die. And I . . . I was terrified!”

“Of course, you were,” Vicky said gently. “But—”

“I would have lost my mind if it hadn't been for Kasey! Even in the dark, we would talk. And she was wonderful, talking about places we had to go together when we were freed. She was always so positive until . . .”

“Until?” Adrien asked.

“This morning. That's when the mean one came.”

“The mean one. Did anyone ever use his name?” Vicky asked her.

She shook her head. “Jimmy fed us and brought us water. We only saw the other guy a few times. Then this morning . . .”

Tears slipped silently down her cheek, but they didn't need to urge her to continue.

“He dragged Kasey out of the hole! Dragged her. He told her her master had come for her, and it was time for her to go. And he warned her again about Trent's dogs, and that he had a gun, and if she didn't behave, he'd have her begging for death. She had best—best!—behave for her new master. And then . . . then she was gone! And I was alone and the darkness was horrible and I was so afraid!”

“Did you see who came for her?” Vicky asked quietly.

“Umm . . .”

“Anything. Anything will help us!” Vicky whispered.

Melissa closed her eyes in deep thought. “I was looking up and . . . I think he was about the same height as the mean one. Same kind of build . . . dark hair. I think . . . I think he was in a suit, maybe? I'm not certain. I'm not certain.”

"That's okay! You've done great, Melissa," Adrien assured her.

There was a commotion in the hall. Adrien turned quickly, ready to draw his Glock. But it wasn't someone ready to hurt Melissa; it was an older woman, frantic to reach her.

A nurse was behind her, apologizing quickly. "I'm sorry, Mrs. Martinelli said she had to see her daughter—"

"Understandable," Adrien assured her, stepping aside. The woman was like a laser-propelled bullet, anxious to reach her daughter.

"Melissa!" she cried, almost throwing herself on the young woman in the bed, her arms cradling her in a hug that might have been dangerous had Melissa suffered any broken bones.

"Mom, Mom, Mom!"

Adrien glanced at Vicky, who gave him a smile. Of course. They both knew it was natural that such a moment would be beautiful and a little heartbreaking.

"Mom, these are the people who saved me!" Melissa managed to say at last.

Mrs. Martinelli turned. She was a lot like her daughter—but older. Red hair turning a bit gray, her size a little plumper, but her eyes as dazzling a green as they shimmered with tears. She hugged Vicky first, words of thanks tumbling from her mouth, and then she turned to Adrien, who accepted her hug a little awkwardly at first, but then returned it, patting her back.

"She's going to be fine!" Adrien assured her.

"I'm going to take her home as soon as I can. I'm going to sleep here tonight, and so is my husband—he's parking the car. We're not going to leave her for a second. He won't come back, right? You got him, you got him, you got him—"

"There will be police on duty, Mrs. Martinelli, here, and when you take her home. We got two men involved in this, but there's a third, and we want Melissa to be safe."

"And Kasey is still out there!" Melissa cried from the bed.

Kasey was still out there.

Adrien looked at Vicky Henderson. She was looking at him.

They might have had a rough start. She'd seen him as a misogynist and jerk.

He'd seen her as a bit of fluff . . .

Really beautiful fluff, but fluff.

Now, he knew, it had changed. They'd earned each other's respect.

And neither one of them was going to stop until Kasey Richardson had been found.

Chapter 3

Vicky lowered her head as they left the room. She was grateful, of course, they had Melissa safe.

"You all right?" Adrien asked her.

She nodded. "Yeah, sorry, I was just thinking. If we'd been a day earlier, we might have gotten both women back safely. If—"

"We didn't have everything we needed. And we do have leads on how we're going to find Kasey."

"We do?" Vicky asked.

"We have an unknown man who must know something. He's apparently the salesman. And we have Jimmy Trent. And we have . . ."

"What?"

"Well, a slew of officers and agents and the two of us," he said, nodding and lifting a brow to her.

Vicky smiled weakly. He wasn't such a jerk at all. He knew how to be nice; how to try to make her feel better. She was stronger than that. She'd earned her way into her position, and she knew how to handle herself when things went right—and when they went wrong.

"So—"

"So. It will be an hour before our unknown guy is out of surgery," Adrien said thoughtfully. "We can get to the station, talk to Jimmy Trent, and then get back to the hospital. In all honesty, I don't think Jimmy Trent is going to be able to tell us much. We need to speak with the guy in surgery."

"Let me call Hank, see if he's gotten anything," Vicky said. They'd ended the communication with their earbuds when they'd left Melissa's room. But even as she drew her phone out to call Hank, she saw that Hank was calling her.

"He wants to talk to you," Hank said dryly.

"What?" She glanced at Adrien as she said the word. "Hitting the speaker button, Hank. Adrien is with me. We were going to come in because our unknown guy won't be out of surgery for at least another hour. We both think he's going to be our best bet, but we don't want to just sit around driving one another crazy, either."

"You do know it's night, right?" Hank asked her, laughing softly.

"Uh, yeah. Sure."

"Well, I'm glad you're in for the duration—though you will need to sleep somewhere along the line. And hey, you're my partner! Never mind, the Fed did good."

"Thanks," Adrien added, reminding Hank they were on speaker.

"Right!" Hank said. "Anyway. So, Jimmy Trent is playing it like a kid, or he's smarter or meaner than we suspected. He'll only talk to 'the redhead.'"

"We'll be there soon. We got a ride with patrol here—"

"You'll find a police vehicle is waiting for you right out front," Hank told her.

"Okay, thanks."

"Yep, thanks, again," Adrien added.

"You got it," Hank told them.

And as Hank had said, there was a patrol car waiting for them at the entrance.

"Once we get to the station, we'll have my car," Vicky told Adrien, smiling as she opened the rear door; the front was occupied by two officers Vicky knew, Lyle Cavanaugh and Betty Woods, both solid and caring, in their mid-thirties and dedicated to the job. She greeted them both, thanking them for the ride and introducing them to Adrien.

"Hey, we've got the easy part," Betty assured them, turning around to see them as Lyle drove. "We hear you two had quite the day, Vicky."

"And not over yet," Lyle said, glancing at them through his rearview mirror. "We've been driving the streets, looking for anything and . . ."

"The problem is Kasey Richardson could be in an airplane out of the country right now," Betty added. "But Eames is working with DDLE and the FBI, U.S. Marshals, you name it. They've covered the airports, the train stations. . . . We just don't know how much of a head start this man has had—or even what his endgame might be with his captives."

"Two things—he wants redheads," Adrien said. "So, he's either got a revenge motive going if a redhead wronged him; or he is trafficking, and he's been asked for redheads."

"Hopefully, we can learn more when we get to the station," Vicky said.

"Jimmy Trent said he'll talk to Vicky," Adrien added.

"Right. We'll get you there and get back on the road, searching," Lyle assured them.

"It's the senator's niece who is still missing, right?" Betty asked quietly.

"It is. And, yes, they forced federal involvement because of her, but whether it had been Kasey or Melissa who had been discovered, I wouldn't be leaving," Adrien said.

"That's good to hear," Betty murmured. "Sorry. I'm a mom.

And I think my kids are just as important as kids in a politician's family!"

"I'm with you on that," Adrien assured her.

"Good to hear it!" Betty said, smiling.

"We're here. We can wait—" Lyle said.

"No, no, get back out there," Vicky said. "My car is here."

"And it may not be a car we need," Adrien murmured.

"What?" Vicky asked him.

"If this man hasn't hopped something that will get him out of the country, he's gone into hiding. And that may well mean he's gone into the wilderness. We're right on the edge of the Everglades, areas that are state, federal, and tribal lands." He looked at Vicky and shrugged. "Horseback may be the best way to go."

"You think he could have dragged a protesting woman—" Vicky began.

"Or one he's drugged, knocked out, or is forcing along at gunpoint," Adrien said. "I can go it alone in there, and you and Hank—"

"We'll see," Vicky told him.

She thanked Lyle and Betty as they got out of the car, feeling ever so slightly resentful again. So, he was a cowboy—assuming she couldn't ride a horse.

Okay, she didn't own one, and certainly not an amazing buckskin running quarter horse, but that didn't mean she couldn't sit in a saddle!

"That's your plan?" Vicky asked him. "What if—"

"Let's see what you can get out of Jimmy Trent," Adrien told her. "Then I'll decide on a plan. Right now, I have ideas, nothing more."

They headed into the station; Eames was there, aware they were arriving. She had always respected him; he was a man who had arrived at his position by working his way up. He was almost sixty now, tall, dignified, with a cap of thick white hair and a well-sculpted face, with deep grooves in his lean cheeks that betrayed the scope of his experience.

He was quick to introduce Adrien to the desk sergeant and a few of the other officers in the area; then he led them toward the rear of the station and the interrogation and observation rooms.

"You ready for this?" Eames asked Vicky. "She's good," he told Adrien. "But this time, the wretch took you—"

"I'm fine. And we think that time—" Vicky began.

"Is of the essence," Eames finished. "Come on. Hank is in the observation room, keeping an eye on him. He's been just sitting, not trying to pace, not fighting his restraints . . . just sitting."

"He knows his goose is cooked," Vicky murmured.

"I suspect he knows he's going to prison. Hank tried explaining that cooperating was going to be his best option, but . . . he said he'd only talk to the redhead."

Vicky gave them a nod, aware Eames and Adrien Anderson were heading into the observation room as she went in to speak with Jimmy Trent.

"The dogs!" Jimmy said anxiously. "They aren't bad dogs. Blue . . . please, don't let them put her down. None of this is her fault. Hercules is just a puppy, really. He's a big shepherd, but he's not even a year old. I know you were honest about one thing. You care about the dogs."

"I'm going to do everything I can for the dogs," she told him, sliding into the chair across the table from him. "But my first concern has to be for a human being. Who is the man who took Kasey Richardson? Where was he taking her? You work with me, and—"

"They're going to want to kill my dogs," he said. "You let me know my dogs are going to be okay, and I'll tell you anything I can."

"I'll make sure the dogs are okay."

"What? You're going to take them to some shelter where they'll *humanely* put them to sleep?"

"No! There are no-kill shelters—"

"And they'll never make it to one. They'll say the dogs were vicious!"

Vicky was surprised when the door opened and Adrien walked in. "You said you wanted to talk to the redhead. Well, she's here. Now, what you are worried about is the dogs. Guess what? Vicky has been worried about them, too. But I have a solution. I have family here with a nice spread of acres not far from your place. I'll take the dogs, and I'll promise you—and Vicky—that the dogs will be all right. My brother has two teenaged sons who work with animals and know dogs, how to train them, how to make them feel at home. I promise you. The dogs will be okay."

Jimmy Trent stared at him a long moment.

"You're telling the truth? I think it's legal for you to lie to me in interrogation!"

"I'm not lying, and you also have a right to an attorney—"

"No, I just want to talk to her," he said, looking at Vicky.

The door opened again. Hank was there. "Animal control is taking your pets over to Special Agent Anderson's family's property. It's happening while we speak," he said, looking from Adrien to Jimmy Trent.

"Really? Are you lying now?" Trent asked.

His face was twisted with hope and concern, making him look very young. Vicky had a feeling if they looked into his background, they would have found something very sad. He'd been used by stronger individuals.

But a young woman was still missing. And he had been the one to lure her into whatever fate was awaiting her.

"Listen, Jimmy!" she said. "You're right. I love dogs. And obviously, Special Agent Anderson isn't lying. You saw him with his horse. He loves animals. We'll take care of the dogs, I promise. In the best way. But you need to have the same compassion for Kasey! Please, help us!"

But Jimmy shook his head. "I—I don't know more. I just know Richard told me we had to deliver redheads to Carlos or else he'd see that they killed us and the dogs."

"Deliver redheads to Carlos. Okay. Did he tell you what Carlos wanted the redheads for?" Vicky persisted.

"He . . . he was working upstate before, for someone else, I guess. I heard him talking to Richard one day. He was laughing and saying, 'It's redheads this time.' But he's bad, really bad. Richard was in with him on some kind of a drug deal, and it went bad, and if Richard didn't do what he said, he was going to see we all died. Horribly."

Jimmy Trent seemed to be telling the truth. He was a broken man.

Vicky nodded and rose, looking at Adrien and Hank.

They had what they could get from him. Except for one thing.

"What's Richard's last name?" she asked Jimmy Trent.

He looked at them curiously. "His last name? Trent. He's my cousin. That's why . . . he always looked after me. I'd get beat up at school, and Richard would make sure it never happened again. He's my cousin. And I swear, he never killed anyone! He just . . ."

"Just gave young women to this Carlos so he could kill them?" Vicky asked softly.

"No, no, no . . . just, um . . ." He paused and looked up at her, shaking his head. "I don't know! I just know I owed it to Richard to help him stay alive!"

"Okay, thank you," Vicky said. She looked at Adrien. "We must get back to the hospital and see what Richard Trent can tell us. Hank— "

"You two do that and keep in touch. I'm going to be out on the road—searching," Hank said. "I swear, I think we had the airports, train stations, and even the major docks on alert. But I think this Carlos fellow may know we're on to him. If so, he'll lay low for a bit, which means he's out there. We have renderings now, pictures of Kasey Richardson up everywhere. This Carlos is going to need to find a way to change Kasey's appearance if he has any hope of getting her out of here."

"Move, everyone move," Eames said, entering the room. "We don't know how much time this poor girl has! Oh, and thanks, Trent. We found your cousin in the system. You repaid him. He disappeared off the grid almost a year ago—after the cops lost him when they were looking to arrest him in the matter of a drug bust. He hid all that time. Thanks to you!"

Jimmy Trent sobbed softly.

The man was far from being a hardened criminal.

Vicky quickly left the room and didn't pause to speak with anyone else as she hurried out. Her car was in the lot, and she knew Adrien was following her as she walked hurriedly toward it and clicked the doors open.

She wondered if he was going to protest and insist that he drive.

He didn't.

He slid into the front passenger seat and was silent for a minute, looking out the window.

"Are you uncomfortable with someone else driving?" she asked him.

"No. Why?" he asked with a frown.

I don't know! Wincing inwardly, she also knew what she might have said—*Because I'm being ridiculously defensive because . . .*

Why? Because he was the epitome of masculinity? But he had never acted as if he felt the least superior in any way!

"Sorry. Just some people get nervous when someone else is driving."

He laughed. "I assume you're a good driver. No, I was thinking it was almost midnight."

She glanced at him. "Past visiting hours? They'll let us in. We're law enforcement."

He nodded. "I wasn't afraid of not getting in."

"Then?" she asked.

"Just thinking."

"And you think that. . . . ?"

"I think he's holding her somewhere near the Trent ranch, and he is going to need to leave her alone long enough to buy some makeup and hair dye," Adrien said. "Unless, of course, he came prepared."

"We don't even know that he knows we have Melissa."

"I have a feeling he does. And he's holding Kasey somewhere."

"Maybe just a nearby house," Vicky suggested.

"Yeah. Maybe."

But he didn't think so; she could see it. The one thing she'd discovered about the man was that he was professional. He wouldn't rule anything out until he had a fact or, at the very least, a lead.

He looked over at her and smiled. "We're inching forward. Only inching, but . . . after we speak with Richard Trent, we can inch even further."

"At midnight," she murmured.

"Sadly, criminals don't tend to keep nine-to-five hours," he said with a shrug.

"Too true," she agreed. She paused, frowning. "Was that the truth—about the dogs?"

He nodded, staring ahead. "My brother does have teenage boys, and they're pretty amazing kids. Josh is into horses and dogs, in that order, and Jordan is into dogs and horses, in that order. They're great students, too. He and Mandy are what parents need to be, I guess. I mean, they're kids. They love video games and all, but Jordan is going to graduate this year, and he wants to go to FSU and major in criminology and work with canine units."

"They do sound like great kids."

"I should be so lucky one day."

"Me, too," she murmured.

They were quickly back at the hospital, producing their credentials, and being led to the room where Richard Trent was recovering from surgery.

He was sedated, but awake. His arm and shoulder were bandaged and in a special cast that kept him from making any movements with it.

He stared at them balefully as they entered the room, knowing immediately who they were.

"You have security for that girl!" he said. He shook his head. "You don't understand. I'm the one in danger here. And Jimmy . . . you may be holding him, but they'll get to him somehow!"

"They? Who are they?" Adrien asked.

He shook his head miserably. "Who knows? Carlos has . . . a small army. And he means it; when you fail him, he sees to it you're killed."

"You know more about him. You were working with him before," Vicky said. "As we explained to Jimmy, the more you help us, the better it will be for you when charges are filed and you go to trial."

He almost smiled. "What difference does any of that make if you're dead?"

"If this is as big as it's beginning to sound and you help us, there is the Witness Protection Program," Adrien told him.

He frowned. Then he almost smiled. "So, Red. You're a local cop? And you're something else—with the Feds, huh?"

"Something like that," Adrien said. "I'm telling you, help

yourself. Your poor cousin is a mess—he was a good guy, right, caught up in saving you? Here's the thing—let us stop Carlos. Then you won't have to worry about being dead."

Richard Trent, so much harder and resolved than his cousin, lay back wincing and closing his eyes. "You could have killed me today. You didn't."

"We try not to kill," Adrien said flatly. "You will heal—"

"And Carlos will kill me," he said.

"Not if we get Carlos," Vicky persisted.

"I don't know his real name. He goes by Carl when he's being Anglo to get what he wants, and he goes by Carlos when he's trying to work someone with a Cuban, Colombian, or other Hispanic background. He's good, and he knows how to get what he wants. I don't . . ."

"You don't what?" Adrien persisted. "Look. I'm going to warn our guys to watch out for you as well as the victim. I believe they're already on to that."

"And they'll care?" Richard asked dully.

"They will protect and serve—yes. Even you," Vicky said.

"He's not going to kill her. I think . . . all right, he was making it pretty big in the drug trade. Then he had a stash, and the cops got wind of it, and millions of dollars of stuff was taken off the market—and away from him. We both evaded capture and then he found me. He's changed what he's doing . . . he just wanted redheads, said there was a huge market for them."

"So, he's human trafficking. Where will he be taking her?"

"I don't know. But I do know he was . . . close. I think he was close enough to watch Jimmy's ranch and the house and . . . that's how he found me. And . . ."

He paused, frowning.

"What is it?"

"He was never the kind for a heart-to-heart talk, but one day he said something about hunting out in the Everglades. They have this thing called 'the Great Florida Python Challenge' where people go out and try to bag the biggest invasive snake. He was laughing and saying with his experience, he could have won the whole thing if he wanted. I figure . . ."

"You figure he has something out there, deep through the marsh, out on a hardwood hammock somewhere?" Adrien asked.

"Yeah. Close to Jimmy's place. He sits right on the eastern edge of . . . of nothing but gators and sawgrass."

"All right. That is a help," Vicky told him.

"Don't forget boats," Richard said.

"Boats? He's got a boat out there, you think?" Vicky asked.

Richard Trent looked at her, a far different man from the one who had threatened her earlier that day.

"No. Don't forget little boats, or not-so-little boats. Grab a solid motorboat and you can be in the outer Bahamas from the ports on the coast in a matter of hours. If it were me, that would be my first thought. Get the hell out of the States and get anywhere from there."

"All right. Thanks," Adrien said. "And don't worry; I'm going to talk to our people watching over the hallways. They will protect you; it's their job."

"Yeah, we'll see," Richard said dully. "At least I'm sedated. Can't hurt much more to die than it did to have this shoulder shattered."

"Sorry about that," Adrien said. "Necessity at the time."

They turned to leave. As Adrien had promised, he stopped to speak to one of the officers on duty in the hallway.

"They've got four of us on and one undercover keeping an eye on everything," the young officer assured him. "We've got this."

"Thanks!" Adrien said, with Vicky echoing the word.

They headed out.

"You can drop me at my brother's, my old homestead, if you don't mind," Adrien told her.

"Drop you?" she said. "Hell, no."

He sighed. "All right, I'm going out—"

"Yeah. And I'm going with you."

"You know, we have jobs that aren't nine-to-five. But Vicky, you don't have to indulge me and go riding into a swamp when it's past midnight—"

"You've got a horse for me?"

"Vicky—"

"I won't slow you down, I promise. I'm telling you, I know how to ride a horse. No, I don't own one, and I actually learned when we did summers up in the Blue Ridge Mountains. I don't like the Everglades in the darkness, but I'd like to believe you have animals that can help me avoid any of the creatures that prowl by night. Even human ones."

He smiled at her.

"Shiloh."

"Pardon?"

"Shiloh. She should be perfect for you. She's a mustang rescue. My brother is into rescuing things, too, so . . . well, you can say hello to old Blue before we head out!"

Chapter 4

Adrien gave Vicky directions to his family's old homestead, now his older brother's home, and she frowned as they arrived.

There was nothing palatial about the place. But Adrien was one of four siblings, so the sprawling ranch house, built circa the early 1940s, stretched out in a long ell. The gated estate wasn't that much different from the one owned by Jimmy Trent. They had large stables, several paddocks, ten horses—last time he'd been "home"—and a massive kennel.

He hadn't lied to her. His brother and his family were huge on rescuing animals, placing them when they could, but giving them a loving "forever" home when they couldn't.

She was staring at the place, still frowning.

"What?" he asked her.

"I can't believe we're here already! Before, heading from Trent's to the hospital and then to the station and back to the hospital . . . short distances, but long drives. First, I should drive at midnight more often—the traffic is way better," Vicky said.

He laughed softly. "Well, let's face it—yes. This time of

night is much better. Once you head this far west, you're in a rural area, and that helps, too. I loved growing up here—close to major cities, 'Far From the Madding Crowd.'"

"Ah, quoting from Thomas Hardy, eh?" she teased. "Still . . ." She smiled. "Think about the Riverwalk in Fort Lauderdale, South Beach, Brickell . . . we're not far at all, and yet a world away."

"That's what I always love. Ah, there's Jeremy!" Adrien said, getting out of the car as he saw his older brother step out of the house.

"Hey! So, your pups arrived a while ago. Nice animals," Jeremy told him.

Jeremy was eight years older than Adrien. Their sisters, Geneva and Charlotte, were in between the two, with Geneva now an attorney in Palm Beach, and Charlotte happily married with two kids of her own in St. Augustine, where she owned a tour company.

They were all grateful Jeremy had chosen to keep their old homestead. Their mom and dad had found it too much to keep up as they aged. And every holiday, when possible, they all gathered at the ranch. Of course, he'd been living in Virginia for the last several years, and work situations had sometimes kept him away. But he was always grateful there was still a "home" for him to go back to.

"They're good?" Adrien asked. "It didn't appear there would be a problem. From what we discovered, no one was ever attacked by any of them—"

"They're doing great!" Jeremy said. "And Chaparral is back, too. All seems well. Except that you're here now . . . with a friend?"

"Yeah, sorry. I know it's late," Adrien told him. "And this is Detective Victoria Henderson. Jeremy, we're still looking for Kasey Richardson."

His older brother was a lot like him; they were the same

height, and had similar features, except Jeremy's hair was a lot darker.

"Welcome, Detective!" Jeremy said.

"Just Vicky, please," she said, smiling. "And thank you."

"You want to go out now?" Jeremy asked Adrien.

"She's still missing."

"And you think she's just west of here, hidden in the wilderness?" Jeremy asked.

"Jimmy Trent's place isn't far from here. All we know is that a Carl or Carlos has her. We believe he intends to sell her, as a slave, as a victim for some sick bastard to cut to pieces, we don't know." He hesitated, shrugging. "Everyone is on it. Rangers, local police, FDLE, deputies, tribal police . . ."

"All smart enough to take it slow in this kind of darkness," Jeremy said. "I have the trailer hitched. I can take you and the horses close to the wilderness, but I'm going to suggest you grab a few hours' sleep. And I'm also going to suggest you choose the airboat over the horses."

It would be a sensible choice, and Adrien knew it. First, wandering around in the pitch darkness that could conceal the wetlands might not be at all a profitable use of time.

And it was true, too; it would be far more sensible to wait for daylight when they could easily access the hardwood hammocks where someone might be keeping a woman prisoner.

He couldn't shake the fear that the man who had Kasey Richardson might move by night.

"You have an airboat?" Vicky asked.

"Yes, ma'am. Seriously, it will be light in a little more than five hours, just breaking light, but that's what you'll need," Jeremy said. "And by the way, I talked to Mike. His people are all over this."

"Who is Mike?" Vicky asked.

"Mike Buffalo. We're close to Miccosukee tribal lands here, and no one knows that area—and the National Park—like

Mike," Adrien said, looking at his brother. "All right; I think you're right. But at first hint of light— "

"I'll get you to the airboat," Jeremy promised. "Come on in. Mandy thought you'd be reasonable. She has the place set for you."

Adrien turned to look at Vicky.

"I'm not going anywhere!" she told him.

Jeremy grinned and opened the door. Adrien swept out a hand, and she walked into the house.

As Jeremy had said, Mandy was waiting for them. His sister-in-law was a tall woman, perhaps six-one or so, with short, stylish dark hair and a quick smile.

"So, you come home for less than twenty-four hours, and we have five new dogs and a slumber party going on," she teased. "As you can see, you're set up for a few hours. Jeremy assured me you weren't an idiot, and you'd listen to reason."

Adrien laughed. "I'm not an idiot, I'm just feeling desperate to save that woman's life," he told her. He turned and introduced Vicky to Mandy, who immediately offered them something to drink or eat.

They hadn't eaten. Adrien realized he was famished.

"You have any power bars or something easy?" he asked Mandy.

"Better than that. I saved two plates. I'll just heat them up quickly," Mandy assured them.

"I'll give you a hand," Jeremy told his wife.

They headed for the kitchen. Adrien turned to Vicky. She was looking around the room, noting the living room offered a convertible sofa, but one with the legs extending in three sections with a foldable section in the middle with cupholders and phone chargers.

The two end sections had been supplied with pillows and sheets.

Vicky turned to look at him. "Wow. Um, nice. My family is great, but . . ."

He shrugged. "I was called in on this for a reason," he reminded her. "You're all right with all this? I don't think your job description calls for treks through snake-infested territory—"

"My job description says I go where I need to go. And I love airboats. And yes, I've been on them many times. Still, one day, I'd love to meet the horses."

"I'm sure we can arrange that," he told her. "But you're on board with this—"

"Yeah, I'm just going to call Eames and Hank and bring them up to speed," she said. "And yes, they'll still be up."

She pulled out her phone and spoke quickly. When she finished the call, she looked at him with a grimace. "Hank will be here by a quarter of six. He thinks you're right, and we need to join those who are searching for Kasey in the Everglades."

Jeremy and Mandy returned, carrying trays. "Lasagna. Easy to reheat," Mandy said. "Hope it's okay—"

"Okay? No, it's brilliant! Thank you!" Vicky said, accepting the tray Mandy offered her.

"All right; we're going to get our five hours," Jeremy said. "You'll notice you're eating on paper—just toss when you're done. See you in the a.m."

"Thank you!" Vicky called again, as Jeremy and Mandy waved and headed down the hallway that led to the bedrooms.

"Of course!" came a reply from Mandy.

"Okay, so, eat, sleep," Adrien said.

"And it's delicious. I must admit, I forgot all about food today," Vicky murmured. "And I do suppose this is the right thing to do. And I even suppose people who know the Everglades better than I ever will are out there, but . . ."

"We're doing the right thing," he assured her.

She smiled, glancing his way. "You're right. And this is . . . well, you do have family in the right places!"

"The boys have school tomorrow. I'm kind of sad you won't meet them. Ah, but I did promise you were going to get to meet Shiloh and the rest of the horses, so . . ."

"Where are all the dogs?" she asked.

"They have a kennel. It isn't full of cages. It's a little house with dog beds all over. They close it up at night; bad things do happen now and then—for dogs. Creatures come out from the waterways, animals can break fences . . . they just make sure they're secure for the night."

"But not protecting the grounds?"

"If someone who didn't belong here drove in, you'd hear them."

"They didn't bark when we came!"

"I guess they like you."

She grinned at that. Then quickly covered her mouth as she yawned. They'd been talking, but he saw they'd both cleaned their plates.

"Let me take your tray—water? You want some water?" he asked her.

"That would be great."

He dumped the trash, wiped the trays, and took two bottles of water from the refrigerator and returned to her and handed her a bottle.

"Thank you!"

"Okay, so . . ."

"Wish I had a toothbrush," she said. She grinned at him. "For your benefit."

"Well, head into the bathroom. Mandy keeps extras in the cabinet beneath the sink."

"You're kidding me."

"I'm not. If you wanted a new outfit, I'm sure she could provide that, as well."

Vicky laughed. "If I'm going to go prowling around in the Everglades, I'll just stick with this. But I will brush my teeth!"

She set her water in the holder and headed toward the hallway.

"First door on your left!" he told her.

"Thanks!"

She returned in a few minutes and curled into her chair.

"We've got five hours," he told her, leaving her to head to the bathroom himself.

"Right. I hope we can sleep."

They could. When he returned, she was already curled into the chair, red hair spilling around her. It might have been a hell of a long day, but she still somehow managed to look like a sleeping princess. Fluff. Nope, she wasn't fluff. The more time they spent together, the more he liked her and admired her. The more . . .

The more he realized he was growing more—and more—attracted to her.

No. They were both mission-oriented. They had shared tense situations and hours. With more to come.

He closed his own eyes. But it took him a few minutes to sleep. He was simply and acutely aware she was there, so close to him.

But sleep did claim him. And then the buzz of his phone and the slowly dawning light of day came far too soon.

"This is amazing," Hank said, settling into the seat of the airboat next to Vicky.

She grimaced and nodded. "Go figure, the Fed can provide, not through a government agency, but through his brother. I realized we could have requisitioned—"

"Yeah. An airboat. And it would have taken forever, and I don't think I'm the airboat captain this guy is!" he said, his words for her ears only, which wasn't difficult; the motor was loud.

Vicky smiled and nodded. Yes, her cowboy had turned out to be an asset. Who knew they'd find an agent with so many workable properties when they'd been told they were getting federal assistance?

They'd heard from Mike, Miccosukee police, who had told them they'd searched during the night. He had given Adrien several locations where he'd already searched; but Vicky had to admit, she didn't know what the locations were or where exactly they might be, though Adrien had.

Mike was giving up the ghost for a few hours, grabbing sleep as they had.

Despite their mission, the morning was oddly beautiful. The sun was rising high in the sky, surrounded by a few light and puffy clouds. They could hear the occasional call of birds over the sound of the airboat motor, and the air rushing by them felt damp and cool.

The airboat motor suddenly cut off. The boat drifted toward a hammock, and Adrien expertly maneuvered it in closely to the hardwood hammock that had suddenly seemed to loom before them.

"Sorry, no way out of getting our feet wet," Adrien said.

"They've been wet before," Vicky assured him, glad that while they weren't the right kind for a hike through the wetlands, she had worn knee-high boots with the little sundress she'd chosen to lure out the kidnappers.

"Yeah, true, but still, honestly? Yuck!" Hank said, but he stepped out of the airboat with a shrug, ignoring the shallow rush of water that greeted him before he could step to the dry land of the hammock.

"There's a kit in the boat, but obviously, watch out for snakes," Adrien advised.

"And don't go pulling any alligator tails!" Hank told Vicky.

"I'll do my best to resist," Vicky promised.

They began to move through the cypress trees, with Adrien taking the lead.

Vicky did love the Everglades, but when she usually came out, it was to Shark Valley. It was part of the park, a place with walking and biking trails, a tower from which one could see forever—and park rangers. She had always thought it was pretty wonderful that such a natural habitat could be so accessible to massive cities, and it was a place to leave the concrete world behind. The cypress trees were beautiful, the mangrove swamps were haunting, the birds were exotic and stunning and . . .

Yeah, well, the alligators. But unless someone accidentally disturbed a nest or, seriously, tried to grab a tail or play with the beasts, keeping a distance from them provided decent safety. Then again, the creatures did wander onto golf courses and even into pools. And after one of the storms, a slew of the creatures had taken refuge in the downstairs of a Fort Myers bank.

Snakes.

Okay, she wasn't so fond of snakes, and she did keep a wary eye on her surroundings as they made their way through trails that weren't really trails—just areas less heavily foliaged than others.

"We have a destination in mind?" Vicky asked.

She remembered thinking at first that Adrien was a showman, a braggart out to strut his stuff at the rodeo to prove his manhood. . . .

"We do," he said. "There's a chikee out here that dates back to the end of the Seminole Wars, that was redone by hunters in the 1950s. It was taken over by the state when they out-ruled such structures in the area, but it was so well built in the 1950s that weekend warriors still like to come here, drink beer—and shoot beer cans."

"And you know about it because?" Hank asked him.

Adrien paused a second, looking back. He shrugged. "My dad went with friends to shoot beer cans a few times."

"And you think this Carl guy would know this old shack—" Hank began.

"There are actually a lot of these old ruins around. The park wasn't established until the 1930s, dedicated in the 1940s, and it's the third-largest in the U.S. It protects the ecosystem, about three hundred species of wading birds, the American crocodile, the West Indian manatee—"

"And the coral snake and other creepy crawlers!" Vicky added.

"Hey, except for pythons and boas, the snakes were here first," Adrien said lightly.

He stopped abruptly.

Vicky, between him and Hank, almost crashed into him.

"What?"

"There is someone there," he said quietly, drawing his Glock.

"How—"

"The sawgrass is overgrown except for there . . . leading to the door. I'll take the direct route," Adrien said.

"I'll take the back," Vicky said.

"And I'll cover you both," Hank advised them.

Adrien was right about the old chikee/shack. Obviously legal or not, those who knew about it had made use of it through the years. It was a structure mainly composed of cypress, Vicky thought, and for something that should have decayed years ago, it appeared to be in excellent condition.

He was also right about the sawgrass. She treaded carefully, trying not to let the field of saw-edged foliage tear into her while hurrying around at the same time.

Massive cypress trees provided shade. The rear of the cabin was almost completely surrounded by them.

Vicky made her way around the house with her gun drawn. There was no door in the back, but there was a window opening, and she hurried to it.

"Found her! And it's clear!" Adrien shouted.

Vicky ran around to the front of the house. The door hadn't been burst open; Adrien had simply pushed it, and the old wood had given.

Hank had joined them.

Even as Vicky entered, Adrien was hunkering down to the floor.

Kasey Richardson lay there, red hair now dyed black. She had been chained to an old structural post and appeared to be . . .

Not dead, not dead! Vicky prayed.

"She's got a pulse!" Adrien said. "She hasn't been harmed, I don't think. I don't see blood—"

The girl opened her eyes. And staring up at Adrien, she began to scream.

Vicky moved forward quickly, assuring her, "Hey, Kasey, it's all right, we're the good guys, I promise, we're here to rescue you—"

"He's coming, he's coming back. He'll be here. He . . . he . . . said they'll kill me if I'm not obedient, and it will be worse than being torn apart by dogs!" Kasey cried. "He's coming back, he's coming back!"

"We need to get her to a hospital," Hank said. "And quickly. I'll call it in—"

He had his phone out.

"Good luck getting a signal," Adrien told him.

"We must get her to a hospital and back to safety," Hank said.

"No!" Kasey shrieked. "We must hide, he's coming back! He told me to behave, that he'd be back and . . . I don't know when he left. I fell asleep. I . . ."

"It's okay, it's okay. We're here, and we're not going to let anything happen to you," Vicky assured her.

She looked at Adrien and Hank.

"We need to get her out of here."

"Wait. Stop!" Adrien said. "Get down!" he ordered.

Vicky obeyed instantly, watching as Adrien made his way to the front-facing window. He turned and nodded at Vicky and Hank.

They nodded. Hank took up a position where he could look—and fire—out the door. Vicky was about to take the other side of the window.

Kasey grabbed her ankle.

"Don't leave me!" she pleaded.

"It's all right; we're here. I'll be right there," Vicky assured her.

She joined Adrien at the window.

They saw someone coming along a trail, not the almost-trail they had just traversed, but one that led from the cabin to the far right.

Vicky thought it might lead toward a road on the eastern edge of the wetlands, close to a road—or something that resembled a road—until the wetlands became untenable by anything short of a canoe or airboat.

A man was approaching. He was wearing jeans and a khaki shirt and a baseball cap. He was perhaps in his early fifties, sporting a full beard and carrying what appeared to be a semi-automatic weapon.

"Hey! Carl, you are no liar! She's in the cabin?" He shouted back to someone.

"Yes. I told you I dyed her hair for you, except it's really a rinse. You can turn her back into a redhead in seconds flat. Once we get her out of here. Of course, no problem getting her to your car, but we'll have to take care getting to the boat."

The second speaker was still invisible. The first stopped suddenly.

He lifted his rifle and aimed at the cabin.

"What the hell are you doing?" the man behind shouted.

But the first man was already firing, shouting in return.

"You ass! There's someone in there. She's not alone. Come out, come out, come out or I'll shoot the entire place down to the ground!"

Wood chips flew. A bullet soared through the window, crashing into the rear wall.

Kasey Richardson screamed and screamed . . .

"She's dead, you're dead, you're dead . . . come out now!"

Bullets flew again.

Vicky looked at Adrien, who nodded.

They had no choice.

It was time to return fire.

They did so.

The man went down. Hank shouted, "Cover me!"

"Carl is still out there, maybe more— " Vicky warned.

"Whoever Carl is, trust me. He's run. He's not stupid; he knows now we've found his little hideout. He's gone."

Adrien was right. Hank was ducked low as he ran out to check on the man who had been riddling the cabin with bullets, but he was down now.

"He's alive!" Hank shouted.

"Yeah, caught him with a glancing shot, he'll have a concussion and one hell of a headache. He needs medical, but . . ." He paused, his jaw clenched as he looked off in the direction that "Carl" or "Carlos" had run. "We have to catch that bastard!" Adrien muttered fiercely.

"Yes, but first, we have the man you shot, and we're obliged to see he gets medical attention. And Kasey needs help. She's terrified," Vicky reminded him.

The girl was curled into a ball on the floor, sobbing hysterically.

"Right," Adrien said.

"So—"

"I'm on it!" he assured her.

He stepped outside the cabin and brought his hand to his jaw. Suddenly, the air seemed to be filled with the loudest bird call Vicky had ever heard.

He stared back at her, shrugging. "Sandhill crane," he told her.

A second later, the call was returned.

Vicky and Hank both stared at Adrien.

"Backup," he told them.

And it seemed that barely a minute later, they saw someone coming through the trees again, this time, from the same direction from which they had come themselves.

There were two men, dressed in the uniforms of the tribal police.

"Mike! Hey, you didn't sleep long," Adrien said, stepping forward to greet the men.

"Well, you know!"

Mike Buffalo stepped forward, a man of about Adrien's age, slightly shorter, Native American, a handsome man with straight dark hair, dark eyes, and a quick smile.

His companion was slightly smaller, but also of the same age, and smiling as he greeted Adrien, giving him a handshake.

Adrien quickly introduced the group.

"Mike Buffalo, Lance Panther, meet Vicky Henderson and Hank Brannigan," Adrien said. "Mike is Miccosukee Tribal Police and Lance is with the Seminole Tribal Police. Reservation land and National Park land and privately owned land butts together here and there—"

"And we're all trying to stop this, but at least you guys got the young woman!" Mike said. He shook his head. "We've heard rumors about disappearances in the state and beyond. But those disappearances I believe involved kidnapping high-risk victims. Those down and out, prostitutes, the homeless, human life every bit as valuable, but without family or friends to insist on help, to persist until they were found, especially when they don't know if people just moved on. . . . Anyway, we've got help coming; I'll send men back out—"

"As will I," Lance assured them.

"And we've got a forewarned group of EMTs coming through with the right equipment to get your injured man and Miss Richardson out of the wetlands and to a hospital. We'll hang in until they arrive—"

"Please! Please!"

They all turned. Kasey Richardson was standing by the door, hanging on to the frame, staring at Vicky.

"Please! Please, don't . . . I need you!"

Vicky lowered her head for a minute. She wanted to be on the chase; she wanted the man who had caused all this suffering to be caught. More. She wanted to know what he'd been doing, and she wanted to find out if there were more victims somewhere who needed to be found.

But she looked at Adrien and Hank and nodded.

She would go where it seemed she was so desperately needed.

"I'll figure out how to catch up with you," she said.

"Not to worry," Mike Buffalo told her. He grinned at Adrien. "I can get you to him. We've been finding each other for years! Did he tell you we were in what might have been the worst rock band ever together?"

Vicky smiled. "No, he didn't mention that," she said. She turned back to Kasey. "I'll be with you to the hospital. I'm sure your folks will be with you soon!"

"Oh, thank you, thank you!"

She was crying again, but she seemed calmer. She walked to Vicky, only staggering slightly, and put her arms around Vicky, who held her gently in return.

"All right, Mike, Lance, thank you. Hank, we're moving that way!" Adrien said.

He looked at Vicky, and she knew that he knew she wanted desperately to be with them on their hunt, but she wouldn't leave a victim in Kasey's damaged state when that victim seemed to need her so badly.

Adrien smiled and nodded quickly. "Mike can find me," he assured her.

He turned and walked into the wilderness. Hank gave her a nod and an understanding smile and followed in his wake.

Vicky, keeping an arm securely around Kasey, turned to Mike and Lance.

"Rock band, eh?" she said lightly.

"They weren't that bad! Honestly!" Lance said, laughing. "They were even almost kind-of-sometimes close to good!"

They heard a groaning come from the ground. The man with the semi-automatic was coming around.

"I've got this," Lance told them. But even as he approached the injured man, more officers and EMTs made their way through the hammock.

"More on the rock band later, I guess," Mike told Vicky. "We'll get this young woman where she needs to be and head back out. Don't worry, I will find Adrien. And we will find the monster who has caused all this!"

She nodded and smiled.

"I don't doubt you in the least!" she assured him.

And her words were solidly honest.

Chapter 5

Hank was a hell of a good man, Adrien thought—he knew Adrien knew the terrain they were traveling better than he did, and despite the case being "his" territory, he was more than ready to step back and let Adrien take the lead.

And Adrien thought Hank had to be in his early fifties, at least. But he must have been one of those cops who hit the gym fairly frequently. He could keep up and he could maneuver like a man half his age.

"Hold up!" he said suddenly.

"What—" Hank began.

"Airboat. He's taken off in an airboat. I just heard the motor. We've got to get back."

"Yeah, well, we can get to your airboat, but if this Carl guy just took off from this direction—"

"There's a shortcut," Adrien told him.

"How the hell do you know this area so damned well?" Hank asked, turning in response to Adrien's shift in direction.

Adrien glanced back at him, shrugging. "My dad was an

ecologist, born in the area, too. He used to come out here with his friends, and sometimes he took us kids on what he liked to call 'bare-knuckle' camping. And Mike Buffalo and I, my family, some of his friends, some of my friends, all became friends, and it was before everyone in the world had a pack of cell phone games, so . . ."

"You got to know the wetlands," Hank said. He laughed. "I grew up in Miami, almost downtown, and it was the jungle of cars that I got to know. Vicky is actually better at all this than me. She spent lots of time out at Shark Valley, her favorite thing to eat was pumpkin bread at the old Miccosukee restaurant that used to be on the trail . . . and she likes most creatures."

"Yeah. Seems she's good with dogs."

"She does love them. She doesn't have one now, though. I mean, we're local, but . . . problems sometimes straddle counties down here," Hank said. He shrugged, studying Adrien for a minute as they reached the airboat. "Too bad you're not staying around. You two have a lot in common."

Yeah, it seemed they did. And, yeah . . .

"She's not married?"

"No, there's a story behind her dedication."

Adrien had started the motor; he wanted to hear the story. But it had to wait. They needed to catch the man who was apparently causing havoc across the state. But he was more than curious about Vicky Henderson. He wished . . .

That they'd met at a party, a bar, even online? Somewhere they might have just met with friends, laughed, talked. . . .

Carl, or aka Carlos. It was imperative they stop the man.

He maneuvered the airboat carefully over a patch of mangroves that were barely below the water's surface.

But once he had done so, they were clear. To his credit, Hank hadn't winced when he'd challenged the risky ground.

"Now where?" Hank shouted over the throb of the motor.

"Northwest—toward the road!" Adrien shouted. "Keep an eye out and . . ."

"I can still hear the other airboat through that cypress stand, I think!" Hank told him.

Adrien listened intently. Hank was right. They were southeast of their quarry, he determined. The man was getting close to the road.

And probably close to a vehicle, and when he reached that vehicle, they'd lose him. . . .

"Hang tight!" he warned Hank, flipping hard through severe shallows again.

The sound of the second airboat was suddenly gone.

They burst into the canal that ran by the road a minute later.

Just in time to see the beige sedan bursting from zero to sixty in a matter of seconds.

But not so quickly he didn't get a partial on the plate.

"Damn!" he swore, pulling out his phone. And to his relief, miracles did happen. He was able to get a signal.

He knew Eames would get the info out to every Florida agency and the bureau, as well. He spoke quickly.

As he finished the call, Eames promised him a car would be along ASAP.

He looked back at Hank.

Hank was grinning. "Impressive. I only got the first two characters on the plate. You got four of them!"

Adrien shrugged. "I was a hair closer," he said.

Hank nodded. "So, we wait. Not long, but . . . I have a few stories I can tell. Now, bear in mind, Vicky is my partner, a damned good cop, but more. She's family. She spends part of her holidays with us, never forgets my kids' birthdays, and reminds me to get my wife flowers on our anniversary. But I can see the sparks flying— "

"What?" Adrien asked. "I mean, she's admirable, yes—"

"Oh, son, there will always be this thing called human chemistry. But! Mess with that girl, and you mess with me. Well, except, you've met her. Mess with her, and she'll mess with you, all on her own!"

"Look, I—"

"Okay, you don't want to hear the stories?" Hank asked him.

He looked up at the sky. Crystal blue now. The air was warm but kissed by the water that lapped gently against the airboat from the canal. The world around them was green with the thick grasses and the trees, and only the cries of wading birds could be heard now and then. Down the canal, an alligator slipped smoothly back into the water.

There was nothing to do but wait. And, hell, yes! He wanted to hear the stories. . . .

He just.

He couldn't appear *too* eager!

"Um, sure," he said casually. "We are just sitting here now. Tell away!"

Vicky paused for a minute, leaning against the wall to gather her thoughts.

Kasey Richardson's parents and her older sister had arrived.

Kasey was now safe in the arms of her loved ones, and Vicky could head back out on the road. She had felt so torn, knowing the victim had needed her, but also determined they catch the man who had caused the trauma in her life. She couldn't resent the time she had spent with Kasey. Of course, the girl had been terrified. She had clung to Vicky like glue until they'd reached the hospital, and she'd still demanded hysterically that Vicky stay with her. . . .

Until her family had arrived.

Vicky reminded herself they had to be thankful. They had

found both women alive. And she had to admit that a lot of the good—and finding the missing women had been very, very good—that had happened had been because of their federal agent, her "cowboy." He was far more than she had estimated him to be. All right, to be fair to herself, she hadn't known he was law enforcement when she had first seen him, and she'd been playing the same game.

She pushed away from the wall. It was time to head back to the waiting room and speak with Eames. She could get back out there—get back to Hank and Adrien. Of course, the entire state of Florida was on the alert, and she was probably the only one who thought it important *she* get back out on the road to pursue the man named Carl. But she wouldn't be alone even in finding her old partner and her strange new partner. Lance had gone back out, but Mike Buffalo was waiting for her, and she had tremendous faith in his capabilities. She was surprised on the one hand that she hadn't met him until now; but in her two years as a detective with the county, the crimes she had worked had been along the coast, in the cities, including the drug-related homicides she and Hank had recently worked. They had been trying, but at least those involved had all been in on the crimes.

Finding the missing women who had been innocent had seemed more difficult, and yet . . .

So far, they'd had the best results.

Except the man causing it all was still out there.

"You want to speak with Richard Trent again?"

She jumped at the question. She didn't need to go to Eames; Eames had come to her.

"I—we already spoke with him. Then—"

"Right after surgery. Maybe he's a little more talkative now. They're going to move him soon, and he knows he's being held and about to be arraigned on many charges."

"I want to—"

"I know. Mike says he's got transport everywhere, and he'll get you to Hank and Adrien. Who, by the way, just lost the perp on one of the access roads. But Adrien caught part of the tag, so we have everyone and his brother out there looking for that tag," Eames told her. "Vicky, we're going to get him. I'm not sure if Richard Trent can help any now that this Carlos guy is on the run, but—"

"He will have something or he won't. I will be quick," Vicky promised.

Eames pointed down the hall. She knew the room. If she hadn't already been there, she'd still know it, because four uniformed officers were standing guard in the hall.

She nodded to Eames, who motioned to the officers, and Vicky walked down to the room, thanking the officer who opened the door for her.

Trent groaned when he saw her.

"You again."

"Hey, I can help you, you know," she told him.

"Oh, right, yeah! You want to help me—after I wanted to make sure you were prepared for a new . . . lifestyle!" he said. He'd moved some, and he winced with the effort. Surgery hadn't been easy on him, she was sure.

And she was human. He might have killed *her*.

And he was lucky. Adrien was a good and decent agent—and a good aim. Richard Trent was down, but not dead because of it. He would do his time.

Vicky was glad, of course, he was alive. Like Adrien, she had sworn an oath to preserve the law.

But she couldn't help being just a little bit glad the man was in pain.

"Hurts, huh?" she asked sweetly.

"You can't play that on me anymore!" he snapped.

"Play that?" she asked. "I'm not playing anything. I didn't say I was sorry that it hurt you."

That actually made the man smile. "How we ever thought you . . . well, never mind!"

"Where did Carlos go? You must have some idea."

"Taking care of business," Richard Trent said.

"Where?"

"I don't know. And you'll never get the girl—"

"No one told you?" Vicky asked him. "We already found the young woman you gave to old Carlos—or Carl. She's safe. And I'm sure she'll have a great deal to say about you!"

He looked scared for a minute—just a minute. Then he slipped back into his mask of hardness.

Maybe he knew that his "goose was cooked."

"You won't find him. He knows the Atlantic, he knows the Straits of Florida and the Gulf of Mexico. He knows Miami-Dade County, Broward County, Collier County. You name it, he knows every county in this state. Oh, yeah, and he must have been a Boy Scout. He knows the wetland, federal, state, tribal, and private like no other out there."

"I wouldn't count on that," Vicky said sweetly. "So, I figure that until he can get to one of those waterways, he'll be hiding out in ye olde Florida-style jungle."

"I didn't tell you that."

"Yes," Vicky said sweetly, "you did."

With a quick smile, she turned and left the room. She could hear him swearing oaths as she left the room. The officers on guard smiled at her.

"You didn't pinch the punk, did you?" one of them asked her.

"Didn't go within a foot of him, or even throw anything at him. I promise," she said.

Eames was waiting for her—as was Mike.

Mike Buffalo had two cups of coffee and handed one to her.

"Anything?" Eames asked her.

"Whatever this Carl's different enterprises might be, I believe he's been practicing them for a long time. Trent said he knows the state and every aspect of it better than we do. He's been drug-running a long time, I believe, and moved into supply and demand when the money sounded so good he wasn't about to resist. Some of that is what I've surmised, of course, but I think I'm right," Vicky said.

"And from what has happened, I agree you're right," Mike offered. "We've heard from Adrien and Hank—he isn't far from where he was. Florida Highway Patrol already found the car—abandoned. He knew he was seen; he knew law enforcement would be after him in that car. So, Detective Henderson, shall we?"

"She needs ten minutes," Eames said, producing a bag. "I had an officer get into your locker and pull out your bag with your fitness training clothing—and your high boots. Better for running around in the wetlands."

"What a great thought, and thank you!" she told him.

"I've been assured that—"

"Yes, I know how to walk through a mangrove swamp, sir, and thank you! I'll be two minutes!"

She was more like five minutes, but she was fast, racing into the ladies' room to change. She emerged realizing she should have thought of better clothing herself.

She figured she couldn't dwell on her lapse; she could just be grateful she was going to be better dressed for the pursuit.

"Ready," she said, reappearing. She turned to Eames. "Sir—"

"Go. I'll see your things are brought to the station. So far, seems you and Hank and our Fed and tribal friends are making a good team. We do need to bring this criminal entrepreneur down before someone else winds up in the crosshair," he said. "Tech is working on this—seems like there are a lot of questions up and down the state about things that have gone on. Time to put it together and tie it down."

She nodded. "Sir, with all of us out there—"

"Just be careful. This may well be more than one man who knows his way around."

"Yes, sir."

She turned with Mike, and they went out to his car. She smiled as she settled into the passenger's seat.

"What?"

"I've never been in a tribal car before," she said.

"Much like any other," he assured her.

"Better than that. It is the first time I've been involved in something that includes every agency in the state—and beyond," she told him. "I like it. But . . ."

"But?"

"I have a feeling that just as we have all kinds of help, so may he."

"A sound possibility. Okay, they're about twenty minutes up—"

"So, great. Time for you to tell me about the rock band," she said.

Looking straight ahead, Mike grinned. "High school. We started off our sophomore year. By the time we were seniors, we were actually being paid to play."

"And you played—"

"Drums. Still play them, still love them."

"Cool. And—"

"Adrien was on guitar," Mike said.

"Ah."

"Have him play for you sometime," Mike said. "What about you?"

She shrugged. "Well, I can't play a guitar or the drums," she said.

"But you knew you wanted to be a cop from the get-go?" he asked her.

She leaned back for a minute. They were on the highway. The drive was smooth, and it felt good just to close her eyes.

"I knew from high school. Before that . . . I wanted to be a veterinarian when I was five—but then I found out you couldn't always save animals that were sick. What else did I want to be?" She hesitated and then shrugged. "Probably the usual things at one time or another, but when I was in junior high, my mom was home alone when a man broke in and nearly killed her—except a cop saw that our front door was ajar and saved her. I was a kid, scared to death about what might have happened, and I became friends with Sergeant Jean Farrell, the woman who saved my mom and arrested the guy who had broken in. I knew she had basically saved my life, as well, and I wanted to grow up to be just like her."

"Now that makes perfect sense."

"I also loved criminology, the science of it, the way that science just continued to grow, allowing us to find criminals through DNA, tiny fibers, profiling . . . except . . ."

"Except?" he asked her.

"Well, we know there is a man out there, and all the science in the world won't really help us right now. I could be partially wrong on that; they may get an I.D. on him through prints or something that he left behind in the car. But even if we know who it is—will that help us catch him?"

"Knowledge is going to help us. Knowledge of the area," Mike assured her. "And we're almost there."

She laughed softly. "There—where?"

"I'll pull off in a few minutes. There's an old—I do mean old—ranger station, from the days when the park began. It was abandoned years and years ago. That's where Adrien and Hank were heading, and I think Lance has already caught up with them." He glanced at her. "Not ESP. Adrien got through to me on his cell."

"Ah."

"Interesting," Mike said.

"What is?" she asked.

He shrugged. "Adrien's story is like yours. He had a friend who nearly died from a drug overdose—Adrien was the one to find him and get him to a hospital. The kid lived, and the dealer—lacing everything heavily with fentanyl—was caught because of an FBI sting. Adrien got his friend to rehab—and became friends with the agent who had orchestrated the sting."

"I guess when we see what good can be done. . . ."

"Yeah. Especially when we get it all together, cover all the bases." He glanced at her.

He turned off the main road to a smaller paved road.

And then on a dirt road that ended in a tangle of trees and brush.

"We're on foot from here," he said.

"Great," Vicky said. But she laughed when he looked at her worriedly. "No, no, seriously, I'm fine. I wouldn't be out here if I thought I'd be a drawback rather than a help! But . . . where are we going?"

"Another lean-to straight out from here, left over from I don't know when," Mike told her. "It's not much, but . . . we need to brainstorm. This man must know half the state is after him. And he must suspect that at least some of us know what he knows about shelters in the area, and maybe places to find help."

Stepping out of the car and into the cypress prairie, Vicky thought about a recent documentary she'd seen on the "river of grass" that was the Everglades. She looked ahead and saw nothing at all—but she followed him as he wound through cypress trees stretching to the sky around them, through a shallow pool, and through more trees to see what remained of a roofless structure.

"And here we are," Mike announced.

Before they reached it, Adrien stepped out to greet them.

"You made it!" he said.

Hank and Lance followed him out.

"Yeah, and you guys are just sitting around?" Mike asked him.

"Hell, no!" Hank said. "This guy," he said, indicating Adrien, "has created a map for us, and we've been weighing the possibilities. All right, Florida Highway Patrol is on all the roads that could really get someone out of here. Carl is going to need to go north or south to reach an area. Of course, we can hope that a python gets him. Gator, diamondback . . ."

"Yeah. We can hope a creature gets Carl—and not us!"

"We are in the rainy season," Adrien reminded them. "Avoid alligator holes, keep an eye out. Come and see the map, and we'll split up to cover north and south."

"Can you be sure—" Vicky began.

"We can be *sure* of nothing," Adrien said. "But . . . come on."

He led the way into what remained of the shack. She was surprised to see there was a truck in it that seemed to have survived the elements for years. There was a large paper spread out on it, and just as Adrien had said, it was a map.

"How . . . ?" she murmured.

"We don't know who or when," Adrien explained, "but this ruin was used by someone we assume to be an ecologist, and he or she kept supplies out here. Flashlights, the map, a few books . . . all right, let's look at the map."

Vicky studied it, seeing the little areas that Adrien had marked.

She shook her head. "If he goes south, he'll have to run into the Tamiami Trail and—"

"Yes, and Highway Patrol is there, but there are also a few places to find an accomplice. And even with FHP all over, there are about ninety miles where he might slip across and find transportation. If he gets across, he could appear to be a tourist at the Miccosukee village. . . ." He paused, looking at her. "Like I said, there's nothing I'm sure about."

"He has a plan; he's had all this in place for years in case of trouble, most probably," Mike said. "And remember, we're not the only ones out here, so . . ."

Adrien looked at Mike. "If everyone is agreeable, I'll take Vicky—"

"Hank, you head out with them," Lance suggested. "Mike and I will move toward the north. You and I know where we are the best. Well, all right, Adrien knows what we know, but—"

"It's good. The places shown are known structures or remnants of structures. We're going to assume he knows what he's doing, but he's still going to need shelter now and then, especially if he thinks he's going to confuse law enforcement or wait us out," Adrien said. "So—"

"Hang on," Vicky said, pulling out her phone and snapping a picture of the map.

"Good idea," Adrien approved. "If we all—"

"How about Mike and I just take the map. Interesting to wonder about the person who left this all here. Someone who wanted to protect the ecosystem," Lance murmured.

"And I've always been grateful to them," Adrien murmured. "So, let's move."

Vicky glanced at her phone. No signal. "How are we going to keep in touch?" she asked.

Lance laughed. "Smoke signals? Just kidding. I picked up a

couple of satellite phones; Adrien has one and I have one. We'll know if anyone else is able to get to him first, as well."

"All right, then," she murmured.

Hank caught her arm as she started to follow Adrien. "Vicky, be very, very—"

"Careful," she finished. With a smile, she started to follow Adrien.

They moved in silence for a while. "That first red mark on the map to the south is what we're trying first?"

"You got it."

"Wow!" Hank murmured suddenly. "Stop, stop! Oh, my God—look!"

They were all still. Vicky turned to see that Hank was staring in amazement at a beautiful cat that had paused through a thin group of cypress near their position.

"A Florida panther! They're so endangered, people can look for years and never see them in the wild, there are only about a hundred and sixty in existence and . . ."

"Python," Adrien warned quietly.

"The panther can outrun it—" Hank began, then added angrily, "if he can see it!"

"Have you run into a python out here before?" she asked Adrien.

"Yes."

"And?"

He turned to look at her, frowning and shaking his head. "I shot it. I never liked killing anything, but we desperately need to solve the invasive snake problem. You used to see a raccoon out here every three feet. The invasive snakes have reduced that population by almost ninety-nine percent."

"We can't let it get that panther!" Hank said.

Her partner was a good shot, Vicky knew. But she was still surprised when Hank took careful aim through the grass and trees.

And shot the python.

The panther flew off; the snake went still.

Adrien winced. "Hank, the sound of the gunshot . . ."

"Oh." Hank looked at them both apologetically. "I just . . . I never dreamed I'd get to see a panther in the wild."

"Right. I'm with you at heart, man," Adrien said. "But now let's hurry. If our guy is out here, he'll be moving again or . . ."

"Or?" Vicky asked.

"Planning an ambush," Adrien said flatly. "Stay behind me, close behind me, and be ready for anything. Weapons drawn."

Chapter 6

"My fault. My fault," Hank muttered.

Well, Adrien thought, it possibly was Hank's fault—but he understood. The area had been overrun by invasive snakes, and several native species were quickly disappearing to the hungers of the giant reptiles. Their nests were massive, causing many naturalists to speculate there might be as many as a couple hundred thousand boas and pythons now finding a comfortable home in the semitropical wilderness of the Everglades.

They reached the remnants of the one enclosure and found it was empty. There wasn't much to it; time had taken a natural toll. Tree branches broke through what remained of the roof, and vines crawled through the one window.

Hank was angry with himself, Adrien knew, thinking his shot might have caused their suspect to move on. And it might have—and might not have. Whoever this Carlos was, he'd planned well ahead for any contingency.

"Hank, this guy is going to be constantly moving. But I think we're heading in the right direction. Someone was here not too long ago."

He hunkered down, studying the splintered remains of the wooden floor.

"There's an actual footprint!" Vicky noted.

Adrien nodded, thoughtful. It might have been made by another searcher. It might have been made by the man they were seeking.

He couldn't help but think that his instincts were right.

He looked at Vicky.

"He was here."

"And I screwed it!" Hank muttered.

"Hank, maybe not," Adrien said. "Like I said, he's going to keep moving, no matter what. And take a step away. There's a snake on that branch. Don't shoot it! It's not even poisonous. It's just a little rat snake, and without those guys, we'd be entirely consumed by the mosquitoes."

"Instead of just half-consumed," Hank asked, swatting at a flying insect. "Then again, we saw—we saw, in the wild—a Florida panther!"

"We did indeed," Vicky said. "Adrien?"

"We've another mile before there's something else like this. There's lots of marshland, and we're still in the rainy season, so I'm glad you got those boots," he told Vicky.

"Ah, but you're still wearing cowboy boots!" she told him.

He shrugged. "Damned hard for a sneaking snake to bite into. I'm okay. Hank?"

"Had a chance to plan for the day," Hank said, lifting his pant leg to show them both the tall and heavy leather boots he was wearing. He laughed. "A little late to ask."

"True," Adrien agreed. He looked at Vicky. She was calm, still studying the footprint. She looked over at Adrien. "He isn't far ahead! Should we let Mike and Lance know we seriously believe he's heading that way?"

"Instinct tells me yes, but anyone could have made that

footprint," Adrien said. "Other searchers, other cops, agents, rangers. I know Eames is keeping a log of who is where, but out here . . . you're not always certain what lines you might have crossed. But I will report to Eames."

Adrien did so. The call took no more than a few seconds. He reported what he believed to Mike, as well, and Mike agreed they wanted to be a little more certain.

"You got the map, Hank, right? We're heading on out to the next position."

"Got it."

When they stepped out of the ruins, Vicky was suddenly dead still, frowning.

"What is it?" Adrien asked her.

She looked at him with deep concern, and that look in her eyes caused a wealth of emotion to suddenly rise in him.

He wanted to take her into his arms, assure her that everything would be all right.

He gave himself a mental shake—not something Detective Victoria Henderson would want at all.

"Someone is out here," she said in a whisper. "I heard . . . something. Like a moan, or a whisper. That way."

She pointed ahead. They were in an area some people referred to as a cypress prairie or a sawgrass prairie. The hardwood hammocks only rose a few feet above the water level, and they were usually full of little streams or rivulets of water; but gorgeous wildflowers could also grow, and the brush could be thick in places.

"There!" she said softly.

They were all dead still for a beat.

"Cover me!" Adrien said.

Ducking low, he started to move, ignoring the sawgrass that snagged his clothing. Halfway from the ruins of the shack to the heavy growth of trees and brush, he paused, listening again. Something was moving ahead.

A gator? A bird? An ibis was stalking the ground near him, seeking insects or worms, and an eagle soared overhead.

Another giant python?

No, there was something different about the movement. Something he wouldn't have been able to explain in words, just something he sensed.

He started moving forward again. It might be the first time he'd worked with them, but he had no trouble trusting his backup to cover his movements.

The sound came again.

This time, he knew it was a moan. It was followed by a whisper he could barely hear.

"Help me!"

He moved swiftly then, shoving aside a swath of branches, and falling quickly to the side of the man who lay on the ground. His bloodied uniform gave away the fact he was a park ranger, but while he lay on the ground, there were no visible signs of blood.

"Hey, hey, I'm here," Adrien said quickly. "Where are you wounded?"

The man appeared to be in his thirties. He blinked, staring at Adrien with hope soaring into his eyes. "Thank God!"

"I'm trying to help you," Adrien told him. He pulled out the satellite phone, reaching Eames, giving him their location, and explaining there was a ranger down. He didn't know the extent of his injuries yet, but they needed medical attention as quickly as possible. There were holes in his shirt; bullet holes, scored by powder. But there was no blood on the man.

"Thank you, thank you, thank you . . ."

"I want to help you. You are wearing a vest beneath your uniform," Adrien surmised. "But he shot you three . . . four times?"

"Ribs . . . I think they're broken. I was alone out here. I went down in agony," the young man said, wincing. "I . . .

went down. I guess he didn't reckon on the vest. He kept going . . . I . . . I should have gotten up, somehow. He's still out there now."

"Be glad you went down; he would have killed you," Adrien said flatly. "And I'm impressed you thought to wear a vest when we all knew this was going on."

Adrien stood. "It's all right!" he called back to Vicky and Hank.

"All right?" the ranger queried.

"Sorry, no, you're not all right. You probably have several broken ribs, but you're alive. Do you have any idea how long you've been down?" Adrien asked.

He'd barely finished speaking before Vicky and Hank came running up.

"No!" the ranger cried.

"No, no, they're detectives on this case. You're fine!" Adrien assured him quickly.

"No, no," Vicky murmured, falling to her knees by the downed man. "Are you—"

"He has a vest on, but he still probably has broken ribs," Adrien explained quickly. "I've called for medical. But please, this can help us a lot. Did you see him, and how long ago did he get you?" he persisted.

Vicky was smoothing his hair back and gently pulling a branch from beneath the ranger's body. He had closed his eyes. He opened them, staring at Vicky.

"Wow! That's . . . better. Thank you!"

"I'm afraid to do anything more," she told him. "But," she added, looking up at Adrien, "help will be here soon!"

"Thank you!" he whispered again. "Um . . . about six feet. He's in jeans and a denim jacket. Maybe forty-five or so. I was just going to ask him what he was doing, if he knew . . . but he saw me from a distance and started firing. He looked like anybody. Not like a criminal mastermind!"

"How long ago?" Adrien asked patiently. "Twenty . . . twenty-five minutes."

Adrien looked at Hank and Vicky.

"No man left behind," Hank said.

"Marines?" Adrien asked.

"Yes, sir. And you?"

"Airborne," Adrien said. "So— "

"Vicky is the better shot; you may need her expertise. I mean, I'm no slouch, but . . ."

"All right, you wait with the ranger, and I'll have Mike and Lance come for you. Vicky?"

She was up instantly. "You're going to be okay, you just may need a few vacation days!" she assured the ranger.

"Go!" Hank said. "Get that son of a bitch who thinks he's smarter than everyone!"

Adrien nodded and used the satellite phone again to bring Mike and Lance up to speed, to ensure they'd catch up heading south, and they would find Hank and the ranger and follow their path.

"Heads up," Mike warned. "This guy is shooting first and asking questions later."

"I'm going to rely on the friends who taught me everything there was to know about this place when I was a kid," he told Mike.

He could almost see his old friend's grin.

"We're moving, south-central," he said.

"Copy that."

Adrien was already walking and moving quickly as he spoke. He was a tall man, and his strides were long; he worried Vicky wasn't going to be able to keep up.

But she was. She glanced at him, arching a brow.

"Just checking."

She gave him a rueful smile. "I could maybe take you at a sprint," she said.

He laughed. "I wouldn't bet against you. Twenty minutes," he murmured. He put up a hand, stopping, listening.

"No. He's still far ahead. Let's keep at it."

"Easier said than done!"

They had reached another patch of watery marsh. She took a step and started to sink. He quickly caught her arm. "This way. You can see the mangrove roots there; a little balance is needed, but . . ."

"Got it and thanks!"

She smiled at him, not at all resentful of his arm, but rather holding on to it as they made their way around the watery mud pit. "Gator hole up there. We'll avoid it."

"I see. We just keep to the side, right?"

"Keep to the side. And hope, of course, that her nest is over there and not over here."

She flashed him a smile, and they kept going. When they reached the next hammock—a tiny island of a hammock—he paused again to listen.

"There is someone ahead," he murmured. "Keep low, use the trees."

They kept moving, slowly, pausing, listening.

Again, he heard something—a whisper in the wilderness that was not caused by any creature other than a human being.

Had Carl found yet another victim?

"Careful, careful," Adrien warned in a whisper.

"Right."

She indicated she could go around a tangle of brush while he moved forward. He nodded his agreement to the plan.

He dropped low to cross an area of sawgrass prairie, gritted his teeth against the snags of the terrain. He was aware Vicky had moved around and was almost parallel to him.

He heard the moaning again. He kept moving, and he saw Vicky had come around, as well.

This time, it was a woman on the ground. Dark hair splayed

around her head. She was curled on her side, crying. She was in dark green pants and a beige shirt with a ranger's hat at her side, but there was something off . . . the uniform wasn't that of a park ranger.

Vicky was moving toward her.

He shouted a warning, drew out his Glock, as he realized the woman was turning, and she was smiling.

Because she was armed.

He didn't need the warning. Vicky hadn't been taken. She was narrowly shielded by a fallen tree trunk, but her gun was aimed at the woman's head, and she commanded harshly, "Drop it!"

"I really suggest you do as she says," Adrien said, striding to stand over the woman, his weapon aimed at her, as well.

The woman dropped the gun, staring up at the two of them. Vicky quickly retrieved the fallen gun, never taking her gaze—or her weapon—off the woman.

She stepped back, looking at Adrien.

"Cuffs?"

He nodded; she covered him while he went to the woman, dragged her up, and commanded she put her hands behind her back.

"No, no, no, you don't understand. I was scared. I was . . . I heard there was a criminal out here!"

Adrien looked at Vicky, arching a brow, smiling. "Really? There's nothing wrong with you, and you're sitting in the bushes moaning, and hmm, someone came to help you, and you pulled your gun out right away."

"Does seem like there's something really wrong with that story!" Vicky said, grimacing and looking at him. But then she stood in front of the woman and demanded, "So. He knows we're after him, knows about where we are, and somehow found you to kill the two of us for him?"

"You don't understand! He'll kill my family!" she cried.

"Who are you and how does he know your family?" Adrien asked.

"He . . . I . . . I . . . okay, I've sold stuff for him. And once you do that . . ."

"Stuff? What stuff?" Adrien asked.

"Pills . . . nothing deadly, I swear! But I was laid off, and I was desperate. I'm a single mom. My name is Gretchen Merton. He called me earlier today and said he might need me, and if I didn't show up, he'd make a phone call and my kids would be dead. And I . . . I know he means what he said. He shot and killed that ranger without even talking to him. He'll kill my kids, please! He can never know I didn't kill you!"

Adrien glanced at Vicky.

"Easy enough to find out. And easy enough to protect your children. But if you're here—" Adrien began.

"My children are at school! Teddy is nine, and Veronica is seven. My husband . . . my husband left me about a year ago, and he . . . he isn't much of a father. I swear, I swear, I swear this is true!"

"But you would have killed me," Vicky said softly.

"Only for my kids!" Gretchen said, tears slipping down her cheeks.

"She's telling the truth," Vicky said. "Call Eames; he can check it out easily enough and get the kids into protective custody. And get someone out here to get her."

"You're sure?" he asked Vicky.

She studied the woman, who was not just crying.

"Yes."

"All right, then."

He got on the satellite; Eames had someone on it even as they spoke. Their answer came quickly. Yes, there was a Gretchen Merton who lived in the North Miami area, and she did have two children at a local elementary school. Eames was damned good. Even before they ended the call, he had police on the way to bring the kids into protective custody.

"All right, Ms. Merton," Adrien said. "How long—"

"Ten minutes. He left me here ten minutes ago," the woman said. "They'll really have my kids. And what about me? Oh, God. You can't just leave me here. He might come back. You don't understand this man. He had connections."

"If he had the connections here," Adrien said dryly, "he wouldn't have had you lying in the grass to try to kill the two of us."

"You have me handcuffed!" she cried.

Vicky glanced at him. They desperately needed to keep moving. But it was true her life might well be in danger if the man's "connections" were alerted to determine if Gretchen Merton had carried out her task as ordered.

"I'll have to stay—" Vicky began, but Adrien lifted a hand again; he felt the vibration on his satellite phone.

Mike was almost there; he had left Lance with Hank while they waited on the EMTs.

"We're good. Mike is going to hang in while we move on. And Eames has people coming in from the south. We're going to get him in a pincher movement, no matter what he's tried to accomplish out here."

"There's Mike! Man, can he move!" Vicky said.

"Yes, Mike can move through the wetlands as fast and easily as a bird can fly," Adrien agreed. "He'll make it to us in about two minutes."

"Wait!" Gretchen cried.

"The gentleman coming will see to it that you're brought in and reunited with your children," Vicky told her.

"And . . . and you won't . . . my God, if I go to jail, they'll have no one!" Gretchen sobbed.

"We'll have to see. Maybe you can help us, and if you do well, the courts can be lenient," Vicky told her.

"I can help you, I can help you more!" Gretchen insisted. "I know his real name. It is not Carl or Carlos. His name is Andrei, and he isn't South American at all. He's originally from Albania, though he did grow up between Colombia and Nebraska. He's got an organization, but he put it all together right here in Florida. He keeps control because he's proven that he'll do anything if people don't do what he says. He got rid of some of his people with fentanyl-laced drugs. There . . ."

She broke off, looking hopefully from Vicky to Adrien.

"Andrei—Andrei what?" Adrien asked.

"Hasani," Gretchen insisted. "Andrei Hasani." Then she began to cry again. "Oh, my God! If you don't get him, I'll never be safe! My poor children."

"You will be safe! We can see to that," Vicky promised.

Even as she spoke, a shot rang out, whizzing by very close to Vicky's face.

Adrien flew to the two of them, encircling them and bringing them down in a pile. He collected himself quickly, rolling to seek out the source of the danger as Vicky did the same.

"Back by that mangrove marsh!" she murmured.

"I see the movement."

He took aim and fired, barely realizing Vicky had done the same. They instantly heard shouts of pain.

Adrien stared at Vicky, shaking his head.

They'd been on the hunt for one man. Somehow that one man had managed to fill an untenable wilderness with lackeys to see to his safety.

Mike had gone flat at the sound of the bullet exploding; he remained low and rushed over to them.

"What is going on?" he demanded. "You want me here or . . ."

"Yeah, I'll head over to whoever that is," Adrien said.

"We'll head over," Vicky added firmly.

"They came to kill me, I told you—" Gretchen began.

"No one will kill you with me here," Mike promised her.

Adrien looked at Vicky. He nodded. Keeping low, they raced the short distance between them and the two who had gone down in the grass. There was no guarantee that whoever they were, they might not still try to shoot them.

But they found the one man with a bleeding shoulder, his gun having flown from his hand about ten feet into the marsh.

The other had been grazed on the side of the head. And he was out cold. Adrien stopped by the first man, the one who was doing the moaning.

"Doesn't matter, doesn't matter, I failed, I'm a dead man!" he moaned.

He looked to be about twenty-five, blond—and bore track marks on his arm. Andrei Hasani had a knack for finding people who would fall under his influence. A junkie was a good bet.

Then again . . .

Junkies weren't always that great at aiming whatever weapon they'd been given.

Vicky looked over at him. "He's just grazed. Concussion, I imagine. His pulse is decent; he's breathing fine. Looks like he's little more than a kid, Adrien."

"Yeah. He's using anyone he can, probably threatening every family out there. He must be stopped." He had his phone out and reported in again to Eames.

More medical services would be there as quickly as possible.

"Maybe easier than driving through some of our traffic?" Vicky asked, trying to speak lightly.

The man with the broken shoulder murmured, "He'll come back, now! He'll come back; he wanted you dead, and he was afraid the woman couldn't act. He'll keep coming and coming and . . . my family, he'll go after my family when he realizes—"

"We need your names. Law enforcement will protect your families," Adrien told him.

"They can't, they can't, they don't know!" the man argued.

"Don't know what?" Vicky asked, glancing at Adrien again.

"He isn't human!"

Vicky gazed at Adrien, and he shook his head and turned to the injured man on the ground.

"Yes. He is human. And he's not going to get anyone, because we're going to get him!"

Chapter 7

You can't judge a book by its cover.

Vicky had heard the saying her entire life, and it almost amused her now that she had thought Adrien to be no more than a blustering braggart of a ladies' man.

She almost smiled as she followed him again through the dangerous terrain. On her own . . .

Well, she probably wouldn't be out here on her own. If it hadn't been for Adrien, she'd have admitted that as much as she loved and appreciated the wild beauty of the Everglades, she was no expert.

But he hadn't treated her once as if she was too delicate, too local, too anything not to be able to keep up. And he knew they were equally determined to stop a man who brought so much fear and misery to so many lives.

They walked quickly along in silence. Ahead of her, Adrien suddenly stopped, bringing a finger to his lips to warn her about speaking. She frowned and watched him, and he indicated she should listen. She heard sounds, but the same sounds she'd become accustomed to through the time they'd already traversed the swamps. The ruffle of wings as birds took to the air. A strange whisper like a sliding sound as an alligator slipped deeper into a pond. Bird calls and the faint rustle of leaves when a breeze drifted on by.

He pointed. He was obviously indicating an area just ahead of them. She wasn't sure why, but it seemed prudent to nod. He knew where they were; he knew what to listen for—and when the simple sound of silence was something to be heard, as well.

"Head slightly southwest, parallel to me around that group of cypress. There's a marsh just the other side of it that isn't far from one of the well-traveled airboat streams. He's trying to get to someone. He's managed to lure help to get him out of here, someone with an airboat that he can hop on and from there . . . anyway, I'm going to make noise and let him come after me. He'll know you're near me, but he won't know where."

"If you let him see you—"

"I'm trusting you're faster than I am. And, of course, I'm going to tell him to drop his weapon."

"You're putting a lot of faith in me!" Vicky said.

He smiled at her. "I am. Let's do this."

She nodded. She couldn't fail him.

She wouldn't fail him. That simple.

"Hey!" Adrien shouted. "Save yourself some pain and misery. We know who you are. We know just about everything you're doing and all about the criminal ring you've got going. But the key thing here is we know who you are, Andrei Hasani. No matter where you try to go, we'll be there. We know your aliases. And I guess you're not that great with history, because officers from both the Miccosukee and Seminole tribes, who know the wetlands better than anyone else, are here. Hell, they're the descendants of those who survived three Seminole Wars by hiding out down here! Andrei Hasani, come out, surrender, and we won't have to shoot you!"

He knew that the only route Hasani could take to have a prayer of getting out of the wetlands and hammocks where he'd been fleeing to take refuge was the route they were on now.

Hasani was before him, close, shielded by the trees.

He could, of course, take a shot at Adrien, but Adrien kept himself crouched low to the ground and moving.

Moving targets were always harder to hit.

And as he had hoped, the man stepped out from the trees, his gun aimed at Adrien.

"What are you, an idiot?" Hasani asked.

He was as he'd been described, a tall man of about six-one with dark hair, a decent countenance, and in fit shape.

Adrien wondered briefly what could have made such a man into a manipulative criminal. He had the look of someone who could make it at anything he attempted.

But Adrien knew he would have needed many more classes in profiling and psychology to understand what made one person's desires so strong they didn't care if they hurt others, down to taking the most precious gift of all from them—life itself.

"An idiot?" Adrien asked. He shrugged. "No, I was just hoping you'd want to stay alive and therefore, you'd surrender to me."

Hasani shrugged in return. "All I need to do is shoot you and keep going. As you've seen, I'm also well-acquainted with the area."

"Again, authorities now know who you are. You won't get far, no matter what you do," Adrien told him. "I mean, come on, just use logic. A man like yourself? If you're alive, you can manipulate your way into the right relationships and perhaps escape from a federal prison. If you're alive. If you're dead, you're dead. No hope for the future."

Hasani laughed. "I'm the one aiming at you."

"Yeah, but my partner is aiming at you."

"The girl? The redhead I may still get my hands on?" Hasani asked, amused.

"Top of her class in marksmanship," Adrien told him, shrugging again. "Come on, Hasani. Live. Give yourself a chance. Just drop the weapon now."

"I don't think I can do that."

"If you don't, you're a dead man. Or, at the very least, an injured man. Maybe she'll sever your spinal column, and you'll be a cripple the rest of your life," Adrien suggested. "Hard to escape then. Maybe not just a cripple. Maybe you'll be paralyzed from the neck down, forced to live in that truly captive state until death does mercifully claim you."

"Your partner is out there, aiming at me? What if I have a few men behind me?" Hasani asked. "Once she fires—and misses me—my people will know where she is. They'll fire back, and she'll be the dead one. Though, honestly, now I'm feeling a little vindictive toward her. I'd rather get her alive and place her with a few buyers who will truly make what's left of her life a living hell!"

"Bull," Adrien said lightly. "Last chance. Throw down your weapon."

Andrei Hasani had what they called a "tell," and Adrien saw it. He was ready to fire.

"Now!" Adrien shouted, as he dropped down into the tall grass.

And Vicky fired. He heard Hasani scream in pain and fall into the grass, as well.

The man was still alive. Vicky could have killed him, Adrien knew. And after what he had said, she'd probably wanted to.

But maybe she wanted him to suffer in prison, injured . . .

"Careful!" he shouted.

The man could still be heard thrashing and moaning. That might mean he was still holding his gun—just waiting for them to approach so he could get off a clear shot.

"Hey, I learn from the best!" Vicky shouted back. "Caught him dead center in the upper chest, shattered his collarbone and shoulder."

"Still—"

"Yeah, yeah!"

He saw her moving carefully through the grass, staying low, as he was doing.

He reached Andrei Hasani first.

Vicky really had to have been top of her class. She had carefully avoided the heart, but the force and impact of her bullet had shattered the man's bone in such a way, his arms and hands had been incapacitated.

"Good job!" he told her.

"Bitch!" Hasani spat out. His eyes had closed and he moaned, but he opened them and stared at Vicky. "I will get you!" he swore. "You will pay for what you've done to me! You have no right, you're supposedly a cop. This is police brutality!"

"Right. I know. I'm going to pay—as you intended the other young women to pay. Right now, I'm thinking you're going to make one heck of a good bitch for some big guy when you go to prison for the rest of your life."

Hasani kept swearing.

Adrien retrieved Hasani's weapon—which had fallen well out of the man's reach—and pulled out his satellite phone. He reported to Eames they'd gotten Andrei Hasani. And yes, he was sorry, but once again, they needed medical attention for the man.

"You didn't shoot to kill?" Eames asked him.

"I didn't shoot at all. We tried to get him to surrender. No dice. But Vicky got him before he could shoot either of us."

Adrien reported their location, and then put calls through to both Mike and Lance to let them know the situation. As he ended that call, he frowned.

He'd thought he'd heard the distant drone of an airboat.

Now . . .

He didn't hear anything at all except a rustle of trees as a flock of ibises suddenly took flight.

"Get down again!" he told Vicky.

She instantly went flat to the earth.

They heard voices coming from the area of the trees directly by the water.

"He should have been there," one man said nervously.

"Hey, I'm not leaving without him. Do you know what happened to Leroy Perkins?"

"That was an accident—"

"My ass it was an accident! We have to find him."

Andrei Hasani tried to moan out a warning; he didn't have the breath to do it.

The two men who had been talking suddenly appeared. They walked into the prairie of high grass where Hasani lay and where Vicky and Adrien were crouched and waiting.

They didn't appear to be armed, but they were at a distance, and the protective grasses also obscured their vision. One seemed to be about fifty, white-haired, stout. The other might have been a decade younger. He was slim and looked frightened and probably been the speaker who had wanted to run.

Adrien nodded at Vicky.

He was going to confront the men, trusting her again to cover him.

"Stop right there," Adrien commanded. "FBI!"

"Oh, God, oh no—" the younger began. "Oh, no—"

"Rather the FBI shoot me than I face Hasani," the older man said, drawing a weapon from behind his back.

"We have Hasani!" Adrien shouted. "Don't get yourselves into more trouble than you need to be in!"

Vicky stood, her weapon aimed at the two men.

The younger one began to sob. "I didn't do anything. I swear, I didn't do anything! We were just told we needed to get him, because he'd been hanging around in the Everglades but his airboat gave out on him. Don't shoot me, please don't shoot me, please, please!"

"Drop the weapons," Adrien said.

"Please!" The younger man begged as he looked at the older man.

And at last, the older man dropped his gun. Adrien and Vicky hurried forward to cuff the two men.

"We've got a bit of a wait," Adrien murmured, looking at Vicky with a grimace. "We need medical for Andrei Hasani—"

"Medical? He's really down? You're not lying?" the older man asked.

"You can hear him moaning away," Adrien said flatly.

"But . . . he's still alive?" the younger man asked.

"He's alive," Vicky said.

The younger man started to tremble. "You can't let him talk to anyone, anyone! He has . . . he has people across the state, and when he wants revenge, he . . . gets it."

"People? Like you? Were you supposed to kill others to get him out of here?" Vicky asked.

"No, no!" the younger man said. "We're not killers. We just . . ."

"The idiot is addicted to pills," the older man said impatiently.

They didn't have a chance to reply. A shout alerted them to the fact that help had come. Mike was walking toward them quickly, followed by a team of EMTs and cops. The EMTs were hurrying along, bearing a stretcher.

"Hey, thanks!" Adrien shouted. "Two to take to headquarters, one to the hospital."

"Yeah, we heard," Mike said. "Hospital, not the morgue, right?"

"These fellows were just out here to give Mr. Hasani a ride, but they've already had a minute or two to warn us about what might happen if he's able to speak with anyone," Adrien said. He left the area where they were standing with the two airboat would-be rescuers and motioned for Mike and the EMTs to follow as he led them to the place where Andrei Hasani remained in the grass.

"Nothing vital," Vicky murmured to the EMTs.

One of them looked at Vicky and arched a brow, but he nodded with admiration. He obviously considered her to be a good shot.

Adrien saw her smile and nod in return to the EMT, but then he saw her frown. And he knew her thoughts exactly.

Was it really a good thing that she was a good shot?

Andrei Hasani would first be seen by doctors, who would patch him back together. Because doctors and law enforcement had sworn oaths, because they were the "good" guys, Andrei Hasani would have his chance to ask for an attorney.

And who knew just what the attorney would do, whom he or she might talk to, and what danger then might lie ahead for others?

"We'll get these two in," one of the cops promised.

"Hey, wait, what are you going to charge us with?" the older man asked. "Walking around the Everglades? Taking an airboat ride? You have no right to—"

"At the very least, we have twenty-four hours," Adrien said pleasantly. "See you later."

The EMTs had Andrei on the stretcher; one was on a satellite phone, listening to instructions from a doctor. They, too, were following the law.

But one of them tripped on something in the ground, causing him to drop his end of the stretcher. Andrei Hasani let out a scream of agony and began to curse the man, shouting with a voice that was down to a hoarse breath of wind, "You did that on purpose; you will pay!"

"Whatever," the young EMT said. "Sorry, I'm not a hiker, and I hate mosquitoes!"

They moved off toward the water.

Adrien pulled out his phone to call Eames again.

"Good work, the two of you," Eames said. "Amazing work."

"Thanks. People are coming into the station who need to talk," Adrien said. "We need—"

"They need to talk, yes. But you and Vicky need to get some rest. Please, take off at least a few hours. Take a shower. I'm sure you need showers. Give it a few hours; shake it off. Mike is with you now; Lance will be bringing in an airboat. He'll get you where you need to be to get back to civilization. We'll let these people sit and stew. You know that's a wise move. We have some time. Take a bit of it to get yourselves back in order."

"If you're sure—"

"I'm not your boss, since you are with the bureau, but this was still left under my jurisdiction, so I'm asking you, please. Come at all this fresh. And as for Hasani, he'll be in surgery for a while," Eames told him.

"He can't be trusted. Even in a hospital, he can't be trusted."

"It's all right; Hank and a few others will be at the hospital. We're all aware that holding him is going to be like holding a wet snake. We know. Tell Vicky what I said. I am her boss. I don't want to see her face here for at least ten hours."

Vicky was looking at him with a frown.

"He expects us in— "

"Uh, no," Adrien said, and handed the phone to her.

Vicky listened to her boss, then said, "But— "

Adrien couldn't hear Eames's interruption, but at the end, Vicky said simply, "Yes, sir."

She ended the call and handed the phone back to Adrien. "Okay, so . . ."

The EMTs had moved on along with the cops and the two men who had been about to aid and abet Andrei Hasani.

Mike walked over to the two of them. "Um, this way—your chariot awaits. Okay, it's not a chariot, but . . ."

Vicky managed a laugh, and she told Mike, "Thank you! Yeah. As much as I love our amazing ecological system, I'm ready to get the hell out of here."

She was silent as they walked through the trees to the water, where Lance was just arriving with an airboat. She was polite and charming, thanking both Mike and Lance, who in turn applauded her and Adrien for finding their suspect in a veritable jungle.

It wasn't until they were alone again, near the car, that she shook her head and said, "I know Eames is thinking like a boss about what's best for the law, and what's best for us, but . . . I don't want to go home. I don't think I can sleep. Okay, the shower thing I get, but . . ."

"Don't go home," Adrien told her.

"What?"

"Come with me back to the ranch. There's plenty of room there. You can shower and play with the dogs. I'll introduce you to the horses. Show you how to play cowboy, or, whoops, sorry, cowgirl!" He frowned. "Okay, I've heard the term *cowgirl*, and I haven't actually heard the term *cowwoman*, or for that matter, I haven't heard the term *cowman*. Just cowboy and cowgirl."

She laughed softly.

"Um, thanks. I don't want to be a burden—"

"Not a burden," he assured her. "I . . . I guess I'm restless, too. And I know my brother and his wife. She'll have clean clothes you can wear. And knowing her, she'll have something that won't fit you too badly at all. Then, if you want, when we get close to interrogation time, we can go by wherever it is you live and get whatever you want."

She was smiling at him. The woman really had the most beautiful face. Was he making a mistake? Was he admiring her a little too much, wanting to be with her. . . ?

Hey.

They had gotten him. *They* had tracked and found Andrei Hasani, and they had taken them down. Maybe it was okay for them to enjoy a little peaceful time together, to laugh and . . .

Oh, bull. He was attracted to her, seriously attracted, and he admired her and . . .

Crazy.

Maybe not so crazy.

After all, he had now been assigned to the local office.

Maybe she was crazy, Vicky thought, listening to the thrum of the airboat motor.

Go home. She should really—really, really, truly—just go home. Get a good shower, wear her own clothing, sleep . . .

Okay, she was never going to sleep. The day had just been far too eventful.

That's what she should do. But . . .

She wanted to go back to Adrien's family's ranch, see how the dogs were doing, meet the horses, relax with good things that existed in the world.

Lie.

She just wasn't ready to leave the strange partnership with

Adrien. Not partnership. She had a partner, Hank, and he was a great guy, a good partner, a solid cop. . . .

And Hank wasn't going to care. He'd be glad she was having a good day—

No, no. Couldn't call it a good day. A successful day, maybe. Partially. They had caught their quarry, but now they knew Andrei had a massive network throughout the state.

"Back to the car and I leave it all to you!" Lance said. "Best work between agencies I think I've seen, and a monster is out of tribal, state, federal, and private land. Thanks!"

"Hey, thanks to you and Mike. I mean, I guess we could have hopped a ride back with the cops and the forensic crew, but this was so much faster," Adrien told him.

Vicky balanced her way over to Lance and gave him a hug. "Thank you!"

He smiled and told her, "Any time! Hey, come for some fun stuff out here, too, huh?"

"I do love the fun stuff out here," she promised him. "Hey, maybe Adrien and Mike can play some kind of a concert out here again."

Adrien groaned. "Trust me. I just wasn't that good. Hey, if I had been, I might have been a rock star instead of an agent."

She laughed softly. "Today, you were a rock star! And thanks," she assured him. "So, you're sure— "

"Not a burden in any way. Eames should know better. The sleep thing isn't going to happen right now. My mind is moving like a bullet. In fact, I very much appreciate the fact you want to hang around. My brother and Mandy had to go straight from work to an event at the boys' school, so . . . we'll have the place to ourselves until just about time to head to the station, so . . ."

"Ah, you could have been alone."

"Yeah, yuck."

"Oh, so, I can't just go prying in your sister-in-law's closet!"

"And you won't need to—she has a closet of extra stuff."

"You're kidding. Why? I mean, who keeps a closet for friends—"

Adrien laughed. "The extra stuff are things my sisters left, and things she bought that don't fit. And since they live out here on a ranch, they get guests who may have come for dinner and just decided to spend the night. Mandy is one of the most social people I've ever met. She loves company, including overnight guests—oh, and any family members who come home at any time. Strange . . ."

"What's strange?" Vicky asked him.

"My parents are great. They were so perplexed. They thought they should sell the place and split the proceeds between us, or even keep them to make sure they had enough to live on throughout their lives. They're very independent people and didn't want any of us having to support them at any time. But we all had a fit, and my brother was already married with a kid on the way, so the rest of us secretly turned the property over to him—he is the oldest, the 'heir,' one might say. But, of course, he didn't want charity from his siblings, so he went and secretly put it back in all our names. But we respect it as his home. He won't leave it, we all get to come 'home,' and it's been . . . well, I guess we were lucky. We all felt the same way."

"Incredibly lucky!" Vicky said. "And nice. You guys must all be pretty amazing."

He shrugged. "I like to think so."

"No ego, huh?" she teased.

"Me? Ego? Hmm. Um, enough to get by?" he mused.

"Get in the car!" she told him.

In a few minutes, they were at the house. She saw several horses grazing in one of the paddocks, and she glanced at Adrien.

"I thought they worried—"

"The horses can be in the paddocks. Old Mac lives in a small place that was a tack room or something else years ago, and he watches out for them."

"Old Mac?" she asked.

"My parents said that he came with the house," Adrien told her. "Seriously, he was a caretaker for the previous owners, and he's in his seventies now, but all my folks had wanted him to do was keep an eye out when they were off somewhere, and he did. Now he does the same thing for Jeremy. You can meet him, too, you know."

She nodded. "But let's start with the showers."

"We'll start with the showers. Oh, hmm. Maybe I should let you choose some clothing first."

"Oh, yeah, maybe!"

Adrien had a key, and of course he knew the alarm code. In a minute, they were inside, and he led her down the hallway that led toward the bedrooms. It was a big, sprawling house.

At the end of the hallway, he opened a door to one of the bedrooms. She saw there was a suitcase sitting on one of the bureaus—his, she imagined.

"The 'family' room for visiting siblings," he said. "But it also has the 'extra' closet. There . . . look at what you will. I mean, I've seen you all professional, and in that cute little sundress, so you ought to be able to find something, right?"

Vicky walked over to the closet. She glanced at him and then started moving hangers around. She found a halter dress that appeared to be the right size, maxi-length and in a black-and-red flower pattern. She drew it from the closet and saw there was a black sweater that went with it.

"Um . . ."

He laughed.

"Well, we'll have to go riding on another day, but I figured I'd just walk you around and—oh, yeah, when we're both set, we'll go meet the dogs."

"Perfect. I really can ride— "

"Will you come back?"

"Will you be here? You're not transferring back— "

"I think I may stay here awhile," he said with a shrug. "It's been . . . odd to say under the circumstances, but nice to be back."

"Okay. Cool. I'm not kidding. I'd love to go riding with you out here."

"Great. Okay, so, for now. There are three bathrooms, but this one is supplied. Mandy is always ready for company, like I said. So, I'll leave you here, and we'll meet in the living room whenever. Take your time, have fun, enjoy!"

"Great!"

Adrien left the room. Vicky collected the dress and sweater and went into the bedroom's private bathroom. As she turned on the water, waiting for it to heat, she found herself thinking again that he wasn't at all what she had first imagined.

He hadn't teased her about the shower. He hadn't flirted. He hadn't tried to do the least thing sexual. Which, of course, would have been crazy. They were professionals working together. That was all. She barely knew him. And yet she felt she knew him better than she did many people she had known forever. She liked the sound of his voice, the look of him, his humor, his strength and his ethic and . . .

She just wasn't one of those people who fell easily into things. She'd never had a one-night stand. She . . .

What was she thinking?

No, no, no, no, no . . .

Walk out of the room. Find him. Suggest they shower together?

And what if he looked at her in shock, refusing . . .

She set the clothing on the little ledge beneath the medicine cabinet and began to strip, seeing as she did so he hadn't lied, there was soap, shampoo, and several big, fluffy towels ready for use. There was also a toothbrush on the sink and a razor, and she remembered she was in the room where Adrien was staying.

She stepped in the shower, inwardly giving herself a firm lecture. She couldn't just assume a man wanted sex . . . they had been on an intense manhunt all day and . . .

Something slithered around her ankle.

And despite the fact she was a trained officer with admirable skills, she let out a terrified scream that would have done a child proud.

And, of course, within the blink of an eye, Adrien was there, clad in a towel, staring and anxious and demanding, "Oh, my God, what's wrong, what happened?"

Of course, she felt entirely ridiculous, standing naked in the shower—staring down at a perfectly harmless little ringneck snake, common in the area, not in the least lethal or dangerous.

"Uh . . . it just startled me!" she said, and she couldn't think of what to do—grab the shower curtain to cover herself?

"I am—so—so sorry!" she stuttered. "So, so, so . . ."

"Let me rescue the little invader!" he said as he reached down and captured the tiny snake, then leaning past her to open the window, manipulate the screen, and toss the snake outside. Of course, as he did so, his naked flesh brushed hers and . . .

He drew back in. They stared at each other.

Then he murmured, "Ah, hell!"

And she winced and echoed his words. "Ah, hell!"

He stepped over the ledge, joining her in the shower, pulling her into his arms.

They hadn't even kissed before . . .

They did then. Kissed, and kissed . . .

Their bodies hot with the heat of the sluicing water, slick and filled with tension and electricity, close, almost as one . . .

And then they weren't kissing. He was smoothing her hair back, their bodies still flush, and he was looking into her eyes. She just smiled and whispered, "I don't want to be a burden!"

His smile went very deep and he assured her, "You're not, not in the least, but . . ."

"Your back. And your front. They need washing."

"And so do yours."

Then they were laughing. In each other's arms. Soap and shampoo did come out, and their bodies were smoother and slicker and closer and . . .

Finally, they were rinsed.

Squeaky clean . . .

And they emerged and dried each other, smiling, teasing, laughing . . .

And then they were in bed. It would be later, so much later, that Vicky would begin to wonder how it all ever happened, when she wasn't the girl who fell easily into things, when she couldn't remember feeling the way that she . . .

If she had *ever* felt the way that she did.

Maybe he was a cowboy. And that was really quite okay!

Chapter 8

Of course, they had to get back to reality. And as Adrien lay by Vicky, staring up at the ceiling, just stroking her hair as her head rested against his chest, he knew reality was coming on fast.

He was about to say they had to rise, but Vicky beat him to it.

She pushed up on an elbow and looked at him. "I'm heading back to the shower. I promise not to scream. Honestly, I'm not afraid of a ringneck. I know the poor little thing is harmless . . . it just startled me."

"Naw," he teased. "You screamed because you didn't know how to invite me in."

She laughed, unoffended. "I really was startled, though the last might be true, as well. I don't . . . I just don't do things like this."

He leaned on an elbow, as well. "Believe it or not, I don't do things like this, either."

"Maybe we both knew that although we don't—it was inevitable?" she asked. She shook her head. "I'm serious. I'm taking a real shower, and you're not invited."

"Let's go back a bunch of hours. Meet in the living room," he said. He stood up and hurried out of the room, not looking back.

Twenty minutes later, they did meet in the living room. "What about food?" Adrien asked.

"Oh, that stuff most people eat on a regular basis?" she asked. "I really did want to see the dogs. Do you think—"

"Power bars," Adrien said, heading to the kitchen. He produced a few boxes for her to choose from, and she found something with caramel and nuts, and chose one. He took several from the box. She looked at him.

"What?" he asked. "You made me use up all my energy."

"All your energy?"

"Well," he said with a shrug, "a lot of it. Come on. I'll take you to the dogs."

Vicky was fascinated and touched when Blue came right to her.

"This is a great puppy!" she said.

"Not a puppy."

"Okay, okay. Great dog!"

Within a minute, seeing the attention Blue was getting, the other dogs—old rescues and new—were wedging around her and wagging their tails. She looked around the kennel, shaking her head. "Your family is amazing!" she said. "Dog beds, a kennel, but like a home—not a bunch of cages. These guys are lucky when your family rescues them."

"They're able to get a lot of them into their forever homes. I think I mentioned that before. Yeah, they're good people. Do you want to meet Shiloh?"

"What's our time?"

"We have another thirty minutes."

"Sure. Are there treats out here? I'd like to—"

"Are there dog treats? What do you think?"

He walked to a cabinet in the kennel and came back to her with a bag of the soft treats Mandy liked to give the dogs. Vicky passed them on to each of the eleven different dogs in the kennel, and he got her out at last.

The night was beautiful as they walked to the paddocks that surrounded the stalls. The moon was out and nearly full. His brother kept enough lights on over the property for movement, but nothing glaring that detracted from the simple beauty of the sky.

Chaparral was at the fence, ready to have his nose rubbed.

"Amazing animal," Vicky said.

"Thanks!" he told her.

"Not you, the horse!"

"I was thanking you for him," Adrien told her. "Now . . ."

He let out a whistle. A minute later, Shiloh came trotting to the fence, also ready to receive some affection.

"Shiloh, meet Vicky. Vicky, meet Shiloh."

"Beautiful!" Vicky murmured.

The horse was a beauty. Perfectly proportioned, a sleek bay in color.

"They're so . . . like dogs! I mean, they know you. They come to you not just for food or treats, but because they're so . . ."

"Most mammals like affection and respond to it when it's given to them," Adrien said. "Anyway, it's time that we head in."

Vicky nodded. "You know, it's so odd! I was angry at first that Eames told us to go home. I thought since we'd done so much of the work, we should get to be the ones questioning our arrestees—finding out more about this massive ring Andrei Hasani has going on in the state—but now . . ."

"Now? We're relaxed, and it would be nice to forget it all."

She grinned. "You did relax me. But, yeah, come on."

"Right. Oh, wait!"

He saw that Old Mac was in the paddock, walking toward them. He walked like a much younger man, with ease and confidence. His hair and beard were both thick and rich, snow-white and long, and he loved to play Santa Claus at Christmas—all he needed was the suit, he liked to tease.

"Hey, Mac!" Adrien said in greeting.

"Hey, there, young fella!" he called, coming up between the horses and smiling at Adrien and Vicky over the fence. "And you, young lady. I'll be happy to make your acquaintance, you know, once Adrien gets around to introducing us!"

"This is Detective Vicky Henderson, Mac. Vicky, Mac, or more properly, Victor MacCoy."

"Mac, nice to meet you," Vicky said. "This is an amazing place!"

"It is. I'm grateful to be here. So . . . detective? Not agent?" he asked, looking from Adrien to Vicky.

"I'm with the sheriff's office," Vicky supplied.

"Ah, nice. Local!" Mac said. He looked at Adrien, and Adrien shook his head, because he knew what was coming.

"I sure hope we see more of you, young lady. Every time this boy comes home, I'm hoping it will be with a bride! He isn't getting any younger, you know."

"Mac, I'm thirty-three."

"Old enough to be married with young'uns!" Mac told him.

"Vicky and I have been on a case together—"

"What? You don't think I have a TV with news stations back there? Of course, I know all about it. Though why aren't you standing there telling the reporters that you're the ones who brought the monster down?" Mac demanded.

"Mac, if I stood in front of cameras, I'd be useless when needed," Adrien explained. "And Vicky and I just got back—"

"Just?" Mac was grinning. "Several hours ago, I'd say."

Adrien lowered his head, wincing. But he realized that, at his side, Vicky was laughing. She picked up easily on the conversation.

"Mac, honestly, we both like it when we're far away from cameras. Adrien is so right. It's not a good thing if you're going undercover again for people to have seen your face. That's one way to get killed quickly."

"Ah, good point. Well— "

"We're headed back to work now," Adrien told him.

"But I am going to come back to go riding!" Vicky assured him.

"I look forward to it. Very pleased to have made your acquaintance," Mac told her.

"You, too, Mac!" Vicky assured him.

Adrien took her arm and led her from the paddock. "Go, go, go, if we want to get out of here!"

She was still grinning, but they hurried to the car, slipped in quickly, and drove out of the property and onto the main road.

"He's delightful," Vicky said. "Mac is delightful."

"He's a fixture," Adrien said, and added, "a good man. A very good man."

"So, it's all over media now that the kidnappers have been caught. We should have watched the news ourselves," Vicky murmured.

"We can catch up at the station."

Vicky nodded. "Yeah. If I know Eames, he did the talking himself. He spent years in the field, but he feels his talent now is organizing, especially when several agencies are involved. And he is good as a coordinator. He knows his people, our strengths—and our weaknesses. But he also feels the same way that you do—better to keep the people in the field out of the limelight. That way, if there's a danger from someone out there with a vendetta against law enforcement, it will be to him."

"He seems like a solid guy."

"He is. A good boss."

"And Hank seems great, too."

"He is. He's a great partner."

"And you wound up stuck with me."

"Quite the different thing," she assured him, flashing him a smile. "Hank is more big brother than . . . more big brother."

He laughed. By that time, they'd reached the station. "Who do you want first?" he asked her. "The old guy, the idiot, the woman—"

"The woman is at the hospital."

"Right."

"Old guy or idiot?"

"Idiot," she told him. "I think he's the easier mark," she admitted.

"Ah, but I think that old guy might know more."

"Fair enough. We'll see, won't we?" she asked.

"Challenge on!"

They entered the station. It was awkward. The desk sergeant just greeted them, but when they stepped into the squad room, those at their desks broke into applause. Eames stepped forward, also clapping.

"Hey, thanks, but not fair!" Vicky said. "Mike and Lance and Hank aren't here, nor all the men and women who helped in the field with capturing our foes and bringing medical help where needed. But thank you, thank you!"

"And we have the two men who were bringing an airboat to Andrei Hasani in separate interrogation rooms," Eames said. "As I promised, no one has talked to them. We've left them stewing in the rooms, pacing, the younger guy sobbing now and then . . . the older one punching the table."

"He's old; I'm young," Vicky told him. "But, sir! Has Hank

gotten anything at the hospital yet? I mean, we have Andrei Hasani, yes. But from what we've seen, Hasani really has a vast network of people out there. He controls them all through each other by threatening family members if those who have fallen into his illegal activities don't do exactly as he says. We need to know just how far that network extends."

"By the way, the younger man is Darrell Chase, the older man is Charlie Keets," Eames told them. "They both have records, petty stuff. Drug bust on Darrell, shoplifting on Charlie Keets."

"That's it?" Vicky murmured. "So, are we going to need to let them go soon?"

"Charges could be fought by a good attorney, but we could charge them with aiding and abetting kidnapping and even stretch it to murder. The great thing is the senator's daughter was Hasani's prisoner, and she's awake and aware and ready to go after the man. She knows what he wanted to do with her, and she's horrified and appalled—and very, very grateful, by the way."

"We're just pleased she's safe," Vicky murmured.

"And we gave a news conference—"

"We've heard," Adrien said. "And thank you for keeping us out of it."

"Of course," Eames said. "So . . . go do your best."

"I'll show you the way," Vicky said.

"I remember from this morning or yesterday or . . . whenever we were here," Adrien assured her. "But the rooms are next to each other—"

"I'll be observing both. Hank is at the hospital, by the way. Now there's more reason for us to have a very heavy presence," Eames told them.

"Right," Vicky said. "But shouldn't Hasani be held at county?"

"Should have been, but they were short a surgeon. He'll be moved as soon as possible."

"Thank you!" Vicky told him. She looked at Adrien.

He nodded, and the three of them started down the hallway. Officers in uniform were at the doors to both interrogation rooms, and they nodded to Vicky and Adrien as they went their separate ways, with Eames stepping into the observation room that separated them.

"Mr. Keets," Adrien said, entering the room and taking a seat at the table and folding his hands before him.

"About time. They've had me cooling my heels in here forever. I should have demanded an attorney. I don't have much money—"

"Your rights were read to you. An attorney would have been provided for you," Adrien reminded him.

"One of your people," Keets said dourly.

"A defense attorney looks out for your best interests, Mr. Keets," Adrien said.

"Like hell. Some cheap trick who squeaked out of law school by a hair and is still a lackey of the state?" Keets demanded sourly. "You have nothing. Nothing to hold me on. They kept telling me they didn't need to charge me with anything, that they could hold me for twenty-four hours before doing so. But all I did was walk into the Everglades!"

"Mr. Keets, we heard you! You were there to aid and abet a man who was taking part in human trafficking! A man ready to murder—a man who demands his followers murder people when he commands it. I don't know how many cold cases we'll be able to put on you, but—"

"What?" Keets demanded, staring at him with concern at last.

"Oh, yes, you didn't know? Yes, you did. You knew. You were the one not about to leave—because you know exactly what happens to people who don't obey Hasani."

"Why didn't you kill him?" the man demanded, slamming his fist on the table.

Adrien arched a brow to him. "You were trying to save his ass—but you want to know why we didn't kill him?"

"If what you're saying is true, I might have had a chance if he'd been dead. But he's alive! And alive . . ."

"Here's what is going to save you," Adrien said, leaning forward. "All the names of all the contacts you know about, everyone who is in his criminal empire."

Keets sat back. "You should have killed him!"

That time, he said the words in a whisper. "If you had just killed him . . ."

Adrien shook his head. "Our job is to bring in criminals, Mr. Keets. We aren't judges, or members of juries. Those are the people who decide the punishments that fit the crimes."

"And people get out of jails and prisons and kill again, and again. Deny that!"

"I'm still not a judge or a member of a jury. I swore an oath to uphold the law."

"And that oath means more than common sense?" Keets demanded. "You know he's not just bad—he's evil. Evil in human form!"

"Mr. Keets, do you want to help me and help yourself?" Adrien demanded.

"Is my name out there? I overheard people talking about a press conference."

"To the best of my knowledge, no names were given out. The press conference let it be known that the senator's daughter had been found and that a kidnapping ring had been broken. That's all."

"As far as you know!" Keets said.

The door opened, and Eames stepped into the room.

"I gave the conference," he told Keets. "No names were given out. It was just as Special Agent Anderson just said. And if you know about others involved in kidnapping and murder and you don't cooperate with us, you're making everything worse for yourself."

Keets sat back, crossing his arms over his chest.

"First off, I had nothing to do with killing anyone. I had nothing to do with kidnapping anyone."

"What is his control over you?" Adrien asked.

Keets let out a long breath. "My wife."

"Your wife."

Keets winced. "She was in an automobile accident. Screwed up her back. Our insurance sucks. But she was put on these pills, and then they stopped giving them to her. She would cry and weep and do nothing but lie in bed. She was still in so much pain. Then, they wouldn't take her at the hospital, and then she went to the county hospital, and they told her to take something over the counter. She was still crying and weeping all the time, and someone told me he knew a guy who could fix it for me. I said I didn't have any money and . . . he said I didn't need money. I just needed to be available to help when help was needed. So . . . I started getting pills for her for nothing, and I should have known that the time would come. So anyway, the buddy who told me about the guy who got the pills for me—Hasani—refused to do something. I don't know what it was. But he said pills weren't worth what he was being asked to do. The next thing, I heard he was found dead. So . . ."

"Men like Hasani feel they need to make an example of someone—it doesn't mean they can carry out every threat."

"So far, he did okay. But . . ."

"Just tell us what you know," Adrien said quietly. "Your name won't go out anywhere."

"We can promise you that," Eames said quietly.

"I know of Darrell—but you've got him in here already. And there were the two guys who, uh, procured for him, but . . ."

"Yeah, we've got them, too," Adrien told him.

"Jeff Nagle and Oscar Benson," the man said flatly.

"And do you know what they did for him?" Eames asked.

"Drugs. You know, too many people get hooked on that stuff they hand out. I don't have other names; I do know most of the people he draws in have to do with promising whatever is needed. I can't tell you what a powerful draw those pills can be!"

"All right," Eames said.

"So, am I under arrest? I'm worried. My wife—"

"Your wife needs a good rehab," Adrien said quietly.

"You don't understand. I was laid off from my job. We don't have—"

"We can set something up," Adrien said. "If you're willing and she's willing, we can help you out of this."

"Oh, you won't get anything out of Darrell. He's new to all this—and possibly the worst coward known to man. He just got his first 'fill' a few days ago. This was the first time he's been called out—I called him. He's the one who owns the airboat we were using to get Hasani," Keets told them.

"All right. I'm going to need a few minutes to process you, and take care of something for your wife," Eames told the man. "And tonight, we'll have a protective detail on you."

Keets looked from Eames to Adrien.

"You . . . you would do that? I mean, protective detail. I'm not under arrest?" he asked, frowning with consternation. "Cops won't be with me to arrest me again?"

"We're pretty sure you're in the clear. You couldn't have picked up a man who had already been taken down by law enforcement. But we'll watch over you tonight. But lest you find yourself in trouble again, the kind that does kill you, we'll see to it your wife does get help," Adrien explained.

"For real?" Keets whispered, almost as if he were a child.

"For real," Eames told him.

Adrien stood to follow Eames out.

When the door closed, Adrien asked, "You really do mean to do these things for the man?"

"I do, unless, as the federal agent assigned, you have a problem with my choice. I have found that when we can, we offer help. Then, when law enforcement needs help, we're a . . ." Eames's voice faded as he thought of a good way to describe his meaning.

But Vicky had come out of the other interrogation room and smiled.

"He wants people to think of us as warm and cuddly. You get a lot more cooperation when the community is supportive."

"Makes sense," Adrien said. "Honestly, I've heard the same thing from some of our higher-ups."

"It's nothing you two need to worry about. Go home. Night tech can work on the names we were given, and hopefully, each person we can get something from will give us someone else. Then eventually, we'll get to the bottom of it all. Or we won't. But with Hasani out of the action, I imagine it will all fall apart rather quickly."

"We can't count on that," Adrien said.

"No, we can't," Eames agreed. "And we may never get everyone who has been involved with him in any way. We'll do our best. Like I said, you've put in more than enough hours—"

"Hasani is out of surgery by now. I want to see him," Vicky said.

"Glutton for punishment. I love it in my detectives," Eames told Adrien. "Vicky, go on to the hospital if that's what you want. After that, please, sleep in!"

"Will do, I promise!" Vicky said. She looked at Adrien. "Hospital?" she asked him.

"I'm in all the way," he assured her.

They started to walk away. but Vicky held back turning to Eames.

"Sir, if anything major happens—"

"I will call you," Eames promised.

Vicky smiled, and they finally left, laughing, waving, and both echoing, "Thank you!" as they were applauded again on the way out.

"I feel guilty. We couldn't have pulled this off without Mike, Lance, Hank, and the others," she murmured again.

"And they couldn't have pulled it off without us," Adrien said. "We're good. Though I was thinking you should maybe give Hank a call. Andrei Hasani is no fool. He has probably already lawyered up and won't agree to speak with us."

She tossed him the keys. "Drive. I'll call Hank."

She dialed as he put the car into gear.

"Hank, I'm putting the phone on speaker," she said when he answered.

"Cool. Vicky, huh? Yah! I still have a partner!" Hank said.

She laughed softly. "Yep, you still have a partner. How is it going at the hospital? I believe Hasani must be out of surgery. Have you talked to him? Has anyone tried to speak to him? Did he get a lawyer?"

Hank was silent for just a second.

"Hank?"

"Yeah, honestly, I was hoping you'd just go home. Now Hasani only wants to speak with you, Vicky. His exact words were a play on the old ride at the theme park—'I want the redhead.' He laughed a lot. Amused himself with his own words."

"But he didn't insist he wouldn't talk without an attorney?"

"No, but Vicky—"

"Hank, trust me, the man is wounded. He isn't going anywhere fast from that hospital bed. And if he hasn't made a phone call . . . well, we're all right. As far as I know—"

"Oh, yeah. Cops are on him. They want him transferred to the hospital at county as soon as possible. Oh, the senator's daughter is gone. They got her out the minute he came in, but then she was really all right. They were just keeping her for observation. She's with her folks. And her dad hired on a new slew of security, so . . ."

"I really want to talk to him, Hank. We're on our way there now."

"I'll be standing right outside, and if he makes a move—"

"He's going to be cuffed to the bed—even if half his body is in a cast," Vicky said. "Seriously, Hank—"

"I know, I know. I just never had to wish you were a brunette before," Hank said. "See you when you get here."

Vicky ended the call and looked at Adrien. "So. He will talk. Let's just hope he'll say something useful."

"About his empire?" Adrien asked. "I doubt it. I seriously have tremendous faith in all your abilities, but I don't think he intends to say a thing. I think he just wants to tease he will—and tease you and promise all kinds of vengeance." He shrugged. "Obviously, the man has a buyer for redheads."

"We need to know who that buyer is."

"And you really think he's going to tell you?"

"No. But I believe I must try to get him to give something away."

Adrien smiled. Looking ahead.

"Ah, come on. Eames said I could."

"Yeah. And he is your superior."

"But you don't like it?"

"The man is a monster, and he wants to play. But I also know you." He flashed her a quick smile. "No, I haven't known you that long, but our hours have been . . ."

"A few have been intimate," she said sweetly.

He laughed again. "Delightfully. But I meant I'm coming to know your tenacity and determination. And if you've decided you're going to talk to the man, you are."

"I do listen to reason," she said.

"Okay, here's my reasoning. He doesn't want to give anyone anything. He finds you appealing, intriguing—and he hates you. He hates that he thought you wouldn't be an incredibly strong adversary, and you proved him wrong. So . . ."

"And here's my reasoning. I understand that. He wants to do anything he can to torment me. He'll tell lies—he'll make up captives he doesn't really have. He'll try to get me to be excited I'm getting somewhere, then shoot me down. And of course, I'm sure he wants to tell me all about the torture he will one day inflict on me. But here's the thing. He may slip. And there's one thing we need—information on his 'buyers' for the women he made the Trent brothers kidnap. I like to believe Andrei Hasani will never see the light of day—and I believe he will receive life without parole. Of course, prisoners do escape. Friends of mine who are guards tell me that usually when there is an escape, it's because someone knew someone on the inside—so that's always a fear. But let's say he does get max security and is locked away for life. Supply and demand. We need to find out who wanted the redheads."

"That's an excellent point. I just don't think he's going to spit it all out."

"Maybe not. Still . . ."

"Guess what?" he asked her.

"What?"

"I don't think it will be successful, but I agree your plan is something we need to try."

She smiled at him and nodded grimly. "And don't worry—

sticks and stones could break my bones, you know, but I can deal with a heck of a lot of words!"

"Yeah. I think we all get to that point," he agreed. "Just know I'll be outside with Hank—oh, yeah, and all the other cops in the place—if he moves a muscle in the wrong direction."

She laughed.

"I think I can take him—even without a gun. He's fresh out of surgery. I'm just not too frightened he can cause me any real harm."

"I'll grant you that. Still . . ."

"You and Hank will be there, and I'm grateful!" she assured him.

They reached the hospital. It was long past visiting hours, but they produced their credentials and were immediately allowed to enter.

When they reached Andrei Hasani's room, they discovered a multitude of officers in the hall including, of course, Hank.

"So, hmm. It's late, you know," Hank told them both.

"Ten o'clock," Vicky said. "We do know how to tell time. Speaking of time—you have a wife and two kids!"

"Yeah, and my wife worries about you more than I do!" Hank reminded her. "Sorry, she worries about everyone. She told me one time it was her part of law enforcement. I'm going home. But I knew you'd show up here, and I wanted to hear what was going on."

"Are you coming in with me?" Vicky asked him.

"No, I set a mic in the room. Apparently, Dr. Aldridge—the fellow in charge of Hasani's case until he's moved—had a prisoner in recovery in Ohio once. There was a crooked nurse on duty, and she managed to get a weapon to him. He almost killed an orderly. Since then, Aldridge discreetly keeps tabs on what is going on. Of course, he assured me, if the man had asked for his lawyer, he would have done the legal thing and gotten it out. But as it stands . . . you can hear what's going on as if it's a nearby conversation, even with the door to the room closed."

"Great. I'm not sure about the morality—"

"Why? Monitoring is important with the man's condition!" Hank said, shrugging. "It's not illegal, since Aldridge wants the hospital staff aware of any change in the man's condition, so . . . oh, and I heard him. He informed the man he was being monitored. He might not have explained how, but . . ."

"All right. It is late. I'm going in."

Adrien watched her walk into the room and moved to stand about two feet from the bed.

"Ah!" Hasani said. "The redhead!"

"I'm here. So, what have you got to say?" Vicky asked.

Hank nodded silently to Adrien. The man had been right; it wasn't loud, but standing just outside the room, even with the door closed, he could hear every word being said.

A glass pane in the door had allowed him to see Hasani. And the man was a mess, half of his body bandaged, in a cast, and held in a sling.

But he was suspected of kidnapping, possibly rape, and possibly murder.

His uninjured wrist was cuffed to the bed.

But his face . . .

Strange, Adrien thought again. The guy looked so *normal.*

As if he could walk into any bar and easily strike up a conversation with just about any young woman who was free. He was intelligent enough to have managed to get away with a great deal for a long time. But the average citizen knew—just as those in law enforcement—that the most evil human being might look like an angel rather than a monster.

"Oh. I wanted you to know I wouldn't forget you," Hasani said.

He forgot he was cuffed and reached out a hand as if he wanted to touch her, stroke her face.

Vicky didn't need to move—the cuff jerked him back.

"Right. Well, your people are being rounded up as we speak, though of course, I did hear there was someone else we'd need to start looking for. You know how gossip runs through jails and all. Seems like there's going to be a new kid in town without you being in on the action."

"I am not out of the action!" Hasani snapped. "You just wait. What? You think I don't have backup?"

She laughed softly. "Your backup turned on you, if rumor stands correct. We have one of your minions—caught up in the middle of the state, actually—talking away. He's telling us the man you were supplying didn't give a damn if you rotted in prison forever. He had someone new, and he didn't need you anymore."

Rage filled the man's face.

"You're a liar!" he said angrily.

She shrugged and turned away. "Okay. I'm a liar. See you in court."

"Wait!"

"What? I'm bored, and I'm sorry, we really don't need you. You don't know anything about the new people working the trade. You're here already, and we need to move on."

She kept walking toward the door.

"Wait!"

"What?" Vicky asked impatiently, pausing with a bored sigh.

"That's my girl!" Hank murmured from outside the door.

"She plays it well," Adrien agreed.

"What? I'm leaving!" Vicky insisted.

"You want something? You want me to give you something that matters?" Hasani raged. "Forget the small fry. Get Rafael Rodriguez—a Colombian visitor who frequents the Bahamas and manages easy access between here and there and then on back to his home. Oh, but do be careful. He loves redheads even more than I do. Then again, maybe I'd enjoy hearing about it if he did get his hands on you!"

"Hmm. There you go. You did give me something. I guess we'll go out and get him—before he attempts to help you in any way," she said sweetly, walking calmly out of the room.

And Hasani went into a true rage as she walked out, screaming and kicking and banging at the cuff that held him chained to the bed.

She walked up to Adrien, smiling. "See? Most narcissists do tend to give it up! Could we go home now, all of us?" she asked, looking from him to Hank.

"Yeah, I think we could all go home," Hank agreed. "Give me a second with our boys—and girls—in blue."

As Hank walked away, Adrien smiled at Vicky. "You are good," he said quietly.

"At everything?" she queried in a whisper.

He moved a step closer and whispered in return.

"Whose home are we going to?" he asked.

She started to laugh.

"Mine. Nice as they be, these are borrowed clothes. Don't worry, I'm not that far—close enough to get back to wherever we need to be come the morning. But . . . hmm, my cell works here, I just need to call Eames and get him on the lookout across the state and in the Bahamas for this Rafael Rodriguez."

"Done already," Hank said, returning to stand by them.

Andrei Hasani was still raging. A confused nurse glanced at them and started into the room.

"Nothing happened to him; I'd let him tire out," Adrien suggested.

The nurse hesitated.

"Yeah," she said, smiling and walking away.

"Hey, um, do you want me to drop the cowboy for you, Vicky?" Hank asked.

"No, no, no problem," Vicky said, looking downward.

And Adrien understood completely.

They'd spent a strange day. They had discovered they were good working together—and discovered a bit more.

But it hadn't even been a full forty-eight hours since they'd met.

And at this point . . .

Neither of them could know if it was . . . real.

Chapter 9

"Hmm. Okay," Vicky said, sliding her car into the drive of the duplex where she lived. "We do have a bit of a problem."

"What's that?" he asked her, arching a brow. "Listen, if you're worried . . . I mean, you can just drop me off if you're beginning to feel—"

"I wasn't thinking—I mean, unless you were thinking that—"

"I wasn't! I was worried about what you were thinking," he protested, staring at her sincerely.

"No, I was thinking you'd be wearing the same clothing—" Vicky began. But he started to laugh.

"Sorry, sorry!" he said. "I thought you were trying to say you'd been rethinking us, what we were doing, and maybe we shouldn't, maybe we should back off. Clothing. Not a problem. You didn't notice the backpack I threw in the car this morning. I'm always prepared—"

"You go home with all your temporary partners?" she asked, lifting a brow. But she knew she had a giveaway curl to her lips. Somehow, she knew he didn't.

"No, I've just been in this for years now and . . . I always have backup clothing with me. I am prepared for the rugged outdoors—and the supposedly cleaner indoors—at all times," he told her.

"Oh, well, good."

"This is your house?" he asked her.

"This is my half of the duplex where I live," she told him. "I like it. Three bedrooms—one is an office now, one is a guest room. I only have one sister, but she and her family come see me sometimes. And one is my bedroom. Rates in South Florida soared over the last few years, but I have a great contract with the retired owner, who is now living near his grandchildren in St. Augustine. I love it. I'm in the middle of everything here, I can get to the beach easily, and I can get to work easily . . . I love it. Oh, and I share a pool with the neighbors, a great couple with a ten-year-old boy."

"A kid in your pool all the time?"

"I actually like kids."

"Do you want a few of your own one day?"

"No more than three," she assured him. "Although my sister believes two is the magic number—we have two hands, so two kids should be just about right."

"So, you have a sister?"

"Two years older, lives in Orlando. She's an actress and works for a theme park up there."

"And she has two children?"

"Yep, boy and a girl. Easy—she managed it in one shot. Twins," Vicky told him, grimacing. "But please, come see my not-so-palatial estate!"

Laughing, he got out of the car, stopping to grab his bag, and followed her as she headed up to the door.

She keyed in the alarm and let them in, then flicked on the lights, and she realized she was ridiculously hoping he liked the place. She had tried to make it like a real home. Her mom had always kept family pictures up on the walls, and she had discovered she liked to do the same. It often reminded her, after a bad day, that the world was filled with good things and with families that truly loved one another.

She had a handsome chesterfield sofa, and thanks to her sister's husband, a true state-of-the-art entertainment system designed to allow music, movies, TV, and games at the push of a button.

"This is great," he said.

"Thanks," Vicky told him. "Where do you live—or where did you live? Or will you get yourself re-transferred and go back to where you were living?"

"Northern Virginia," he told her. "And I love Virginia. It's a beautiful state with seaside and mountains. But no. When the bureau got involved after the senator's daughter disappeared, the situation was studied and evaluated. And probably because of my background, they considered me the best man for what the powers-that-be considered necessary undercover work. When I knew what they wanted . . . well, working in a Florida office hadn't come up before. So I figured . . . my parents aren't getting any younger. I liked the idea of being closer to them, and as you've seen, my brother is here . . . so, I mean, whoever knows what the future will really bring, but I want to stay now."

Now. *Did that mean he wanted a few months here, a year maybe, and then he'd move on again? Or did it mean,* now *I want to stay here?*

She gave herself a brisk mental shake. They had definitely become friends, and friends could remain friends through distances and years. But if it was something more . . .

She was being ridiculous. But then again, work had been her passion for so long. She had been one of the youngest women in the history of the department to earn her detective's shield. Of course, her desire to become involved in law enforcement went back to the time when her mother had been saved by a female cop during a home invasion. Vicky wanted to emulate the female officer who'd saved her mother's life.

He arched a brow. "Vicky? Everything okay?"

"Oh, yes, sorry! I was just thinking that we become so involved with work that . . ."

"That we forget to have lives?" he asked her. "Yeah, I know."

"Well, anyway—oh, food! I do keep food in the house—real stuff, not just grab-and-go. Okay, I'm not a gourmet cook, but I can whip up a mean omelet, and if nothing else, yogurt, fruit, hot dogs . . . that kind of thing."

"Sure. What would you like?"

"I don't know. Come on, the kitchen and dining room are this way."

The dining room was an ell extension off the living room, and a counter with four chairs and a breezeway separated the kitchen from the dining room. Vicky headed on into the kitchen, opening the refrigerator.

"You're welcome to come and take a look," she offered.

He walked around to join her, his body close to hers as they studied the contents of her refrigerator together.

Naturally close. And it felt good.

"Hey, wait!" Adrien exclaimed, smiling at her.

"What?"

"You don't just have hot dogs; you have corn dogs!"

She laughed. "And lots of honey for dipping. Or I also have mustard if you prefer."

"Corn dogs with honey. Sounds great to me. And we also have—"

"Broccoli! I see it. We can heat some up and pretend like we're having a healthful meal," Vicky said.

"Works for me. Hmm . . ."

"What's that?"

"You have an IPA in there."

"Please, help yourself!"

"There's just one."

"I'll have a glass of cabernet with mine—I'm not a fan of IPAs. My brother-in-law left that on their last trip down here."

"I'll pour your wine while you steam or microwave or do whatever you do with food," Adrien offered.

"That will work."

They set about their tasks and were done in a matter of minutes—thanks to her niece and nephew, Vicky knew precisely how to make the corn dogs crispy rather than soggy. Adrien found a glass and her cabernet, then set out their drinks along with forks for the broccoli. In only minutes, they were set up side-by-side at the counter to eat.

"This place is really great," Adrien said.

"Well, I'm not sure about great—"

He laughed. "Not a palatial mansion, no. But a super spot for getting to work. And as you said, not that far from the beach, and not that far from all kinds of great restaurants, malls, nightspots, and still not far from the Everglades and leaving society behind for a bit."

"It's been good. Traffic can be terrible, so it is good to be close to the places I need to go."

"And where are your folks?" he asked her.

She grinned. "South Miami. Close enough, too. Where I grew up. They do, however, like to spend a lot of time in Orlando. Theme parks are more fun than a daughter investigating serious crime."

"But I'll bet they're proud of you," Adrien said, frowning.

Vicky laughed. "Yes, they are. It's just when Liz goes to work, my parents get to go and see what she's doing; and hey, she has kids, too. And . . ."

"And you 'cop' out all the time when they want you to do things with them?" Adrien asked.

"No!" Vicky protested, but realized he knew what she never

wanted to admit, because his life was the same. "Okay. Maybe, sometimes. I try not to! I mean, I really do try to make sure I'm around for Christmas and Thanksgiving and . . . yeah, you're right. I don't mean to."

"I know the story. Not just with my folks but . . ."

"But?"

He shrugged. "Five years ago. I was engaged. She didn't like my hours."

"Ah, got it. And so . . . no commitments!"

"I never made that decision. Just . . ."

"Just happens that way?" Vicky asked.

"No. I just decided at that point if I ever made a commitment again, it was to someone who was willing to understand it wasn't like living with a banker. That's all. Hey, I'm social enough—"

"A cowboy."

He shrugged. "I was happy for the transfer; I love the horses, the dogs, the ranch. And yes, I grew up barrel-racing, heading to the rodeo, so . . . if you want, a cowboy!"

Vicky grinned at that.

"You got something against cowboys?" he teased.

"Only some," she assured him.

He stood and reached for her hand. "Some cowboys can be . . ." He frowned, his voice trailing.

"Yeah?"

He laughed and said, "Good in a pinch. Or after a few days of trailing after deranged narcissists in the Everglades or trying to trick them at the hospital. Or . . . you know. Just good in a pinch. Because this cowboy . . ."

Again, his voice trailed.

"Yeah?"

"This cowboy thinks you're one of the most beautiful women and coolest human beings in general he's ever met," he said softly.

She laughed, rising to slide into his arms.

"I know what this cowboy is good at—eloquence!" she told him.

"And a lot more, I hope," he whispered.

They began to kiss, and he knew how to kiss, and she certainly wouldn't put it into words, but he was not just good at kissing, he was excellent. He could be amazingly romantic, lifting his mouth from hers to look deeply into her eyes and then dramatically sweep her up into his arms. Then he smiled, his face crinkling as he said, "Um, do we need to pick up—"

"It's my place," she assured him. "No one will care if we pick up in the morning!"

"Sorry for the interruption in my sweeping you off your feet!" he teased, as he turned and started for the hallway and paused again.

"Uh . . . which . . ."

"Second door on the left!" she said, breaking into laughter.

"Laugh at me, will you? Laugh at my seduction attempts!"

He nudged the right door open with his knee and ceremoniously laid her down on the bed, then bounced onto the opposite side, immediately taking her into his arms as his lips found hers again.

Then there was no thought for the longest time, just sensation, then laughter again as they struggled with their clothing, a moment when they just looked at each other, and their lovemaking became fierce and urgent and strangely tender all in one.

In time, in one another's arms, they drifted to sleep.

It was during the wee hours of the morning when Vicky awoke. And it was with Adrien at her side with a finger to his lips.

She frowned, but no words slipped from her lips—just a question in her eyes. He made a motion to let her know someone was out there, in the yard of the duplex.

And her neighbors weren't the kind to be running around in the middle of the night.

Adrien was already up, a pair of jeans pulled over his legs, his Glock in his hand. She quickly retrieved the little Beretta she kept in the nightstand, then slid out of the bed and grabbed the robe from the foot of the bed.

She nodded at him; they were ready.

Adrien crouched carefully to look behind the drapes at the side of the room. He shook his head and eased out to the hallway.

She followed.

He indicated he was going to the back; she nodded and headed toward the front. She saw nothing and came back around. Adrien pointed to the hallway, and she slid along it; he entered the guest room, and she went into the office.

And it was there that she saw the man in her backyard. A sense of urgency filled her; she wasn't sure what good it would do the would-be assassin, but was he trying to break into her neighbor's window? Did he have the wrong window? Or did he believe one section of the house would lead to the other?

She slid back into the hallway to find Adrien, who again warned her to silence.

He lifted two fingers.

She frowned; she had only seen one man.

He indicated the other was around the front of the house. Then he whispered to her, "We need to get them both."

She nodded.

"There's a man on the porch, out of sight of the windows and the peephole, playing with the alarm. We get him first, and we can hope the other isn't a fence-hopper to escape through the back."

She nodded. At the front, she hit the buttons on the alarm from her side; they waited until they heard the intruder trying to twist the lock.

Then Adrien drew the door open, and the man nearly fell in.

They both had their weapons on him.

"Don't. Don't draw. I really hate having to kill people," Adrien said.

The man nodded. He opened his mouth as if he would shout out a warning, but Vicky took care of that herself as she sent a knee flying hard into his jaw.

He dropped.

"Cuffs?" Adrien murmured.

She stared at him. Obviously not. She was wearing a robe.

Adrien drew the belt from his jeans and tied it tightly around the man's wrists and dragged him the rest of the way into the house. Vicky ran to grab a kitchen towel; it would serve as a gag for the moment. Adrien was already outside, moving carefully around the house.

Vicky headed straight for the back door. The alarm was off; she could open it silently. Adrien had come around from the front of the house, moving like a wraith. He was directly behind the man, who was inspecting her neighbor's window. Adrien thrust the nose of his Glock against the man's back and warned, "FBI. You're under arrest. Don't move, don't go for your weapon. Put your hands on your head and turn around."

The man spun around, reaching for his gun.

Adrien clocked him on the temple with his Glock, and he fell flat.

"All right, two of them, one a blond, one looks Hispanic, both of them look like they're in their late twenties," Adrien murmured, stopping to inspect the man, who was fallen and who was now unconscious. He looked back at Vicky. "Have you—"

"Called it in. I realize it's about four a.m., but I'm calling Eames; I'll let him get who he wants out here to handle this. The jail is going to be full, it seems." She went back into the house. The first man was on the floor in the living room, struggling to undo his hands and making sounds despite the makeshift gag she had him wearing. She called Eames and explained the situation, and she hadn't even hung up when she heard sirens. In a minute, patrol cars were pulling up in front of the duplex. She realized she was still in a robe, but there hadn't been a chance for anything other—at least she hadn't walked out naked.

No chance to dress. She walked out the front door to greet the first two officers who arrived. She was glad she knew them both, Officers Thomas Talon and Trish Montgomery. "Hey—" she began.

"What is going on with you?" Trish asked, shaking her head. "We all know about Andrei Hasani—I think the whole country does—but—"

"Two men, trying to break in. And they probably gave my duplex-mate a minor heart attack," Vicky told her. Trish had been with the force about ten years, Thomas nearly as long. They were both in their early thirties, good and dependable people.

"Do you know who—" Thomas began.

"Not a clue. But Adrien Anderson was here, and he heard them before they could get started, and oh . . . I'd better handle this! Adrien will fill you in."

She hurried toward the little porch that signaled the entrance to her neighbor's door.

Her neighbor, Eddie Blackstone, had walked out his front door in pajamas and a robe, looking frightened and confused.

"It's okay, Eddie!" Vicky said quickly. She felt guilty. He was so frightened. And it was probably her fault that people had been trying to break in.

"Two would-be home-invaders, robbers . . . I'm not sure. But we've stopped them, and everything is okay."

"Oh . . . you hear about things like this, but you don't expect them to happen to you!" he said. Eddie was balding, nearing fifty, a good guy, friendly and easy to get along with, and from everything that she had seen, he was a great dad, as well.

"But it's all right; these officers will take them in. It's okay. You can go back to sleep. If your kid is awake, please let him know everything is all right. And your wife, of course!" Vicky said quickly.

He looked at her and nodded, slowly managing a weak smile. "Thank God we've got such a great cop for a neighbor! Thank you, Vicky. Thank you. And I'll get back in and let you handle all this," he told her.

She smiled weakly, guilt racing through her. Of course, they didn't know anything yet. The men might have been robbers, regular run-of-the-mill burglars just hoping to break in and steal something valuable while the homeowners slept.

But she didn't think that was true. And the last thing she wanted to do was bring danger to such good and decent people.

"Vicky?" Trish was calling her. Adrien was there; he was leading the second man out to the patrol car. The man was awake—with a good knot rising on his temple—and he was cuffed.

"I'll bring the second man," Vicky murmured.

"Have they said anything?" Trish asked.

"Nothing. We haven't tried to ask them anything," Vicky said. "This has all been happening so fast. One was in the front, the other man was in the rear." She hesitated, taking a breath and shrugging. "I don't think they are the brightest two criminals I've ever come across. This guy was playing with the alarm, and I don't think he had a clue as to how to disarm it."

"Why try to rob a house with an obvious alarm if you don't know anything about alarms and wiring?" Trish murmured.

"I don't know," Vicky replied.

"Unless they were after you specifically. I've heard that Hasani has been spouting vengeance since he was taken in."

Vicky shook her head. "But he hasn't made a phone call. He's been in the hospital surrounded by doctors and nurses."

"We'll see what they say," Vicky said with a shrug. "And still . . ."

"How could anyone have gotten to him?" Trish asked. "Unless we have a dirty cop or a hospital employee who is up for some bribery."

"Or one who isn't real," Adrien said, joining them.

"We need the second burglar," Thomas said, at Adrien's side.

"Right. Let's get him," Vicky agreed. "I hope he didn't crawl his way out."

"Trust me, he didn't. I'm on it," Adrien said.

He headed back toward the house with Thomas joining him.

"Vicky, I'm worried about you," Trish said. "I mean, I know you're a great detective and a crack shot and all that, but no one is an island. I mean—"

"You mean someone could get to any of us. I know that," Vicky said.

Trish didn't reply at first; they both watched as Adrien and Thomas led the man who had been at the front door out from the house.

Adrien's makeshift belt-cuffs had been replaced by real ones.

"Police brutality!" he shouted at Vicky.

"Amazing how every perp who tries to draw a weapon on you shouts that when you clock him instead of shooting him," Trish said dryly.

"If Hasani is out for me," Vicky told Trish, "there's little I can do except watch out for him. And I can do that," she promised.

"All right, all right, we'll take them in and get them booked on these charges," Trish said.

"And we'll get dressed and be in. I want to talk to them both," Vicky said.

"Yeah. You need to get dressed. Both of you," she added with amusement. She lowered her voice and teased, "The Fed is working out okay, I take it!"

"I have a guest room," Vicky said. It wasn't a lie. She did have one.

Trish just grinned and turned away. "I heard about his spectacular riding skills, as well. I wouldn't have let that cowboy go!"

Vicky watched them and turned to see Adrien was right behind her. He was shirtless in his jeans, arms crossed over his chest as he watched the police car drive away.

"It was Hasani," he said, looking at her. "They sure as hell aren't master criminal minds, and I'm not sure Hasani's little bribed-and-threatened army has many brilliant criminals in it. But they were sent out here not to rob the place, but to kill you."

"Adrien, we haven't even talked to them yet—"

"Vicky, the man shouted 'police brutality' at you. Why would he shout that to you if he didn't know you were with the sheriff's office?"

He had a point, and she lowered her head, wincing. Then she lifted her head and told him, "I need to get in there and talk to them."

"*We* need to get in there and talk to them," he corrected. He turned to head back into the house, and she followed him.

He was waiting for her, waiting to see her set the alarm.

"We're all right," she murmured. "Just—"

"Yep. I'll head to the guest shower with my bag, and we'll meet in the living room," he told her.

She gave him a half-smile and agreed.

And maybe it wasn't quite so bad. The first streaks of daylight were beginning to appear in the sky.

They'd almost had a complete, awesome night.

Maybe not complete . . .

But awesome. And in truth . . .

Would she have heard the men attempting to break in? Might they have gotten into her neighbor's place? Hurt the family?

The thought was a frightening one.

And she wasn't sure how to solve the dilemma before her if she was going to be a danger to anyone she was near.

She hurried in, took a quick shower, and dressed.

He was ready in the living room.

"Let's go find out who our idiot burglars are," Adrien said.

"Right. Let's do it."

They had started the drive to the station in silence. Adrien wasn't sure what else he could say, but he knew the two men hadn't selected a random dwelling to attack.

They had come after Vicky. Hasani truly wanted his revenge on her. He wasn't sure why the man wasn't as determined that he pay, but apparently in Hasani's mind, women were entertainment, and Vicky didn't know her place. She had dared to take him down.

She could have shot to kill; she had spared the man's life. But that didn't draw gratitude from him, just hatred.

She was the one who spoke at last. He knew she had been worried. Not for herself, but for her neighbors.

"This is truly a complicated mess," Vicky murmured as she drove. "Here's the thing. It seems that most people who do Hasani's bidding are drug addicts or someone making money on drugs, or maybe there's a petty thief or two in there. And most of the time, they're going to fumble an assignment, and law enforcement will get them easily enough. But I'm afraid of the time that he orders someone to do something, and they are capable as a criminal. In his dealings, he must know people who are associated with the cartels—maybe even contract killers."

He hesitated just a minute and then said quietly, "Vicky, you are in danger."

"We are all always in danger," she reminded him. "It's the job."

"Yes, but . . ."

"Not like this. I know. But we can't back down to this man, Adrien. We can't."

"I know, and we won't stop, but maybe you—"

"Don't say it, Adrien. Hey, I'm the one who got him to spew out angrily last night and give us the name of his buyer!" she reminded him.

"Vicky, I know, and seriously, I swear to you, this is the truth—I couldn't admire an officer, agent, deputy, or any manner of law enforcement more. But did you see the Indiana Jones movies?"

"I did, but what the heck does that have to do with anything?"

"Well, there is this great scene where an incredibly tough guy is twirling swords or knives around in a threatening way that shows no one beats him. Indiana takes one look at him, shrugs, and shoots him. Might have been the toughest ninja or whatever in history—but another guy with good aim took him down in two seconds."

"I'm always armed, and I'm always watching out for ninjas, I swear," she told him.

He leaned back, smiling.

"The thing is, Vicky, right now, you can't be alone."

"I'm not alone. I'm with you."

"Thanks for that. But I think we need to get things and get you to a different place to stay, and maybe we should keep moving around, too. Then we need more officers, deputies, or agents on duty when it comes to sleep."

"What?"

"Trust me, Eames will agree," Adrien told her.

She was silent. "I—I can see slipping around from place to place, but if we have people on guard, that one smart person in debt to Hasani will see them, and they'll just wind up dead."

"Not if we do it right."

"Adrien, I don't know—"

"I don't know how to do it exactly right yet, either. It's something we need to discuss."

"Discuss, yes, fine," Vicky agreed. "Let's see what our guys have to say. Maybe—and even I doubt it—they were random thieves."

"Sure," Adrien murmured.

At the station that morning, shifts were changing.

But Trish and Thomas were still there.

And Eames was there.

"So, you're under attack, Vicky?" Eames said.

"Is that what the men have told you?" she asked him.

"Nothing. We've got their prints, and they have records. Steven Page and Mick Menendez. Steven Page, twenty-seven, did time on a drug charge—selling meth. Mick Menendez also did a short stint, five years for robbery. We haven't interviewed them yet. They've just been processed. Oh, by the way, we have word out everywhere on the name you tricked out of Andrei Hasani yesterday, Rafael Rodriguez. Marinas, airports, train and bus stations have all been alerted, along with all agencies. We found a record on him, too, felony from a few years back; he served his time, but we have his face up everywhere—FBI put him on a most-wanted list."

"Fantastic. I'll take Menendez," Vicky told Adrien.

"That leaves me with Steven Page," Adrien said.

Eames lifted a hand. "Vicky."

"Yes, sir?" she said.

"You talk to both men. I'm not taking you off the case; that could be disastrous in many ways, because I can't even send you to another country. We don't know how far Hasani's influence might go. But we do need a discussion and a plan on how to go forward. Maybe you should start sleeping right here."

Vicky glanced at Adrien; she'd known he was right.

"We'll discuss it all, sir," Vicky said.

"Right after you two finish in interrogation. Hank will be

involved, of course, but since his house wasn't broken into, I don't expect him here until nine."

"Right. Of course," Vicky murmured.

They walked down the hall again, and Vicky entered one room as he entered the next on the other side of the observation room.

The blond man, Steven Page, was seated at the table, cuffed to links on it. He appeared anxious, younger than his years, with his mussed sandy hair and wide eyes.

"This is ridiculous. I was just trying to steal a few things to pawn. I mean, it was wrong, but I should just be given a court date—"

"You didn't ask for an attorney?" Adrien asked.

"Oh, yeah, they read me my rights, but I was hoping . . ."

"That we'd know you were really just a good guy in a bad situation and we'd just let you walk out of here?" Adrien asked.

"I didn't really do anything. I was just fooling around at the door. Right? I mean, I didn't do anything. I didn't."

"Why did you 'didn't do anything'?" Adrien asked him. "Tell me the truth, I'll see what I can do."

The man lowered his head. He started to cry.

"I—I was ordered to."

"Who ordered you, and what were you supposed to do?"

"Kill the redheaded detective. Make her suffer first. Kill her."

"Who ordered you?"

The man looked up at Adrien and said in a terrified whisper, "Hasani."

"How? The man is in the hospital under guard."

Steven Page started to laugh. "People get desperate pretty easily. And trust me, there are a few desperate people at that hospital."

"But how did you receive the order?" Adrien pressed.

"I got a text."

"From whom?"

"I don't know . . . just from the hospital."

"I need your phone."

"They took it when they brought me in!" he protested.

Adrien stood quickly; they needed the phone, and they needed to trace the text. It was probably a burner phone and already tossed. But that it had come from someone at the hospital meant something might be done.

"Wait! What about me?" Steven Page demanded.

"Sit tight. I'll be back, just sit tight!"

Adrien left the room.

He thought he just might have a plan to make it all come to an end.

Chapter 10

There wasn't much information Vicky could get from the man who sat before her, trembling every now and then and shaking his head. Mick Menendez just kept insisting that all he had wanted to do was steal some things to pawn so he could pay his rent.

"You aren't a very good liar," she told him. "We know you were there to kill me. And you know what? You're a lousy liar, but I bet the assignment wasn't something you liked, and I don't think you've ever killed anyone."

Menendez looked at her, surprised, perhaps because she had pegged the truth.

"I'm not a killer! I just wanted—"

"Stop it. You were there because you have a relationship with Andrei Hasani, and he somehow managed to get an order out to you. And even though the man is in the hospital and will go away for the rest of his life, you're all ridiculously terrified of him because he's managed to make examples of a few people who didn't follow his commands," she told him. "You were there to kill me. How did you get the order?"

He was silent, staring at her. Then he closed his eyes. "I'm a dead man!" he breathed.

"No. You're not."

He let out a bitter laugh. "You don't understand how easy it is to kill a man in prison."

"I'm not arguing that it can happen. But if you can help us get to the truth—"

"I can't. And I'm not lying. Steven got the message. He called me, and he showed me the text. The message said I was being called on to pay my debt. He showed me the text, but the number just said 'Florida.' I swear to you, I don't know. I would give you anything if it would help me, but I don't think that anything can help and . . . I don't know. I just don't know. I just . . . I got hooked on the pills and then . . ."

He hung his head low, shaking it, and repeated, "I'm a dead man."

"No," Vicky said, rising. "Mick, I don't think you're a bad human being. What you need to do is rid yourself of this addiction to drugs. And it can be done; I've seen it time and again. You're not a dead man. I was supposed to be dead—I'm not. This man can and will be stopped."

She realized she was angry. Not just because she was a target—but angry because one man could manipulate and ruin the lives of so many others.

She didn't know if he believed her or not. She knew they had to get the tech department to work on Steven Page's phone. Of course, it was going to be a burner. But they might be able to trace a tower, at least.

She got up and stepped out into the hall to find that Eames and Adrien were waiting for her.

"Someone at the hospital—" she and Adrien began together.

"I've had Steven Page's phone sent to our best tech," Eames said.

"And we need to talk," Adrien said. "We must find out now just what is going on there."

"My office," Eames said.

"Look. This is tricky. What the guy really wanted was to get Vicky to the man we've been told is the buyer. And whether this buyer makes slaves of the human beings he acquires or makes snuff films, we don't know. This man has been operating all kinds of criminal enterprises for a long time now, and we only became aware of it because of these last kidnappings. We've already seen just how many people Andrei Hasani has in his network, and there are probably many more. We must get to the head of the snake—"

"And Hasani is in custody, and it doesn't seem like that changes anything," Eames said, shaking his head. "Will we ever stop that man?"

"First, we're going to see that he's charged federally. That gets him out of the place where he seems to have so many contacts. Here's the thing; we're bound to the law. This is one instance when it might have been kinder to the world—and to us—if he'd been killed during our attempt to capture him. But we hold ourselves to high standards that criminals don't follow. And right now, we're looking at a veritable witch's brew of trouble."

"We're going to need to use me," Vicky said.

"Wait, wait, we can't set you up as bait—"

"I am bait already," Vicky said. "It would be better to be bait with a plan. I need to be at that hospital again myself—"

"You need to be under a rock somewhere," Eames said.

"Hasani would find someone to lift that rock," Vicky said. "And we all know it. Adrien—"

"Yes. We set things in motion in the hospital. Bring Vicky there with a select group of people. No one knows yet that we know there is a leak at the hospital, be it law enforcement or medical staff. Since it just might be someone assigned to guard the place, only the hand-picked group we know will be with us. I personally suspect that the mole is someone who is medical—or is slipping in as medical—and is the one taking directions from Hasani. But we need to cover all our bases." Adrien paused, took a deep breath, and looked at Vicky. He didn't like his own plan, she knew.

But it was the best one they could have under the circumstances.

"So, anyone assigned to guard Hasani now is taken off. We go in, sir," he told Eames, "with just you, me, Hank, and two more officers you know to be the best and most loyal. In fact, I'm thinking that we'll pull in Mike Buffalo and Lance Panther, Miccosukee and Seminole police and—" Adrien said.

"But they have no jurisdiction here—" Eames said.

"We throw them in county uniforms. They aren't going to arrest anyone; it's just I'd trust those two men with my life a thousand times over. We wouldn't have Hasani now if we hadn't had their help crossing state and tribal lands while we were after the man."

"You think these men will do this?"

"They will."

Eames was thoughtful. He looked over at Vicky.

"He's right," she said. "With the group of you there—and me challenging Hasani face-to-face, ready to let him know his idiot henchmen didn't get to me—I'll be safe. And we might well trick him into making a mistake. He can be riled. The man truly hates women, and one who is getting the best of him might well cause him to—"

"Try to kill you right there?"

"Exactly. And we'll find the leak, and he or she won't get anywhere, because I'll have the best backup known to man."

"I still don't like it," Eames said.

"I don't, either," Adrien said. "It's just better than sitting around like ducks at a carnival shooting range."

"Get your friends on the line and make sure they agree and that their superiors agree. And, Adrien, while this case has been left with me as lead, I'd like you to clear it with your superiors." He glanced at his watch. "Hospitals get going early. Let's see if we can move all this within the next two hours."

"Yes, sir," Adrien said.

Vicky glanced at him, and they both stood.

"I have one of the little offices; we can go there," Vicky told him.

"Lead the way; I'll make the calls."

"Take the desk," she said lightly, "make your calls. I'll just, um, sit here and think about exactly what I'm going to say to the man."

She listened as Adrien called his supervising director, who immediately approved his plan, she knew, because he made the call on speaker.

Then he put through calls to Mike and Lance, who in turn had to clear their participation in the operation with their superiors.

But there was no one out there who didn't want Andrei Hasani stopped.

When Adrien finished, he folded his hands and looked at her.

"We're a go. Vicky, I— "

"I know. No one likes this, but I do. What can happen to me in the hospital with all of you behind me? In fact, I'm almost afraid nothing will happen, that even Hasani will realize he's in a hospital with law enforcement all over him and— "

"Hasani doesn't give a damn about those he coerces—bribes or threatens—into doing his deed. Whoever he has at the hospital will be told to take a crack at you—if he hasn't figured out a way to do so himself."

She smiled at that. "He's in a bed, bandaged to a tee, and strung up, as well. I don't think that it will be him."

"But we need to be ready for any possibility."

"And you will be. And that's why I do like this plan—it's my way out."

Vicky smiled. Her office was private.

"Come on!" she told him. "You promised me a ride on Shiloh. We can't take that ride until I dare to go out in the open!"

"You're right," he said. "Well, we need to wait for Mike and Lance to get here, for them to wear the right uniforms—"

"We should have them deputized."

"Eames has that power, right? Things are different by jurisdiction—"

"Yes, he has that power. I was about to suggest coffee. And maybe something awful out of the machines," Vicky said.

Adrien grinned. "That will work."

Before they could stand to head out on a search for something edible, there was a tap at Vicky's office door.

Hank had arrived.

And he came bearing a box of donuts and a holder filled with coffee cups.

"So . . . you guys bring in a monster, and we're still on it!" he said cheerfully. "But trust me, I'm not feeling magnanimous in the least. Whoever makes a move—"

"We arrest," Vicky finished for him.

Handing her a cup of coffee, Hank said, "We'll see! Donuts. It was all I could think of, and the donut shop was on the way. And we're cops—okay, technically, you're an agent, most of these guys are deputies, we're detectives, but . . . all cops when it gets down to it. So, donuts!"

Vicky and Adrien both managed to smile, and they tried to keep the conversation light as they ate. Vicky thanked him. She wasn't really big on donuts, but that morning, she had to admit, they were fresh and delicious.

Mike and Lance arrived together; they were deputized, and they changed uniforms at the station.

Then it was time to go.

It was ten a.m. when they arrived at the hospital, and the morning shift was still in place. Federal, state, and local officers on guard duty were released. Eames gave the direct order.

The doctor in charge of Hasani that day was Leonard Miller, a man who had been with the hospital over thirty years. It was unlikely he was involved in espionage with the man, but anything was possible.

He informed them that he intended to sign the paperwork for Hasani to be moved to the infirmary at the jail where he'd await arraignment the following morning.

As those on guard duty departed, they watched to see if anyone seemed distraught that they'd been given the day off or made any attempt to go near Hasani's door again.

None did.

They were then a tight-knit group: Mike, Lance, Eames, Hank, Adrien, and Vicky herself.

"You up for this?" Adrien asked her.

"Of course, with you at my back," she said.

He grinned. "I think you'd be up for this if I was here or not," he told her.

She shrugged. "Well, you know, by *you*, I meant it in the plural. But you're right. I want this over. I want him locked away where the sun doesn't shine—much less allow for visitors! Anyway, by all accounts, I'm ready. And I am hoping whoever his accomplice is, they haven't gotten to him yet. I want to see Hasani's face when he sees I'm alive."

"We're set," he said.

Mike and Lance stationed themselves in the hall on opposite sides of Hasani's door. Eames chose a waiting room that faced the door to the man's room.

Hank and Adrien took the positions at the doorframe.

Eames beckoned to her. "Verify with the doctor that you're fine to go in to question the man. He'll expect law enforcement to still seek to see him. We haven't let out anything in the news whatsoever about the attempt to break into your house last night."

"Right!"

Vicky found Dr. Miller in a room a few doors down. She waited for him to come into the hallway and then asked if she might go in and speak with Hasani.

"Oh, yes, you're fine. I told you, I'm transferring him out of here tomorrow. Don't get me wrong, we are grateful for all the security, but my staff and other patients who figured out he's here in the hospital want the man gone!"

"Of course," Vicky said.

An older brunette nurse was leaving the room as Vicky headed back toward it.

She gave Vicky a nod and a wince and indicated her tray of instruments. "Sadly, the man has the heartbeat of a twenty-one-year-old in perfect shape."

"Thanks," Vicky murmured, and the woman moved on by to reach her next patient.

They were ready to go. Vicky gave them all a thumbs-up sign and entered the room.

When she opened the door, Hasani had his eyes closed.

She walked over to the bed and stared down at him and cleared her throat.

He opened his eyes.

And stared at her with stunned surprise.

No, he hadn't been informed yet that his assassination attempt of the night before had failed miserably.

She smiled. "Good morning, Mr. Hasani," she said.

"Is it?"

"Oh, yes, any morning when I'm alive and well is a good one. Don't you feel that way?" she asked sweetly.

She went and pulled a chair up to his bed. "Of course, any morning when we've taken in a few more members of your pathetic little army, well . . . I don't get it. You're truly an intelligent man—a very intelligent man—but you're also the textbook definition of a psychopath. You kill with no remorse, not a speck of guilt. You ruin life after life, and it means nothing, absolutely nothing, to you. I understand that someone in your criminal enterprise reached you here—came to the hospital. You've been charged and refused bail. So you will be a guest of the state first, as per procedure, but then you will also be charged by the federal government . . . I just do the arresting, I'm not a lawyer. But even without a law degree, I'm pretty sure you're going to spend the next decades incarcerated. So, why do you continue to threaten and haunt people? Especially the people you choose. Come on, you don't order a pathetic addict to go out and commit murder!"

He smiled at her. "Don't worry. I have better people on the job."

"Do you?"

The door opened. A young man in a nurse's uniform came in. He was in his early twenties, and his shaggy blond hair seemed a little long for the uniform. He had fine features and freckles and couldn't have been more than twenty-five. Vicky rose from the chair as he came closer to the bed.

"I'm sorry to interrupt. It's time for Mr. Hasani's medication," he said to Vicky, before turning to Hasani, looking as if he were almost in tears.

"Excuse me, Mr. Hasani, it's time for the special medication you requested," he said.

"Of course. And I am ready for my medication!" Hasani said.

Vicky thought of the nurse she had passed in the hallway just moments ago. And she knew instantly, of course.

Hasani had called in a major debt. This young man was supposed to kill her then and there and die himself. Hasani had something major on the man. Most likely, a valid threat against a wife or children.

Even as the thought raced through her head, the door opened, and Adrien stepped in.

"Stop," Adrien ordered, with his gun pointed toward the young man.

Hank walked in behind Adrien. He also had a gun aimed at the man.

"Do it or your daughter is dead!" Hasani shouted.

"I can't kill, I can't kill . . . I . . . can't!" the man sobbed.

"No, you're a coward. Do it! Die like a man yourself. Or she will die. Think of it. Your daughter's brains spilled everywhere!" Hasani shouted.

The young man reached beneath the snowy towel covering his tray and produced a gun.

"Drop it!" Adrien ordered. Vicky saw his Glock was aimed at the young man.

It looked as if he would drop the weapon, but he held on to it and started shaking. "You don't understand! She's just six, my baby girl is just six and . . ."

"We do understand," Adrien told him. "And we can help you."

"And we can kill you before you can kill her," Hank advised.

"My life for hers . . ." the man whispered.

"His people are like you—they don't want to kill! He has them terrified. If we can reach the network—" Vicky began.

"Like hell, I have some seasoned killers out there, and his daughter will die!" Hasani roared. "Your life for hers!"

"Seasoned killers like this man?" Vicky mocked.

"Damn you, die!" Hasani raged at her.

"Sorry!" Vicky told him. "No, not sorry! Sir, trust me, we can help you!"

The young man's shoulders slumped. He twisted around,

facing Hasani, his hand trembling, the gun about to slip from his fingers.

"Do it!"

"I—I can't!"

Hasani let out a roar of fury, suddenly rising, ripping the needle from his arm, and lunging over at Vicky.

She knew Adrien was ready to shoot, even though she instantly fell backward, out of Hasani's reach.

But another shot rang out.

The bullet hadn't been intended for Vicky.

The sobbing young man had struck Hasani.

Adrien had known he could have gotten a shot off before the man turned his gun toward Vicky.

He hadn't expected what had happened, except that once again, Hasani's big mistake had been in not seeing his terrified squad of soldiers were not necessarily natural born killers. He hated to admit it; the shooting of Hasani had taken him by surprise. And while the man would be charged with something—since apparently, he had provided the communication system Hasani had needed—Adrien doubted that he'd be charged with a crime for shooting Hasani. What he had seen was Hasani trying to kill Vicky. So it could be said he shot the man to save her life.

Whoever he was, the fellow had refused to kill Vicky, despite the fact he had been beyond terrified for the life of a child. His child. And if he hadn't killed Hasani . . .

Adrien couldn't think of the morality of it all then.

Because it was pure chaos in the hospital the second the gunshot rang out.

Adrien grabbed the gun from the shaking man's hands, while Vicky rushed to Hasani on the bed. She looked at him, shaking her head. But he could see for himself.

There could be no help for Hasani. The man's shot had

caught him straight through the heart, and blood spilled copiously over his chest.

"Young man," Adrien said quietly, "you're going to need to come with us."

He nodded. "I will take whatever I deserve. I just need for Ellie to be okay!" he whispered.

The real nurse came flying back into the room, looking from Hasani to the group of them, frowning as her eyes lit on the young man.

"Who are you?" she demanded.

"It doesn't matter," Vicky said, setting an arm on the nurse's shoulder and leading her back out. "I'm sorry, this is a crime scene now, and the room is off-limits to everyone but law enforcement. Please—"

Of course, the hallway had come alive with many of the doctors and nurses on staff, along with terrified patients.

But Mike and Lance had control of the hallway. They hadn't known exactly what had happened yet, but they could see Vicky, Adrien, Hank, and Eames were fine, and that was what mattered to them. They managed to clear the hallway, and when they did, Vicky looked at Hank.

"We need to get him to the station. Quietly. You and I walk out with him and down to the car, and we'll let the others—"

"Deal with the scene. Come on. Young sir, if you will . . ."

"Vicky was in the room. Does she need to—"

"I'm here," Eames said. "Vicky didn't discharge a weapon. She and Hank . . ." He paused, looking at the young man. "She might be best with this fellow. You two take him."

Vicky nodded, ready to leave with Hank. She glanced back at the bed. At Hasani. Eames had the feeling that she was feeling badly.

She wanted to regret the loss of a life.

She couldn't.

She glanced at him quickly, nodded, and left the room with Hank and the still unknown young man.

"So, to tie things up here. Doctor to pronounce him dead, and then forensics," Adrien murmured.

"We need it for the paperwork," Eames told him.

By then, Dr. Miller had come back. He looked at the bed and then at Adrien and Eames. "There is nothing I can do for that man, you realize."

"Just pronounce him dead," Adrien told him.

"You shot him?" Dr. Miller asked.

"I did not. Your pseudo nurse did when he attempted to stab Vicky with a needle from his arm," Adrien said.

"I must admit, the man was . . . I was frightened every time I was here. Kept the door open and had one of the guards from the hall come in right behind me," Dr. Miller said. "Well, yes, we'll get him down to the morgue."

That took a bit of time. He excused himself to Eames for a minute and went out to the hall. Mike and Lance were still there, speaking with assurance to those who continued to look out and slip from their rooms to ask them what was going on.

"So, Hasani is dead," Mike said. "Hate to say it about human life, but good riddance. We weren't all that much help," he told Adrien.

"But you were. You were the assurance we needed that allowed us to be watching out for Vicky."

"He wanted to kill Vicky, and he came up dead himself," Lance said, shaking his head.

"Live by the sword, die by the sword?" Mike suggested. "Exactly what happened?"

Adrien explained the best he could. "We were so focused on Vicky, it didn't occur to me he'd fire at Hasani. And yet at that moment—Vicky had the situation under control, but the young man may not have realized it—Hasani had lunged at Vicky. His temper always seemed to get the better of him. So . . ."

"Criminal or hero?" Mike asked lightly.

"Maybe most of us are a little bit of both," Adrien said.

"Hey, speak for yourself!" Lance protested.

Adrien grinned. He thought about all the time they had spent together growing up. Mike and Lance from different tribes, and Adrien from neither; and yet they'd managed even as kids to get together because of their shared love for horses, music, and their ecosystem.

"We really should get the band back together," Mike teased, as if reading his mind.

"Ah, yeah. Probably not today. So, thanks. Eames is calling men in, and you two will be free from this commitment. Again, thanks. I am not stupid; I know that dirty cops—agents, deputies, whatever—do exist. I just think it's rare, and the huge majority of the time, we are the good guys. We needed to be certain. So, thank you."

"Not at all; we had the easy end of the gig," Mike said.

He gave Adrien a wave, and the two of them started out.

Adrien headed back to the room, where Eames waited with the body of Andrei Hasani. But as he arrived, more officers were getting off the elevator, along with a forensics team and a couple of orderlies from the morgue, who were ready to take the body.

It seemed like forever that they were at the hospital, but he knew all about procedure.

Finally, Eames said they could leave, and he remembered he'd been getting around in Vicky's car. So it was good to have the ride with Eames.

As they drove, the older man glanced over at him.

"You've been a true asset here, you know."

"Thanks. And I'm happy to say, the work here has helped my bureau coworkers amazingly, as well. They're busy mopping up across the state. Though now . . ."

"You don't think Hasani had people who would want revenge, even with him gone?"

Adrien was thoughtful for a minute; then he shook his head. "Men like Hasani—anyone with the power to strike back—don't give a damn about others. They're not going to risk their own lives or 'enterprises' for a dead man. And seriously, look at the fellow who was in the room—Hasani's revenge on others failing to kill Vicky. That fellow was a mess."

"Right. He will be charged; from the reaction to him that we saw, he was never a hospital employee; he acted as one to get in to Hasani," Eames said slowly.

"How do you think he made the initial contact? And why? If he wasn't in the hospital . . ."

"Hopefully, Vicky is going to find out how everything was achieved. That man was terrified of Hasani. So if he wasn't a real hospital employee, why was he there?"

"Let's really hope Vicky gets it all figured out," Adrien said.

Chapter 11

"Cocaine."

The man's name was Eric Cafferty. He didn't have a record, but his driver's license verified his identification. He didn't seem to want to tell lies.

His only concern was for his daughter.

Vicky was amazed by the fact they were arresting people who pulled at her heartstrings—such as this man.

He was simply a mess.

The good thing was it wasn't hard at all to get him to talk.

"I should . . . I should have known better. I mean, you know, it starts out that you're at a party, just having a good time, you've got a few drinks down, and someone says you should do a line of cocaine, and you do. Next, you're doing a few lines, and then . . . then you get the nights when you don't even remember what you did. I was at a meeting—I mean, I tried to get clean once—before my wife divorced me; and then it was, you know, what the heck? Maybe we shouldn't have been married anyway, but Marci was pregnant, we were just nineteen . . . she wanted the baby, and we both gave up college. I started working for a transit company. Then . . . I mean, it was all right. But we were both still young, we went to parties. . . . I meant to clean up. I went to a party where there were no drugs—guy having it had a brother who was a cop. And his brother told him a story about a guy who started with pills because of an accident. He was kept on them, and suddenly the doctor wouldn't give him any more. He started trying to get more, doing cocaine, whatever, lost his job, lost his wife, lost everything—and went to a hospital with a gun—not to hurt anyone else, but to shoot himself so that they'd give him more pills."

"Addiction is truly a horrible disease," Vicky said.

He looked up at her with damp, hazel eyes. "I guess I'll get clean in prison," he said. "And I don't care. I really don't care. As long as . . . as long as my baby is all right. I'm divorced, but oh my God, I love that little girl! She is everything in the world to me, and she doesn't deserve to pay for me being such a horrible human being."

"Eric, you're not a horrible human being. You have a disease. And I think you're going to be all right, but—"

"I won't be charged with murder? I mean . . . that would be incredible. I hope they believe I had to do it. Oh, man, he wanted me to shoot you—"

"You did have a gun."

He sat back. "Not even my gun."

"All right. There are just guns in hospital supply rooms these days?" she asked dryly.

He shook his head. "Well, not usually. I was told in the text to go to the restroom on the first floor. There would be a nurse's jacket and ID there, and then I could get up to the third floor, where they had Hasani. Then I was to go to the supply cabinet and sign into a locker there. A tray was there that looked like the kind a nurse would walk around with, and there would be 'items' necessary on the tray. I about died when I saw the gun, but . . ."

He leaned back, shaking his head. "The text came with a picture of my little Ellie being dropped off at her school. The picture and a warning. I didn't even know about the gun, but . . . when I had it . . . and then he lunged at you with that needle. . . ."

"You're not going to be charged with homicide," she told him. "I don't even know what they will charge you with, but I promise, we're all going to help you as much as possible. What we need to know is who you were getting these messages from."

He shrugged. "They were signed by Hasani," he said. "I—I never saw the number before."

"Was the picture of your daughter recent?" she asked him.

"Recent?"

He seemed puzzled by the question.

"Hang on," she told him.

Hurrying to the evidence locker, she procured his cell phone and made her way back quickly to the interrogation room.

She handed him the cell. "Find the message and show it to me, please."

He keyed into his phone and then handed it back to her. The directions for what he was supposed to do were just as he said—along with a warning that Ellie would die a brutal death if he didn't. And there a picture of a little girl, adorable, in a little school uniform that included high socks and bows in her pigtails that matched the navy blue of her shirt.

But studying the picture, Vicky frowned. It was giving her more than she had hoped for. There was a sign behind the child that welcomed parents to a back-to-school night—with a date that was at least six months in the past.

"It isn't a recent photo, Eric. I believe this was taken immediately after you got your first free fix from the man, so he could let you know he had you under control when the time came he needed your help."

"Yeah, maybe."

"I don't think your daughter is in any danger. I sincerely believe Hasani's power over people died with him. But when we arrived, Hank saw to it that patrolmen will be watching over her and your ex-wife. Eric, there's no guarantee, ever, that we're safe, but . . . I don't believe your Ellie is going to be in any danger."

"Even if people find out that I killed Hasani?"

"We will never let that news out. And I believe any competition he has is simply going to be glad he's out of the way." She looked at him and offered him a weak smile. "There will be charges, but you may even get away with probation—and court-mandated rehab."

"I will go to rehab, and I'll stay in rehab, and . . . but whatever my punishment, it's worth it for my daughter!"

"Well, your decisions haven't been the best," Vicky told him, "but I believe you must be a great dad."

She smiled and rose, taking the phone with her. "Let me see how things are progressing," she told him.

Hank had been carrying out some of the necessary communications while she had spoken with Eric. He had been in the observation room since he had finished, and he met her in the hallway as she exited.

"There's a basket case for you, I'm afraid," Hank said.

"I really hope Eames is into helping him, too," Vicky said. "Hank, this picture he sent as warning is several months old. Not enough for the child to really change, but . . ."

"He didn't have anybody on the kid. Not yet, anyway. He just got insurance on everyone with whom he ever did any kind of business. But you don't need to worry. We sent patrol out to watch over her and the ex-wife. They live in a gated community, but as we know, anyone can get into any kind of community when they want. But it makes it a little easier on the cops."

"What have they told the ex-wife?" she asked.

"Just that he was involved in a situation, that he was fine, and—as I know you wanted—he was involved in saving the lives of others."

"Am I crazy? I just feel so sorry for that guy."

"You're not crazy. His heart is in the right place. Like many young men and women—and older men and women—he became a victim of his own addiction. Anyway, let's get tech on this number."

"Burner, I know it's a burner."

"Of course. But maybe we can learn something. Hey, sometimes crooks get stupid and buy their phones with credit cards. Let's get this traced and hope that maybe our man—or woman—was stupid."

"Or arrogant," Vicky said thoughtfully, "certain that they would never be caught, and they were above suspicion!"

"That's possible, too," Hank said. "I'll take this to tech. I sincerely believe other people are safe now, but I wonder if we should get something out there in the press. The man did die from injuries sustained in the Everglades, and anyone who was under his thumb because of drug addiction should come in, talk to us, and be guaranteed access to help."

"That would be great. But that's going to be—"

"I don't think that's even a call Eames can make. It's a federal situation."

"Right. Okay—"

She broke off. Eames had returned with Adrien, and seeing them, Vicky looked at Hank and said, "And here they are. I'll wait for them. You get the phone to tech."

Hank headed off.

Eames looked weary. "I've called a press conference—"

"I had an idea," Vicky said.

Eames groaned, and Adrien grinned.

"Of course you do. I was going to run it through with you both . . . I've got fifteen minutes. But I suppose I will listen to your idea, Vicky."

She nodded, smiled at Adrien, turned, and headed to the office. When they were there, she put forth her idea about offering anyone who had been involved with Hasani to come in for help—no charges rendered for the drugs.

"I'll call my people," Adrien said, rising. He paused, looking at Eames.

But Eames actually smiled. "I like it. If we start getting a slew of people, we can feel more confident that we've really ended things. Vicky, what did you find out about our friend with the gun?"

Vicky relayed the conversation she'd had.

"He really was trying to save my life," she told him.

Eames still appeared happy. "We'll see what we can do for the man."

Adrien ended his call. As he did so, the door burst unceremoniously open.

Hank was there.

"You're not going to believe this!" he said.

"What? Tell us!" Eames said.

Hank glanced at Vicky.

"You were right. About arrogance and someone thinking they're above suspicion. The phone was a burner—yes, pay as you go. But they traced the serial number, found the convenience store, and found the credit card with which it was purchased."

"Hank, spill!" Vicky cried.

"The good doctor. Dr. Leonard Miller—the very man treating Andrei Hasani!"

"We need to arrest him, now. I'm going to call ahead. We

have a few men at the hospital still; they can get him before he leaves," Eames said.

"I'm going to head over in case—" Hank began.

"Hell, I'm going, too." Vicky stared determinedly.

"Make it a threesome," Adrien said.

They were headed out of the office without waiting for a go-ahead, but Eames just called after them, "Hopefully, he'll be in cuffs by the time you get there."

They hurried out to the parking lot, and Hank shouted, "I'll drive!"

At the car, Adrien opened the front passenger door for Vicky. She grimaced and jumped in, while he quickly took the back seat. Hank went for the driver's seat. He maneuvered the car perfectly, and they were soon at the hospital.

They barely flashed their credentials at the entrance and hurried up to the floor where Hasani had been shot, and Dr. Leonard Miller had last been seen.

They ran into the two guards left on duty on the floor almost immediately.

One was Sadie Jenkins, another coworker Vicky knew well, and she hurried over to her.

"We've been searching; hospital security has been searching—we haven't found him yet," Sadie told her. "And no, he wasn't due to leave yet. His shift doesn't end for another hour or so."

Vicky thought about her conversation with Eric, how he had been told to find the nurse's jacket and then go to a storage room.

"Storage, we need to search all the storage rooms," she said. "It's where he stashed the gun for Eric to get earlier," she explained.

"We need hospital help," Adrien said, and he quickly stepped in front of one of the nurses stepping down the hallway, asking her for directions.

The young woman instantly looked worried and a little frightened, but not so much so that she couldn't point out the several rooms on the floor.

"Split up," Adrien said.

"Heading down the ell," Hank said.

"I'll go left," Adrien said.

"Fine. I'll go right," Vicky agreed.

They moved quickly. Vicky reached the first storage room. She tried the door, and it was locked. She saw the young nurse had chosen to follow her.

"Do you have a key?" Vicky asked.

"I can get one," the woman murmured.

She ran off to do so. Vicky thought she could hear movement in the room, but she wasn't sure.

"Why would this be locked?" she whispered when the nurse returned.

"It, uh, shouldn't be," the nurse replied.

"All right, thank you. Get back, please," Vicky said.

The young nurse obeyed her. Vicky waited, twisted the lock as quietly as she could, and threw the door open, then stepped back.

Gunfire ensued, but she was well out of the way.

Naturally, once again, the halls suddenly filled with screams and people.

You don't run toward gunfire! Vicky wanted to shout.

But among the people hurrying her way were Hank and Adrien. She warned them to stop.

"Stop it, Dr. Miller. We all know who you are. There's no way out for you now. You should have never used a credit card to buy that phone, sir. What I can't understand is how you came under the influence of such a man!"

"I . . . I just bought the burner and gave it to him!" Miller cried from within the storage room.

"And you bought a gun to leave for another man to kill me?" Vicky asked.

"I—I thought he wanted to kill himself. He told me that all was lost and that . . ." A deep sigh followed his words. "I don't know how he knew, but he knew I'd helped myself to some medications, and he was going to turn me in."

"You're making it a hell of a lot worse, Dr. Miller," Vicky said. "Just come out. He probably never had anything true on you. It sounded like a good ploy to him. And you fell for it. Come on now—make it easy on yourself!"

They waited. She looked at Adrien, who nodded.

"Dr. Miller, just come out," Adrien added. "We know where you live. We can freeze your bank accounts. Please. Like she said, don't make it harder on yourself. You haven't hurt anyone yet. Don't hurt us, and don't hurt yourself any more than you have already!"

And to Vicky's amazement, it was just that easy.

Dr. Leonard Miller walked out of the storage room with his hands over his head.

Hank moved toward Dr. Miller to do the honors and cuffed the man.

"Let's go, Doctor," Hank said.

Dr. Miller hung his head as they walked out. The hospital administrator on duty came running up to them on the way out. Adrien hung back to speak with him and explain the situation. He explained that forensics would be back, but it appeared that trouble for the hospital would be over.

Adrien sat in back with the prisoner, and they returned to the station, where Eames awaited.

"I'm taking this one myself," Eames told them, as he led the doctor to an interrogation room. "And, not to worry, Vicky. We're working with young Eric. We have patrol watching out for his family, and we're working with an attorney. He's getting leniency, probation, and court-mandated rehab. I think this experience will have taught him something. We can only hope."

Eames started walking away but stopped. He turned back to the three of them.

"Go home. It's been one long day, and there are other detectives here, you know."

"Yes, sir!" Hank called.

"Wait, sir!" Vicky said.

"Yes?" Eames paused, and she walked over to him. "You, too, sir. You finish with the good doctor, and you go home. Oh, your press conference—"

"Over and done with while you were at the hospital," he told her. "With federal blessing and cooperation, we have the invite out for anyone involved with the man. So—"

"You will finish this and go home," Vicky told him.

He shook his head, looking over at Hank and Adrien. "Be careful of this one!" he warned, but he smiled at Vicky. "I promise I'll go home after, Detective. I promise."

He went on, and she returned to Adrien and Hank where they stood in the hallway.

"So . . ."

"It has been a really long day," Adrien told her. "We haven't eaten—except for the donuts Hank so kindly brought this morning."

"I know a great restaurant on Griffith Road. The Field. Irish, lots of great food. And some great beer," Hank offered.

Vicky laughed, and Adrien looked at her. "The Field! Yeah, I've been there with my family. So, let's head on out for food!"

They did. It had been a long day; they needed to wind down. They talked in general as the waitress took their order. An Irish band was playing, and they enjoyed the music.

But when they were finishing up and coffee was being served, Hank grew serious.

"Do you think it's really over?" he asked.

"Snake's head," Adrien told him. "I do. I believe there will be a mop-up, and I believe people will come in. Vicky's idea was a good one. And trust me, the federal government is always happy to see illegal drugs off the market."

"So, are you going back to D.C.?" Hank asked him.

Adrien grinned as he glanced at Vicky.

"Actually, I live in Northern Virginia," he said.

Hank waved a hand in the air, rolling his eyes. "Whichever! When do you go back?"

"I don't. I was transferred down here. We have several field offices down here—here, Tampa, West Palm . . . more. I was transferred here, in Broward. I grew up here."

"You're staying?" Hank asked.

"I am."

Hank looked perplexed.

"What is it?" Vicky asked him.

"Am I losing a partner?" Hank asked.

"Hank, you couldn't lose me if you tried," Vicky assured him. "You're— "

"Like an extra dad?" Hank asked.

Vicky and Adrien both laughed.

"Big brother!" Vicky told him.

"All right, then. But I do imagine we'll work together in the future. It's amazing how well this worked because everyone was working together. And thanks for that great relationship I feel I've got now with Mike and Lance, and that can be so important, too," Hank said.

"Oh! Yeah, they're going to bring back the band, and we're going to see them play one night!" Vicky said.

Adrien groaned. "Only if you guys sing."

Hank laughed. "Only if you know classic rock!"

Their waitress brought the check.

"On the county tonight or on the Feds?" Hank mused.

"How about just on me?" Adrien suggested. "Truly, my pleasure. My thanks to those with whom I was privileged to bring in a case."

"Well, we could—" Hank began.

"Yeah, but so can I," Adrien said.

Hank looked at Vicky. "I guess I don't need to offer to bring Adrien home, since he's staying at your place."

Vicky glanced nervously at Adrien, but that look she gave him might have given Hank the greatest amusement of the night.

"Oh, come on, Vick, you're a grown-up who works all the time and tends to live like a nun. You two . . . yeah, not a long acquaintance, but man, do the two of you click!" He leaned closer, addressing them both. "That doesn't happen all the time in life. Met my wife at a Halloween party. And I knew then that it was just right. That's not always true, but sometimes it is. We were married by Christmas, and it's been almost twenty-five years. So . . . whatever the future brings, grab happiness and the great human touch when you can!"

"I'm so glad we have your blessing!" Adrien told him, and Hank laughed again.

"Go home! And rest well."

They managed to leave, Hank in his car, Vicky and Adrien in hers.

"I do have a car," he told her. "It's at my brother's house."

She smiled. "Well, I think we may have a day off soon, and when you take me riding, we can pick up your car."

"We may need a drive-by before then," he told her. "My 'quick' bag, or grab bag, or whatever you call the overnight thing I always have packed doesn't have that many articles of clothing in it."

She grinned. "And I need to return that dress."

Adrien was silent for a minute.

"That was presumptuous of me," he said.

"What?"

"That I was going home with you."

"Actually, it was presumptuous of Hank!" she said, smiling. She turned to him, frowning. "Maybe it was presumptuous of me, too. I mean, you probably want to figure out how to really establish yourself here and— "

"I found a great place to live," he told her. "Assuming the current occupant likes my idea."

"Where?" she asked. In all the time they'd been together, he hadn't said anything about being interested in a place.

"You do have an extra room, though, of course . . ."

She grinned.

"We've really only known each other for about three days," he said seriously. "And that is presumptuous of me, but . . ." He looked at her again. "I don't want to go to any home that isn't where you are."

She smiled and nodded. "I do have an extra room. We're not far from the ranch. We can spend plenty of time riding and playing with the dogs and, oh! One condition!" she told him.

"And what might that be?"

"I want a dog. I want Blue. I love dogs, and I've wanted a dog for so long, but I was worried about my hours. Okay, we're still both going to be working all the time, but with two of us . . . there's a nice yard here, and the kids next door are good kids and can help and— "

"It's okay. Blue is yours if you want her. Or," he added, smiling. "Ours."

"Do you think . . ."

"Think what?"

She glanced his way quickly and then gave her attention back to the road. "Do you think Hank is right, that maybe . . ."

"Yes," he said simply. "I do."

They reached her house and went in quickly. It was only about ten o'clock, but it had been a long, long day.

Showers were a necessity.

And fun.

As they began peeling away their clothing, Adrien teased her again.

"At least tonight you're not going to have to pretend you're afraid of snakes."

She made a face at him and shook her head.

"Only the human variety," she assured him.

"Ouch! Did you just call me a snake?"

"No! Why, did you think I was afraid of you?" Vicky asked.

"I'm a little bit afraid of you," he returned, grinning.

And then he had her in his arms, and he added, "Afraid you'll decide I'm not at all the Florida almost-cowboy you just might not want into the future."

She smiled. No one knew what the future would hold.

She did know she wanted to give it every chance in the world.

She rose against him to press a kiss against his lips and whispered, "This cowboy feels a little long-day icky right now . . ."

"Oh, but I will fix that!"

He caught her hand and led her to the bathroom and turned on the water.

"I'm going to try the romantic thing again," he said, sweeping her off her feet.

"Just don't fall! It's a shower, slick!" she cried.

He didn't drop her. And the shower was *slick* and wonderful, and after, it was the same incredible mixture of urgency, sensation, and laughter, too.

The night stretched ahead . . . and it was incredible.

Nothing interrupted them until the sun had been up and Eames called.

"Oh, no, what now?" Vicky asked.

"I'm calling you to tell you to take the day. Some of Adrien's coworkers up in the Tampa area arrested Rafael Rodriguez. He didn't have any redheads with him, but they did find a truckload of cocaine that was in his car when they found him and pulled him over for being impaired. Better yet—Vicky's idea is paying off. We've had ten calls from people asking for help who had at least met Hasani and received pictures of loved ones with warnings they would pay their dues when asked. Tie-up is happening fast. You guys will both get some time off after this."

"Both," Vicky murmured, glancing at Adrien.

"Oh, sorry—all three of you. Hank has been wanting to take his kids to Disney. Now he'll get the chance. And you and Adrien . . . well, you two just enjoy. Do not come in today. Do you hear me? Do not come in today," Eames said firmly.

"All right, sir, but—"

Eames laughed. "Don't worry; I'm setting a few things in order, taking care of a little more of the paperwork, and I'm going home. I'm taking my wife to Hard Rock for a day at the spa, a little poker, and lots and lots of hours just soaking up sun at the pool!"

"Great! I'm glad to hear it."

"Oh, Adrien will call in, I imagine, but tell him he's been given the day off, too."

"Um . . ."

Eames ended the call.

Vicky looked at Adrien, grinning and shaking her head.

"Eames knew about us, too! How? I mean, we didn't go near each other when we were working, and we didn't . . ."

"Chemistry," he said.

"What?"

He laughed, folding his hands behind his head and staring up at the ceiling.

"Sparks were probably flying all around us!"

She batted him on the arm and lay down next to him again. "Seriously . . ."

He curled toward her. "Maybe they all just saw the admiration in my eyes every time I looked at you." He shook his head. "I don't know. But I'm glad. And I'm glad that two of the most important people in your life seem to think it's great. Now I just need to meet your folks and your sister and her family."

"Hey! At least I have only one sister—I need to meet two more of your siblings and your parents and . . . wow."

"All in good time," he assured her, but he kissed her lightly on the lips and rose above her and reminded her, "We have the day off."

"I'm going to get to ride that horse!" she said.

He grinned, nodded, and said, "All in good time."

And she smiled, too.

It was actually going to be their first real morning together.

Epilogue

Their wedding was far different than most. Well, maybe not that different. They were married in a church. Vicky's father proudly gave her away, their siblings were all wedding attendants, and both their mothers cried.

There was little danger of anything going wrong at the wedding, since the attendees included deputy sheriffs, police from the Miccosukee and Seminole tribes, and plenty of agents.

Nothing went wrong. It was a simple and beautiful service.

Vicky had wondered if it would make a difference; they'd lived together from the second day they'd met.

And yet it did. They'd written their own vows, and she knew, as they spoke, that they were truly joined for life, and it was a beautiful feeling. Her "cowboy" was someone who respected her for her abilities, loved her for her strengths and weaknesses, and was the rare and unique human being who had no problem letting her be her. And it was incredibly nice, too, that their families were both so happy. She even found it amusing their mothers were whispering about just how happy they were—they'd been afraid there might never be that right person for their incredibly dedicated and complicated children.

She could never put her finger on exactly what it was, but when they said their vows, it was just there, that beautiful feeling, knowing ever more surely that she loved and was loved in turn.

It was the reception that was a bit different. They held it at the Anderson family ranch. They arranged for pony rides for the little kids, with Adrien's nephews happy to be in charge.

They had gotten a large tent from the caterer in case of the rain that so very often came in the afternoons. But even the weather seemed to want the day to go perfectly for them.

Their guests were spectacular, too. All were so different, all so fascinated by one another.

But there was one thing Vicky wasn't about to let go. She'd made a few arrangements that were going to be a surprise for Adrien.

She'd hired a band, but the band knew what was happening.

And after they'd cut the cake, she made the announcement.

"And now, dear friends and family, we have a special treat; I bring to you two new members of the band, my very new husband and his dear friend, Mike Buffalo, bringing back the music of their youth!"

"What?" Adrien protested.

But Mike was laughing. "Get up there, you!" he said to Adrien.

"Only if Hank comes up, too, and my beautiful bride chimes in!" Adrien said, staring at Vicky.

"Um . . ."

"Classic rock!" Hank called out as they went up. They all went up. And within an hour, most of the guests were singing. Lance Panther proved his part, grabbing Vicky for a rendition of "Stop Dragging My Heart Around." But the best was in the end when Adrien, the agent, the cowboy, proved his lighter side and chimed in to sing at last, his number specifically for her, "Can't Help Falling in Love."

And then they were off . . .

They were headed for a weeklong cruise to the Bahamas.

And that would be fun.

But the greatest thing would be that it wouldn't matter when the cruise was over.

Because she'd be spending the rest of her life with him.